CHRIS COPPEL
LUCK

Matador
9 Priory Business Park,
Wistow Road, Kibworth Beauchamp,
Leicestershire. LE8 0RX
Tel: 0116 279 2299
Email: books@troubador.co.uk
Web: www.troubador.co.uk/matador
Twitter: @matadorbooks

ISBN 978 1800460 003

British Library Cataloguing in Publication Data.
A catalogue record for this book is available from the British Library.

Printed and bound in Great Britain by 4edge Limited
Typeset in 11pt Minion Pro by Troubador Publishing Ltd, Leicester, UK

Matador is an imprint of Troubador Publishing Ltd

TO D.T.

None of this would have been
possible without your constant
and unwavering inspiration.

PART I
THE BEGINNING

CHAPTER
ONE

Daniel Trapp had always been lucky.

*

His parents had died between the level-crossing gates, just outside the town of Glenwood Springs in Colorado. The GenRail Starliner hit their car at over ninety-eight miles an hour, giving the eight-year-old Ford Focus and its occupants little chance of survival.

Witnesses seemed to agree that the car was driven carefully onto the tracks by Ellen Darnell. The automated gates then lowered on either side of it. Onlookers claim to have seen the couple look at each other and smile, seconds before the impact.

Ellen was thirty-five at the time of her death. She grew and sold her own strain of lavender, loved cooking, reading crime novels and was seven months pregnant.

When the car was ripped into two halves by the impact, Ellen was somehow thrown clear of the fiery carnage. Instead of dying like her husband, from massive blunt-force trauma, decapitation, and the fire, she survived an additional few seconds while airborne, before crashing head first through the windscreen of a beer delivery truck.

Miraculously, other than her head being cracked open like a melon, her body sustained little damage.

Her husband, Zeke, incurred enough damage for both of them. The coroner was never able to decide which of his catastrophic injuries had been the primary cause of death, as they appeared forensically, to have all occurred simultaneously.

*

Her unborn baby survived the accident and was extracted from Ellen's lifeless body, via emergency C-section at the side of scenic State Highway 134.

Nobody at the crash site could believe the baby's good fortune to have survived such a horrible accident.

Later, the attending doctor at the Glenwood Springs Hospital neonatal intensive care unit looked down at the preemie cocooned within the incubator, and uttered to himself: "You must be the luckiest motherfucker on this planet."

CHAPTER
TWO

Mary Trapp hated her husband. Not all the time, but when he did something totally dickish, she just couldn't help herself. She never really understood how someone could be super smart one minute, then head-up-ass stupid the next. Yet Mr PhD in Particle Physics managed it almost every day.

On this occasion, he had somehow managed to dribble superglue across their brand-new granite countertop.

Their twenty-three-thousand-dollar goddamn countertop.

All that while trying to glue a pencil back together.

A twenty-frigging-cent pencil!

"What the hell is wrong with you? Have you seen what you've done in here?"

Henry Trapp wandered into the room wearing a set of over-ear Bluetooth headphones. He smiled at Mary then proudly held up the repaired pencil.

"Pretty good, huh?" he bellowed, compensating for the Grateful Dead music blasting through his phones. He looked to her for some sort of praise. Instead he got Mary's famous glare of doom. He held his hands out, palms up, in a gesture of 'what did I do?'. The glare of doom continued until he removed the headphones. The glare still continued, but seemed now to be focused on the phones themselves. It took Henry a moment to get the hint, at which point he finally switched them off, bringing silence to where a millisecond prior, Jerry Garcia and the boys were in the middle of a seemingly endless jam.

"Look what you've done," she said.

Mary pointed a shaking finger at the glue dribbles.

Henry looked suddenly relieved. "Oh, that."

He stepped past his fuming bride of almost fifteen years and opened the freezer. He removed a small steel canister and carried it to the site of the controversy. After a brief examination, he unscrewed the cap and poured a thin line of liquid from the cylinder over the glue droppings. The glue immediately crystalized and the counter frosted.

Mary looked on in horror and screamed.

"No!"

Henry smiled smugly back at her before reaching for a stainless-steel spatula hanging with other implements next to the stove. With surgical precision, he slid the spatula's blade between the frosted glue and the countertop then grinned proudly as the adhesive separated from the granite as if by magic.

"Liquid nitrogen. Nature's little helper."

He knocked the glue clumps off the spatula and into

the trash, dropped the utensil into the dishwasher, and turned to face his wife.

Mary looked back at Henry in complete shock. With a disbelieving shake of the head, she nudged him aside and carefully inspected the granite.

"You got lucky."

"Nothing to do with luck. The extreme cold reacts with the acrylic resin in the glue and basically undoes the bonding."

He walked back to the freezer to return the liquid nitrogen canister.

Meanwhile, Mary grabbed a sponge from the sink and held it under the faucet.

Henry still had his face in the freezer. "Yup, works every time. Just so long as no water gets on the counter…"

Mary lowered the sponge to the counter.

"…top," Henry finished.

A sound like a cracking ice floe filled the room. Henry slowly closed the freezer door and looked to the countertop. Mary was also staring down at the crack that had appeared. It went from the sink all the way to the Viking Range.

"You know I might be able to—" Henry offered.

"Not a damn word!" She cut him off.

"But—"

The kitchen was suddenly filled with the strains of Tom Jones belting out the eternal question, '*What's new, pussycat?*'. Mary grabbed her phone. "What!"

"Yes, this is Mary Trapp." Her expression lost all its anger.

Henry watched with growing concern as the colour drained from Mary's face and she began to swoon. He helped her to a stool as she continued to listen. Tears cascaded down her cheeks. For a brief moment, she looked up at Henry and tried to offer him comfort while at the same time shaking her head.

Henry was starting to get a bad feeling. "What's wrong?"

*

The flight from Burbank Airport to Vail's Eagle County Airport was uneventful.

The crew always worried about the passenger behaviour on this route as Vail, being for the most part a vacation destination, seemed to promote a highly festive on-board atmosphere. Booze and all. It didn't take much to turn the narrow cabin of the Bombardier commuter jet into an uncomfortable (for the crew and sober passengers) party zone.

On this flight, however, the passengers were, for the most part, quiet and surprisingly well behaved. The crew assumed that this was probably the result of the woman in 9A, who boarded the plane sobbing, and continued crying throughout the entire flight.

Henry had tried everything he could think of to console her, but to no avail. He had made varied attempts at distracting conversations, offering her a large gin and tonic which was comped by the crew and even offered one of his highly prized, yet rarely used, Clonazepams to 'take the edge off'.

She declined all gambits. Henry was forced to take his precious pill himself, washing it down with the gratis Gordon's and tonic.

By the time the captain announced the beginning of the descent into Vail, Mary's raw sobs had matured into a more peaceful mewling. Even as the tears continued to track across her cheeks, she spoke for the first time since learning of her sister's fate.

"I'm sorry, Henry. I'll be okay. Thank you for being so strong."

Henry took her hand and gave it a gentle squeeze. She patted his, then returned it to her lap to join the other one which was clutching a tear-soaked napkin in a near death grip.

Henry, meanwhile, was doing everything in his power not to doze off. The gin and Benzodiazepine had not made him in the least bit strong, rather, had made him clinically mellow. Every fibre of his mortal existence wanted to go to sleep, yet a more primitive consciousness told him that a snooze at that point in his marriage could be terminal. He wasn't wrong.

Thankfully before leaving Los Angeles, he had had the good sense to book a car and driver to take them from Vail to Glenwood Springs.

True to the limo company's promise, the black Suburban was waiting for them kerbside once they deplaned. With hand luggage only, it was mere minutes from jet to car.

Probably a good thing, as neither was in a state to produce any more mental dexterity than was absolutely necessary.

Their driver met them at the gate and practically snatched their hand baggage from them, such was his focus on pleasing his passengers. He even tried to grab

Mary's designer (fake) handbag, but after a gentle slap on his wrist from a stunned Mary, gave up on that option.

Doug was twenty-four, lanky, dirty blonde and looked almost exactly like Shaggy from *Scooby Doo*, wispy goatee and all.

Once on the road, Doug made his one and only attempt at small talk. "So, what are you folks doing up here in Eagle country?"

"We're here to claim my dead sister's body, then go to the hospital and see if her premature baby is going to survive," Mary said.

The driver looked devastated. "I am so sorry. Nobody told me. I would have—"

"What's your name, son?" Henry interrupted the man's apology.

"Douglas, sir, and again I really am—"

"We don't know this area well. Would you be available to be our driver while we are here? We're not worried about the cost. It'll be for a couple of days."

Mary, suddenly concerned, turned to her husband. "But we might—"

"I know, honey." He patted her hand. "If we have to stay longer, we'll get a rental, if needs be."

"I'll have to go home at night. I live about thirty minutes from here," Doug said. "We have a newborn ourselves, but I can be yours from dawn till dusk."

Henry smiled back at the driver's reflection in the rear-view mirror.

At the mention of the driver's newborn, Mary again dissolved into tears.

"Oh heck," Doug mumbled.

CHAPTER
THREE

The drive to Glenwood Springs passed without a word. Doug, still mortified, dared not utter anything. The Trapps stared out of their respective windows in complete silence. They passed through some of the most breathtaking scenery in the country, but were too deep within their own dark, colourless worlds to notice.

*

Doug pulled in front of the Glenwood Police Station and sprang out of the SUV to open the door for Mary. He then started heading to the other side of the car, but Henry had already managed by himself.

"Don't worry about me." Henry stepped out of the vehicle. "I'll call you when we're done here. Okay?"

"I'll just wait here."

Henry handed him a twenty. "Go get yourself something to eat."

"Wow! Thanks, Mr Trapp."

"The name's Henry. We are gonna be part of each other's lives for the next few days, so – just Henry."

Doug nodded as Henry joined his wife on the station steps. He took her hand as they walked into the building.

After spending about five minutes in a modern yet utilitarian waiting room, a uniformed officer walked in. Sheriff G. Massey introduced himself to the couple, then escorted them to a small conference room on the second floor.

The sheriff was in his mid-fifties and looked exactly that. Not a young man, but not yet old. He carried his six-foot frame well with only the slightest trace of a paunch. He felt that as God had let him keep his hair, a little extra weight round the middle was a fair trade.

"Coffee, tea, soda?" His deep baritone filled the small space even at low volume.

"Thanks, but no. We're fine," Henry replied.

Massey was just about to take his seat.

"I wouldn't mind a glass of water?" Mary asked.

Massey opened a credenza behind him revealing a small fridge filled with bottled water and soda.

"You sure, Mr Trapp?" He gestured to the contents of the fridge.

"Is that Dr Pepper in the back there?"

Massey laughed. "Sure is. I try to hide them as it's my favourite as well." He noticed Henry's look of concern. "Not to worry. I got cases of the stuff on the first floor. In fact, I might as well join you."

He found a second bottle, well hidden behind an untouched RC Cola. After distributing the drinks along with a paper cup for each, he sat at the head of the table and took a long pull at the Doctor P before focusing on the Trapps.

"It goes without saying that I am truly sorry for your loss, and wish that wasn't the reason you were both here today, but dammit, it is."

Mary gave him a weak and forced smile. "Thank you. Can you tell us what happened?"

Massey took a deep breath, and was clearly looking for the right words. "Like I said on the phone, they were both killed on the level crossing, eight miles out of town. They were in their car when they were hit. Unfortunately, it was the Starliner."

They both looked questioningly back at him.

"The Starliner is an express."

Mary seemed frustrated by the statement. "Why does that make it more unfortunate?"

"Most of what we get on that line is freight. Trains half a mile long. On the stretch where your sister and her husband were struck, they would be doing less than twenty miles an hour. Plenty of time for the driver to see them and maybe even slow down a bit."

"Maybe even stop?" Mary asked.

"No. Sadly a half mile of train takes a hell of a long time to come to a full stop. Something to do with inertia. The damage to their car could have been a lot less though, maybe even survivable, but with an express doing just short of a hundred, well—"

"Not survivable?" Henry said.

Massey simply nodded.

"But it was a gated crossing, right?" Henry asked.

"Yup." Massey took another swig from his drink and was about to put it down again, then drained the balance.

"How the hell can anyone get stuck between the gates? And even if they did, there must be time to get out of the car? Hell, you'd drive around or right through the gates if you wanted to!" Henry stated.

The sheriff took a long look at the two facing him, their features reflecting their need for some concrete fact or answer.

"Yes, you could, if you wanted to, unless maybe if the car was broke down," Massey added.

Mary stared hard back at him. "Was the car broken down, Sheriff?"

"There's still a lot of things being investigated. We don't have all the pieces of this puzzle yet, and I don't want to spin you folks a web of conjecture, just to try to give you the answers you need."

Mary tried to keep her voice calm. "Was the car broken down?"

Massey looked her straight in the eyes. "No! There were a baker's dozen witnesses out there at the scene and all agreed that the car's engine was running right up until impact."

The Trapps looked anxiously back at him. They wanted more.

"It appears they weren't even in the traffic lane until just before the accident. They were in a lay-by just a short spell down the road.

"Seems like they were waiting for something. Then they pulled into the street, drove onto the tracks and sat there with the engine running till the crossing gates came down."

The only sound in the room was the battery-operated clock on the wall moving the second hand in one-second increments.

Tic, tic, tic.

After what seemed like a week of silence, Massey rose from his chair. "I booked you in at the Glenwood Plaza Hotel. It's late. You've had a long trip and I think we should continue this in the morning. It's not something we need to finish talking about tonight.

"Let's get a fresh start first thing. The restaurant in the hotel is open late and the food's pretty good."

He waited for them to make a move.

"What about the baby?" Mary asked.

"He's fine. He's healthy, even though premature. He's one lucky kid."

"Lucky? His parents are dead," Mary said.

"True, but he isn't. I consider that lucky."

Mary looked about to add something more, but Henry got to his feet and held out his hand to Massey.

"Thank you, Sheriff. This has been a long day for everyone." They shook hands as Mary rose, and after a brief nod of agreement, headed for the door.

"You'll be able to see him tomorrow if you're ready. It's too late tonight. Hospital rules."

Mary stopped in her tracks. "Why wouldn't we be ready?"

"He's two months premature. He's got a heap of machines plugged into him to keep him alive. It's never an easy thing to see."

"I still don't see why you think I wouldn't be ready. That's my sister's child!"

The stress was starting to show.

Massey gave her a patient and understanding nod. "Goodnight, Mrs Trapp, Mr Trapp. Let's say nine a.m. tomorrow. Okay with you both?"

"Yes. Thank you, Sheriff," Henry answered for the pair. He then led Mary out of the conference room.

Massey watched them go. He was not looking forward to the second part of the conversation.

CHAPTER
FOUR

Douglas pulled up just as they exited the police station. He had downed a pair of chicken tacos and a Pepsi. He had done the best he could to air out the SUV before getting back to them.

"Sorry about the food smell."

Henry smiled. "Never apologise for the smell of good food, son."

"It was good, too!" Doug added. "Where to now, folks?"

"Somewhere called the Glenwood Plaza Hotel," Henry replied. "Any good?"

"Oh man! It's the best in town!"

Mary rolled her eyes, soliciting a nudge and mini glare from Henry.

The two didn't say a word as he drove them the quarter mile to the hotel. He was hoping that they would be impressed when they saw it.

Dusk was falling and pretty faux oil lamps lit up the town's main streets. Doug knew it was almost too 'postcard' pretty, but he still got a kick when folks saw it for the first time.

He stole a quick glance in the mirror, and was disappointed to see that both of his passengers seemed to have closed their eyes. Whether in sleep or just to avoid seeing any more reality for the moment, they were gonna miss the view.

Halfway down the main drag, Doug pulled the car into a sweeping drive that curved up to the Glenwood Plaza Hotel.

Built in the late 1800s the massive European-styled period structure looked down over the surrounding town. Twin bell towers dominated the central part of the hotel. The hotel was built as a giant U. In the centre was an extensive manicured garden.

Doug smiled, knowing his passengers could not ignore the grandeur of this place. Especially now, as its red tile roof took on a dark purple hue as dusk became night.

He checked the mirror and saw that they were both fast asleep.

"We're here."

No reaction.

"We're here, Henry." Louder this time.

They both opened their eyes and after a moment getting their bearings, looked out of the window.

"Quite something, huh?" Doug offered proudly. "It was built in eighteen—"

"Holy shit! It's the Overlook Hotel!!" Mary interrupted. "Perfect! Just bloody perfect!"

Doug cringed and drove the rest of the way up to the majestically arcaded entry in silence. He knew that it did look a little like the hotel in Stanley Kubrick's psychological horror film, *The Shining*, but most people thought that was kind of cool. Her reaction was a first.

*

Once checked in, they found that the sheriff had not been entirely honest –the restaurant didn't stay open late. However, the Skyview lounge bar was still open.

Clad in gleaming dark woods with green leather armchairs, the feel was more like vintage Atlantic Ocean liner rather than a hotel bar in a small town in Colorado. The room was empty, save for the bartender who gave them a warm smile as they entered.

"Evening, folks. What can I get you?"

Neither could answer as they were both trying to digest the fact that the bartender looked, though younger, just a fraction too similar to the one in *The Shining*. He noticed their expressions. "How are things going, Mr Torrance?"

The bartender's impression of the infamous Lloyd, the movie's bartender, was spot on. He then immediately noticed that the Trapps had not seen the humour and were both looking a bit creeped out.

"Just kidding, folks. A lot of people think I look like Lloyd. Plus, this big old hotel, and you being the only ones in the bar tonight! I promise you, I'm no relation and as far as I know, there isn't a single ghost in the place. I'm Brad and I'm here to serve."

He gave them an open and warm smile that instantly dispelled the earlier creepiness.

"But I still wouldn't stay in room 237!"

"You're a funny guy, Brad!" Henry said as he wagged his finger at him as if he'd been a naughty child.

Mary had seen nothing amusing about the recent exchange. "Is the kitchen still open?"

"Not fully, but we can do sandwiches, salads or a hot dish."

"What's the hot dish?" Henry looked hopeful.

"This late it'll be whatever the night guy can scrounge around and put over a flame. Probably pasta." Brad seemed almost apologetic.

"Great sales job there, Brad," Mary said. "I'm starving and certainly don't want a damn salad. Put me down for a pasta. Actually, we'll both have the same."

Henry was about to say something but he changed his mind.

"What can I get you to drink?"

"Wine," Mary said.

Brad reached for a wine list.

"Do you have a 'Stag's Leap Cab'?" Mary got straight to the point.

Brad smiled at her ordering efficiency. "We sure do. It's a 2012. That's supposed to be—"

"Is it alcoholic and drinkable?" Mary was direct.

"Yes, it is."

"Then get one opened!" She looked around the empty room then back at Brad. "Anywhere?"

"Yes ma'am. You can sit at the bar if you like."

"We'll grab a table. We have to talk over some stuff," Henry smiled.

Brad gestured to the twenty-two empty tables dotted around the bar.

*

The wine arrived and the two downed their first glass as if it were a matter of life or death.

The bottle was empty by the time their dinner arrived. The service was not by any means slow. Their drinking was just that fast. They weren't imbibing for pleasure. They were after the blessed deadening effect the alcohol would offer them. They could have gone with a couple of Jägermeister boilermakers to speed up the process, but felt that would have been pretty low class.

Getting smashed on expensive wine however, now that was classy!

As Brad placed their dinners before them with great panache, Henry signalled that the empty bottle in the wine bucket needed a mate. A full one.

Having both ordered the pasta which was the only hot option, they hadn't held up much hope, considering the late hour and that the head chef had probably gone home some time ago.

What arrived was nothing short of spectacular. Plain white over-sized bowls held glistening portions of bucatini with multicoloured vine tomatoes, charbroiled shrimp, mini mozzarella balls and basil leaves that had all been tossed in a chilli and sun-dried tomato oil. The result was a melee of colour and aroma.

They both took their first bite at the same time then stared at each other in shock.

"Oh my God!" Henry mumbled, his mouth full.

"I know!" Mary agreed, her mouth even fuller.

Not another word was attempted until their bowls held no more than a thin sheen of chilli oil.

Mary drained her wine glass (again), and flopped back into the soft leather. "That really helped. I feel almost human."

Henry nodded. "Me too. Albeit, a very full and somewhat inebriated human." Mary looked like she was trying to work out how to say something.

"Out with it." Henry prodded.

Mary took a deep breath before proceeding. "Did you pick up anything odd about the sheriff?"

"Odd how?"

Brad appeared tableside. "Can I get you anything else?"

"No, thank you. That was really fantastic. If that's what comes from a quick scrounge around, I can't wait to see what the kitchen can do with a little forethought!" Henry replied, patting his happy tummy.

"Actually, you got lucky. The exec chef was still here planning the menu for a big banquet next week."

"Well, please thank him for a truly uplifting meal. You have no idea how much we needed it," Henry said.

Brad removed their plates and other post-meal detritus then left them alone.

"He didn't seem to want to be very forthright with the details, did he?" Mary asked.

"I think he didn't want to hit us with everything all at once. I'm sure he's gonna tell us everything tomorrow," Henry replied.

"What about the fact that they just sat there until the train hit them? Does that sound like Ellen to you?"

"No. But we don't have all the pieces yet, do we?"

"According to the sheriff, they drove onto the tracks, left the engine running then waited for the train," Mary insisted.

"I know, but let's just see what tomorrow brings, okay? There's nothing we can do tonight, and there would be nothing worse than for us to start hypothesizing about it without all the details."

"Evening, folks!"

They both almost jumped out of their chairs.

"Whoa! Sorry if I gave you two a start. I wanted to bring you both a little glass of Calvados to help you digest those pastas. I'm Jerry White. I do the cooking around here."

Jerry placed a couple of snifters of amber liquid in front of Mary and Henry. He was the exact opposite of one's expectation of an executive chef. He was thin as a rail and must have been over six and a half feet tall.

Though clearly nudging the post middle-aged years, his voice was still youthful with an almost sing-song quality to it. He was casually dressed in jeans and a grey fleece top. He had changed out of his executive chef tunic after the main dinner service.

"I really didn't mean to interrupt, but Brad mentioned how much you enjoyed my food and that deserves a reward in my book."

Having regained his composure, but not his sobriety, Henry got shakily to his feet and shook the other man's hand. "On the contrary. We owe you. That was a truly delicious meal. May just be the best pasta I've ever had."

Mary nodded in complete agreement.

"Well thank you, both. I hope you enjoy your stay."

Jerry started to walk away. He hesitated, then turned back to the table again. His face had taken on a far more serious expression.

"I really don't want to pry, but I couldn't help overhearing a snippet of your conversation when I walked over here. You were talking about that awful accident a few days ago?"

They both looked up at him with a mix of curiosity and concern at being overheard.

"I was a friend of Ellen's. I give a cooking class up here every Monday afternoon. Have done for almost twelve years. Ellen's been coming to my class for ten of those. We became friends. Both her and Zeke. They used to cook for me every so often. It was a real pleasure dining with those two. They just loved life."

"Ellen is…was my sister," Mary said.

"Oh crap!" Jerry paled still further. "I didn't mean to intrude. I just—"

"Please." She gestured to the chair across from her.

Jerry eased himself into the offered chair. "I didn't even know she had family beyond Zeke. To be fair, I never gave it much thought and she never brought it up."

He reached across to the next table and grabbed a linen napkin from an unused place setting. He used it to wipe his brow. He suddenly looked ten years older.

Henry looked on with concern. "You okay?"

Jerry offered up a half-hearted smile. "I'm fine." He searched for the right words. "Just a little sad and a little troubled."

He looked over at the pair staring back at him.

"Listen to me talk such nonsense! Here you are, in full shock and mourning, and I'm telling you about my feelings. That's what age does to you. You start thinking that everyone wants to hear about your own problems."

"Clearly you haven't spent much time on social media. Narcissism is the new humility," Mary stated. "You said you were troubled. Care to elaborate a little?"

Jerry seemed to give the request deep consideration. Having reached a decision, he looked to the bar. "Brad, would you please pour me a Calvados as well?" They all waited for Brad to deliver the drink before continuing.

"Brad, would you be so kind as to take your break now? I'm gonna have a little conversation with these kind folks."

"No problem, Chef." He placed the snifter in front of Jerry. "Everything all right?"

"Absopositively!" Jerry looked up at him and gave him a stage wink. "Gonna divulge the secret to my pasta recipe."

"You mean the chipotle paste you add at the end?"

Jerry laughed. "Why, you cheeky little SOB. Go take your break."

"Sure, Chef. No problem." He started to head back to the kitchen. "Want me to bring over the bottle?"

Jerry looked to the others questioningly. They both shook their heads adamantly.

"I guess that's a no," Jerry smiled as Brad left the room.

"Jeez but that boy takes after his father. I hope he gets himself together earlier in life than his dad did. All he cared about were girls, pot and skiing."

"What happened to his father?" Henry asked.

"He finally grew up around thirty-five, got himself into the CIA—"

Henry and Mary both looked wide-eyed back at him.

"Not that CIA, the Culinary Institute of America. It's the gold standard for learning the culinary arts in the US. If you survive there, you can cook pretty much wherever you want. Like right here in Glenwood Springs!"

It took a moment for the penny to drop.

Jerry raised his snifter in a toast. "To my wayward son!"

They all clinked glasses then drank.

The moment of levity quickly drifted away leaving an awkward silence in its place.

"Please understand—," Jerry began hesitantly. "What I am going to tell you could easily be the ramblings of someone who has spent too much time in overheated kitchens. In fact, I don't know what it is that I am trying to tell you."

He looked to the others for some sign of patience, or at least understanding of his situation.

He got neither.

"I think something happened to Ellen and Zeke."

"That we know!" Mary remarked sarcastically.

"That's not what I mean. Something happened to them before the accident – or whatever you want to call it." He took a serious gulp of his drink before continuing. "They were the most carefree couple I have ever known. Free-spirited, non-conventional—"

"That's for sure!" Mary couldn't help herself.

"Obviously you knew them, at least Ellen, better than anybody."

"I used to know Ellen. I knew the driven, ambitious Ellen. I cannot in all honesty claim to know the woman who ran off, quit her job, her friends, and her family, just to live in a log cabin and grow sage or whatever."

Jerry smiled. "Lavender. She grew lavender. Sold it online too."

Mary's glare let Jerry know that she had no interest in the minutia of her sister's cottage industry.

Jerry should have done a better job at reading his audience and stopped there. Maybe it was the Calvados but for whatever reason, he chose to swim further into the rapidly chilling waters.

"Whether you agree with her choices or not, doesn't change the fact that the two of them were incredibly happy."

"They were hippies! Of course they were happy. Jesus!" Mary replied.

Henry tried to hold her hand to calm her down, but she shook his off without even looking at him.

"Please understand, I am not trying to condone or change your personal opinion about Ellen and Zeke's lifestyle. I'm only telling you what you already knew about Ellen, before—" Jerry looked for the right words, as he forged bravely (and blindly) on.

"About seven months ago, things changed. She became – detached! I guess that's the best way to describe it. She still came to my classes, at least for a while, but she seemed to be doing so out of habit rather than enjoyment. She'd lost her sparkle." He glanced nervously at Ellen in case his choice of adjective brought on another attack.

Mary simply shrugged her tacit acceptance.

27

"Shortly after that, she and Zeke had me over for one of their chef-night dinners. It was one of the most surreal evenings I think I've ever had. They weren't themselves. They talked like they used to talk but – there was no passion or even focus. Even the food was incredibly average. It was as if they had done the least possible, just to get it on the plate."

"Sounds like every dinner at our house." Henry winked at Mary.

"Fuck you, darling." She winked back.

"Then about six weeks later," Jerry continued, "she took me aside after the class – the last one she attended by the way, and told me that she was pregnant and wouldn't be able to come to the hotel any more.

"I tried to find out why one negated the other, but Ellen couldn't seem to find the words. The more she tried to explain what she was feeling, the more distant she became. I suggested that maybe she should talk to someone. Someone professional. She just glared at me. I mean really glared! Before I could do or say anything, she grabbed her bag and ran out of the kitchen. That was the last time I saw her."

Silence filled the bar as the Trapps digested Jerry's words.

"Depression during pregnancy isn't that unusual. Neither is nesting and wanting to just stay home," Mary offered, breaking the silence.

"Five months later," Jerry continued, "I ran into Zeke at the market. He looked twenty years older. He'd grown a beard. Grown his hair. He was wearing his usual clothes, but – they just – looked kinda dirty. Also, I couldn't swear to it, but I think he smelled – stale.

"I asked him if everything was all right, and he just nodded. I asked about Ellen, and he did the same. Just nodded. I told him that if they were having problems, there were people, myself included, who could help. He laughed at me. Not a jolly laugh. It was kind of creepy. I told him that they could call me any time to just talk or whatever. He then gave me the same long stare that Ellen had given me. Then he said, 'There's no point. We're not meant to be part of it.' Then he walked out of the store. Left his shopping cart in the middle of the aisle and just walked out. "I spoke to the sheriff the next day," Jerry continued. "He basically told me that I was worrying for nothing. He felt that they both, having been a couple of stress-free stoners, had simply been hit smack in the head with reality. He thought that parenthood had probably just freaked the hell out of them. The thought of having to turn into normal, boring people with real-life responsibilities was a lot for them to cope with.

"I decided the sheriff was probably right. What he said made a lot of sense. I stopped worrying about them and gave them their space. Then I heard about the accident."

Jerry looked from Mary to Henry trying to gauge their reaction to his words. They seemed uneasy, but he wasn't sure if it was because of the story or because of him.

"I'm not sure I understand what you're trying to say." Henry spoke for them both. "Do you think that Ellen being pregnant played a part in what happened?"

"As I said before, I don't know what all of it meant. I just thought you both should know that something was off. The way they were acting was just weird."

"I don't wish to be rude, but I think I knew my own sister a little better than you. If you ask me, Ellen and Zeke began acting weird the moment they met. No mystery – just a couple of messed-up people."

Jerry looked mortified. "I didn't mean to – I just thought—"

"No. I don't think you did think!" Henry joined in.

"I can't apologise enough to you both. I just thought you should know."

"Know what?" Mary's expression was glacial.

"I was just trying to help." Jerry reached for the leather folder with their dinner bill inside. "I hope you will at least let me comp your meals."

"Not tonight." Henry gently took back the folder and signed the bill without checking it. "I think you've done enough tonight."

Henry helped his wife to her feet.

Henry gave him a tight-lipped smile. "Still the best pasta ever. Stick to cooking!"

Jerry just stared after them. He was trying to decide why he had said what he had.

He finished his drink, but instead of returning to the kitchen and his office, he just sat there. He couldn't work out why he had done that. To complete strangers! Finally, tired of his own self-recrimination, he rose from his chair.

Then it hit him. Hard. He suddenly knew why he had felt the need to tell them his story. It wasn't that he felt they should be informed. It was that they needed to be warned.

CHAPTER
FIVE

The next morning, Mary and Henry were back in the police station waiting room.

Henry was reading an article about the new Hybrid Porsche SUV.

Mary was sitting bolt upright, her hands clasped in her lap. She kept glancing over to her husband, but he was too engrossed in the car's specs.

"Are you ready to talk about last night?" she whispered.

"There's nothing to discuss."

"I disagree."

Henry put down the magazine and turned to her. "Okay. What's to discuss?"

"You heard him. They were both acting pretty freaky. Could that have something to do with – what happened?"

Henry turned so he could look directly at her. "I have never said this to you before, and I don't want it held against me, but as you alluded to last night, your sister and Zeke were always pretty freaky."

"That's not true. I was just making a point for that chef guy. Besides, he was talking a whole different type of freaky. They were happy, even goofy freaky. That chef—what he was saying sounded like something much darker."

"Oh please! What does he know!?"

"He was a friend of hers," Mary said.

"Did Ellen ever mention him? Have you considered that the guy might just be full of shit?"

"God, I hope you all aren't talking about me," Sheriff Massey exclaimed as he entered the room. "Come upstairs and we can finish our little chat."

He led them to his office on the top floor. Other than asking how they slept, no other words were shared until they were all seated. Though certainly not what one would call large, Massey's office was both functional and somehow cosy. The walls were dotted with family pictures, Native American art and a surprisingly expansive collection of awards, accreditations and certificates of achievement.

They sat in a small seating area, furnished with a studded leather sofa and two matching armchairs. A can of Dr Pepper and a bottle of water were already in place on a small coffee table. It was obvious that he was trying to put them as much at ease as was possible.

Massey grabbed a file folder from his desk, then sat in one of the armchairs.

"How's the hotel?"

"It's a hotel," Henry said.

Massey raised an eyebrow.

"Sorry! It was fine. We're just a little off today."

"Quite understandable." He looked to each of them in turn.

"Right then." He pushed ahead. "There is a whole heap of forensics that still need to be completed, but I do have a preliminary report right here." He waved the file folder.

"May we see it?" Mary held out her hand.

"'Fraid not. As I said, this is just a preliminary report. We don't make those public. Too many suppositions!" He paused. "What I can do is tell you verbally the gist of the findings so far. I hope that will suffice."

"And if it doesn't?" Mary wasn't giving an inch.

"Let's hear what the sheriff has to say, okay?" Henry suggested.

Mary reluctantly nodded.

"Right then." He opened the folder. "Basically, the initial findings show that Ellen and Zeke Darnell were both killed as a result of having had their car impacted by a passenger train travelling at a high rate of speed.

"Ellen Darnell had been driving the car. Zeke Darnell was in the passenger seat. The car was stationary between the level-crossing gates, which had both descended, as is normal when a train is approaching. The engine of the car, a 2012 Ford Focus, was functional, and powered on at the time of the incident."

Massey took a moment to check on his audience. They were both literally at the edge of their seats. Paler than when they arrived, and clearly dreading, yet craving, any additional details.

Massey continued. "After taking a total of fifteen witness statements from other drivers waiting at the crossing, two hikers standing at the crossing, and the train engineer, it is clear that the vehicle was intentionally driven to the area between the crossing gates, bridging both sets of railway tracks.

"The vehicle, once in position, was placed in park, and the occupants intentionally remained within the vehicle. There was no attempt to drive or move the car. There was also no attempt made to exit the vehicle prior to impact.

"Due to the position of the vehicle on the tracks, the vehicle was struck on the right, or passenger side. The impact was substantial and devastating to the vehicle and the passengers within. The gas tank was ruptured and the resulting explosion—"

"Stop. Please." Mary pleaded.

Henry reached over and held out his hand. She took it and held it tightly. "Does this have to be quite so clinical?"

The sheriff placed the folder on the coffee table and looked to both of them. "No, it doesn't. I apologise. I thought you would have wanted to hear the specifics. I should have warned you."

"How about skipping to the end?" Henry suggested.

"Do you want to hear the causes of death?"

"Other than the train?" Mary shot back.

Massey picked up the file and flipped to almost the last page. "The preliminary finding is that Mr and Mrs Darnell drove intentionally onto the railroad tracks for the sole purpose of ending their lives.

"At this time, the investigation into the reasons for such action is ongoing, however after initial investigation, it appears that both Mr and Mrs Darnell had been suffering from long-term depression and general malaise. A cause or trigger for these conditions has not been formally confirmed. Investigation has shown, however, that the symptoms may have started at roughly the same time as Mrs Darnell's pregnancy. There is no record of either victim having sought treatment or counselling for their conditions."

Massey flipped the file shut then studied the pair. "I'm really sorry, but everything so far indicates that this was a double suicide."

"Ellen was a Buddhist! She would not commit suicide," Mary insisted.

The sheriff held his hands up in mock surrender. "I can only interpret the facts as presented to me. Let me say though, speaking from long experience, we don't know shit when it comes to understanding what people are really thinking. None of us knows what goes on within the minds of our family and friends. We only see the thin veneer that they permit us to see. Behind euphoric joy, there can lurk horrendous suffering.

"I hope that we can find out what caused these two people to feel they only had one alternative on that day, but you have to be prepared for the fact that we may never know what led them onto those tracks.

"One thing I do know is that by some joyous miracle, a child was born from that horror. That is who we should be focusing on now. Not on those that can no longer be helped. Rather, on someone who needs all the help we can give."

He looked over at Mary who returned his gaze unwaveringly. Her eyes were red-rimmed and ready to tear. "Thank you, Sheriff. What do we need to do now?"

"Nothing. Your sister's body won't be released for at least a couple of weeks until the inquest winds down, and a judge has ruled on the verdict. We can talk about arrangements closer to that time."

"What about Zeke?" Henry asked.

"His mother is going to make the arrangements. His ashes will go back to Vermont."

Mary looked surprised. "They won't be buried together?"

"They are both to be cremated and returned to their places of birth. It was in their living wills."

"Thank you very much for your time." Henry shook Massey's hand then started to lead Mary from the office.

Massey stood by the open door. "The hospital is expecting you. Go spend time with the child."

Mary seemed reluctant to leave. "May I ask one more thing?"

Massey nodded.

"Don't I need to identify – the body?"

"No. That is being done forensically."

Mary looked at him questioningly. "May I at least say goodbye to her?"

"The accident was, as you know, severe. The injuries were—"

He had no more words.

"I know she was badly hurt, but please understand, I would like to see her face one last time," Mary gently pushed.

"I really am sorry, Mrs Trapp, but I cannot permit that."

Henry tried to usher her out of the door, but without success. "Please, Mary. We should go."

"I don't believe you have that authority, Sheriff," Mary insisted.

"Actually, I do. When I believe that an action will cause undue pain or damage."

"I already know she's dead. How much more pain could my seeing her one last time actually cause?"

Massey looked almost pleadingly over at Henry.

"Sheriff! I want to see my sister's face one last time!"

"No. I can't allow it," he replied as gently as possible.

"Why?" she demanded angrily.

The sheriff took a while to respond. "She doesn't have a face any more, Mrs Trapp."

*

They sat alone outside the police station on one of many brightly painted wooden benches that were sprinkled around the town. Henry had his arm around her as she stared, unseeing, towards the distant mountain peaks. "You know he was right, don't you?"

She turned to him. "Yeah. I do. I just didn't—"

"I know." He gave her a squeeze.

"What did he mean by forensically?"

Henry took a moment to gauge her current stability.

"Dental records, DNA—stuff like that."

Mary nodded and offered him as brave a smile as she could muster. A thought suddenly hit her. "Maybe it's not Ellen. They haven't confirmed that yet, have they?"

She looked hopefully over at Henry.

"It's her. You know it is."

Mary stared down at her lap. "But isn't there a slim chance?"

"I really would love to tell you there was, but she was known by half the witnesses to the accident. It was Ellen."

Mary took a deep breath and nodded her acceptance. The two sat in silence for a good few minutes.

"You feeling up to seeing the baby?" Henry broke the silence.

Mary bit her lip as she again nodded.

Henry looked to his left at the small parking lot and waved his arm. Doug flashed the SUV's lights then started the engine.

CHAPTER
SIX

The hospital was clearly new. It was spread across acres of manicured wooded land. Real money had been spent on making the functional form of the building blend into the high Colorado terrain.

Doug pulled up at the main reception area. He opened the vehicle door for Mary, but she just sat there. Doug looked to Henry for direction.

"You okay? We don't have to do this." Henry held her arm as he spoke. "We can come back later if you want, or not at all. It's up to you."

She offered him a forced smile. "Come on then. Let's do this."

She exited the SUV, followed immediately by Henry. They walked through the automatic glass doors and headed directly to the reception desk.

The inside of the building was as pleasantly designed as the exterior. Earth tones and natural building materials abounded. Very expensive and clearly custom-commissioned art hung from every wall.

The dark wood reception desk was topped with black granite. It held specs of gold within its surface. Against the cold darkness of the slab, these shone almost like little stars.

The receptionist was Native American. She had long, straight hair that reached her waist.

"Good morning." She welcomed the couple with a brief but dazzling glimpse of whiter than white, perfect teeth.

Henry returned the smile, minus the extreme bleaching. "Hi. I'm Henry Trapp, and this is my wife, Mary. I believe you were expecting us?"

Her smooth receptionist demeanour unravelled just a fraction. "Yes, we are, and may I say how sorry I am about what happened."

"Thank you," Mary replied.

"If you'll take the elevator to the third floor, the duty nurse will meet you and take you to the neonatal unit." She gestured towards the elevator lobby just a few feet away.

"Thank you," Henry smiled. "I think we can find our way from here."

It took the receptionist a few seconds to realise he was joking. Her sparkling white teeth parted, releasing a surprisingly loud snort-laugh.

Henry tried to keep a straight face as he led Mary towards the elevators. Once inside, Henry immediately noticed that the usual intolerable Muzak had been replaced with eerily beautiful Native American flute music.

He would have happily stayed and listened to more, as even the few seconds of it had brought on a sense of inner peace.

He realised, not for the first time, that living on a diet of Rush and The Killers, did little towards helping him gain any inner relaxation.

Then again, it would be a bitch to try to rock out to flute music, Jethro Tull being the obvious exception!

As the elevator doors opened they were greeted by a very fit-looking man in green scrubs.

Amos Carter gave them both another ultra-white dental experience. Judging by his physique, hair, and of course, teeth, it was blatantly clear that Mr Carter took his appearance seriously.

"Hi. I'm Nurse Carter." His voice matched the overall scheme. Manly and precise.

Henry was about to make a quip about him being a male nurse like Gaylord Focker (*Meet the Parents*), but Mary's radar for perceiving Henry's tendency for a verbal faux pas, was at full power.

"It's nice to meet you." She dove in just in time.

After the introductions, they were led to the small ICU for preemies.

There was something sad about a room filled with mechanical wonders, all designed to keep the tiny, premature babies alive. Not sad that they were keeping them alive, just devastating that such tiny, innocent beings should have to start their lives in such a clinical way.

On that day, there were only two incubators in use. Henry hoped that maybe, up in Eagle country, there were fewer babies brought into the world too early. That wasn't actually the case at all. It was just a quiet day.

Nurse Carter showed them to one of the incubators.

Every attempt had been made to swaddle the poor infant in layers of snuggly blankets. Most of him had to still remain uncovered so the machines that were keeping him in this world had access to prod, poke and oxygenate.

He was so incredibly small. His skin was wrinkled, and just a few shades too red. His little face was scrunched up tightly, as if trying to remember something vitally important.

Henry suddenly realised that the baby looked way too like Mr Magoo. He felt his face beginning to form into a smile, but realised that nothing good could come of his sharing the Magoo revelation.

"My god, he's so small!" Mary whispered.

"He's pretty average for seven months. He'll grow like a sapling starting in a few weeks," Carter explained. "Are you planning to adopt him?"

There it was. Out in the open for everyone to see and hear. The subconscious spectre had been lurking in the dark recesses of both their brains since they heard about the accident.

They both looked at the nurse with a mix of shock and guilt.

Henry was the first to break the silence. "We really haven't had a chance to give that much thought."

He looked to Mary for some sort of acknowledgement. She ignored him and kept her eyes on the infant.

"We're not the parenting type." Mary's voice held no emotion.

"That's a load of crap, pardon my French," Nurse Carter exclaimed. "Everyone has the parenting gene somewhere."

"We traded ours in for red wine and non-child-friendly furniture," Henry shot back then looked to Mary for a reprimand.

Instead she raised her eyebrows, and nodded tacit approval of his statement.

"It would be your loss," Carter added as his final comment on the subject.

A silence ensued, interrupted only by the ticking, pumping and whirring of the various machines.

Mary couldn't take her eyes off the baby.

"Can I hold him?" she uttered, much to Henry's complete surprise.

"Sadly no," Carter replied. "At least not outside of the incubator. He can't leave it, but you can use the access ports so long as you are gloved."

Mary looked to Henry for reassurance. Henry was still shocked by her wanting to hold the child in the first place. Mary had always been almost child phobic.

Carter helped Mary put on a pair of long purple nitrile gloves. He then opened the twin access ports and Mary hesitantly reached both arms into the incubator.

"It's really warm in here!" she exclaimed.

Carter smiled. "That's kinda the point."

Henry looked on with an expression of wonder. This was way out of type for his wife.

With butterfly-like gentleness, she stroked the baby's arm. He rolled slightly towards her hand. This momentarily freaked her out, until Carter explained that that was completely normal.

"A baby craves the human touch."

Mary felt the arm again, then moved her hand towards the child's. Almost in slow motion, the baby closed his entire hand around one of Mary's fingers.

Mary let out an involuntary gasp and gently tried to pull her hand away. The baby kept hold.

"He likes you," Carter said.

Mary kept her hand in place until he slowly released her finger. He then yawned contentedly.

Mary withdrew her arms and turned to Henry. Tears were streaming down her cheek.

"You okay?"

All she could do was nod. Such were her emotions, she knew if she tried to speak, she would burst into tears.

"You're not. Are you?"

Henry looked into Mary's red-rimmed eyes for a long time.

Finally, Mary managed one word.

"No."

"Oh shit! Well, I'm not gonna drive a damn minivan," Henry stated as he approached the incubator. "Right, Gaylord. Glove me." He held his arms out to the nurse. Carter was grinning from ear to ear.

CHAPTER
SEVEN

Once in the SUV, they sat close together in the back, holding each other's hands.

Doug took a quick glance at the couple in the rearview mirror.

"Hope you don't mind my asking, but I was wondering if you knew how long you'll be staying in Glenwood Springs?"

"Getting bored with our company, Doug?" Henry asked.

"God no, Mr— sorry, Henry. Just wondering if you'll be here long enough for me to show you some of the sights?"

"You have sights here, Doug?" Mary joined the banter. "We most certainly do. The hot springs alone are amazing."

"We are actually leaving first thing tomorrow, but I'll make you a deal. When we come back in about six to eight weeks, if you agree to be our driver again, you can show us these hot springs of yours."

"Deal!" Doug replied. "Remember to bring swim suits!"

Henry and Mary both did mini cringes at the concept of public bathing.

"We had some good news today, Doug. I think it's fitting that you be the first to know, considering what a miserable pair we have been." Mary leaned forward in her seat.

"No way! You guys have been great. You want to talk miserable – try driving some of the Kardashians around for three days straight."

"Which ones?" Mary was curious.

"Haven't got a clue. Not a fan."

"Why were they here?" Mary prodded.

"Apparently, one of them wrote a book," Doug replied. "I was surprised any of them could even read. Unless of course it was written on a mirror."

All three laughed.

"We are gonna be parents!" Mary announced.

"Nice one, Mrs Trapp! I gotta tell you, I think I knew. When I picked you guys up from the hospital today you were glowing. You just had that look. Pregnancy is a wonderful thing."

The two smiled at each other, but didn't correct Doug. He seemed so proud of his ability to sense her 'condition'. Why take that away from him?

*

After spending the rest of the day arranging their flight

home, talking to their lawyer regarding adoption, and, without warning, having an X-rated shower together, they decided to stay in the hotel for dinner and give the restaurant a try.

They both knew they had one more thing to do before leaving.

*

After an invigorating couple of martinis back in the bar (there was no sign of Brad), they weaved themselves to the main dining room. They had booked earlier and had a table for two overlooking the arcade and gardens waiting for them.

The dining room was reminiscent of the grand hotels of western Europe. The cream walls were draped with heavy green curtains and matching swags. The tables were set with bright white starched linen. The place settings were antique Sheffield plate, and the glassware, delicate crystal.

Unlike their first night in the hotel bar, the menu in the restaurant was varied and, at least to the Trapps, droolworthy. There was an astonishing array of fresh game making up the daily specials.

Mary went for the venison filet with red wine and loganberry reduction. Henry opted for the boar with sage, sundried tomato and onion stuffing. They ordered a bottle of Opus One Overture. A splurge, but they felt they deserved it.

They were halfway through the bottle when their food arrived. Two servers appeared, each carrying a silver domed plate cover. In unison they placed one in front of each of them, then whisked the tops away revealing their dinners. Then both servers vanished. Their single task completed. As the Trapps stared down at their plates in delighted wonder, the maître d' appeared and checked if there was anything else they needed.

"A million dollars would be nice," Henry joked.

"Yes. Wouldn't it?" The man's expression never changed. He probably had heard that crack close to a million times. "Please enjoy your meal."

"We will." Mary smiled at their host before then giving Henry the infamous glare.

Their food was delicious. Fresh, impeccably prepared and artfully presented.

"Why didn't we know about this place?" Henry asked.

"Because, my love, it's in Colorado."

"Maybe we should do a little research on Colorado and come back for a vacation. I mean, this food is fantastic," Henry suggested.

"Uganda probably has at least one good restaurant too. Does that mean you would like to go there as well?"

Henry did a mini spit take, having just sipped a little of the Opus One.

"Careful, honey," Mary quipped. "You just dribbled about thirty dollars' worth."

He was about to retort, when a familiar figure suddenly loomed over their table.

"How was it?" Jerry asked.

Henry smiled back. "After adding a little ketchup, it was quite tasty."

"I'll have to add that to the sauce." The chef was clearly

48

amused.

Jerry grabbed a chair from a vacant table and pulled it up to theirs. "May I?"

"Of course," Mary responded. "We came here tonight hoping to see you."

"Well I'm glad you did. I have been feeling terrible about last night. I had—"

Mary held up her hand, palm out, to stop him. "No! We are the ones who should feel terrible. Everything you told us was in the police report. It seems everyone knew about their—" She searched for the right word. "Depression. Or whatever."

"Still. I didn't have to hit you both over the head with it." Jerry tried to explain. "My ex-wife used to say that one of my biggest failings was that I never seemed to be able to read the room correctly."

Henry took a sip of wine. "The fact is, if you hadn't told us what you did, when you did, we would have been hit with it without advanced warning. You gave us some background that really helped us digest some of what Sheriff Massey said today. So, thank you."

"Wow!" Jerry was clearly surprised. "Thank you very much for saying that. I still think I was a dumb ass for talking the way I did, but I really am glad you stopped by."

Jerry rose from the chair and started to slide it back to its designated table.

"You may be interested in knowing that we are going to be adopting Ellen's baby," Mary advised.

A darkness crossed Jerry's eyes. Just for a millisecond, but they both saw it.

"Something the matter?" Henry asked.

Jerry forced his brightest smile. "Absolutely nothing. In fact, that maybe the best news I've heard all year. Ellen will be looking down at us right now and be feeling very proud of her sister."

Mary was sincerely moved by his comment. "Thanks, Jerry."

"No. Thank you. And congratulations."

With that, Jerry gave them a perfunctory nod, and headed back to the kitchen.

Henry looked long and hard at Mary to see if there was more to say. She looked right back at him. "Nope. Not a word."

Relieved, Henry signalled to the maître d' for the bill. He came immediately over to the table. "There won't be a bill. The chef has you covered," he whispered. The last thing he wanted was for other diners to hear about comped dinners.

This time they didn't refuse.

*

In the chef's office, Jerry was staring at a picture on his wall. Ellen stood together with six other culinary students, waving happily at the camera.

He felt he should have said something when he heard they were adopting the baby. Then again, he couldn't make that mistake twice. And maybe there really was nothing to tell them.

But inside, he knew different. He recalled the last words Zeke said to him. 'We're not meant to be part of it.'

Jerry's office was right off the kitchen. It must have

been close to a hundred degrees in the small, windowless room, but Jerry sat there alone, feeling suddenly cold as he began to shiver.

CHAPTER
EIGHT

The return trip was uneventful. Their decision to adopt the baby had completely changed their thought patterns. They were having to think of someone else for the first time. Mary especially seemed different. She had gone from being distraught, to being suddenly excited about the prospect of a new little person in their lives.

The sadness over Ellen's death hadn't been vanquished. It was still there just under the surface, but was just cached for later access.

Their heads were now full of all the things they had to tackle in advance of bringing a stranger into their lives.

They wanted their home to be perfect. Not that it wasn't already. Tucked away in the hills of West Hollywood, their remodelled ranch-style house was their pride and joy.

The interior was peaceful and cosy just as they had planned. Black stained and distressed oak floors juxtaposed against the bright white matt walls. Paintings and self-taken photos were everywhere. Overstuffed couches flanked the natural stone fireplace. White plantation shutters covered every window, breaking the sometimes-harsh Los Angeles sun into equidistant, stacked strips of light that played over their furniture and large indoor palms.

*

The next day the two of them stood in the entry hall, clipboards in hand, trying to determine what needed baby-proofing and what could be tweaked enough to be baby-safe, without going to the extreme.

The list was getting longer by the day.

"Are we overthinking this?" Mary asked.

"Probably! Then again, we don't have a clue what we are doing."

"Well that's a nice start," Mary said.

"You think we do?" he threw back.

"Not remotely, but some things should remain unspoken."

"I need to go to work. I can hardly call myself the CEO if I never show up."

"I'm still not clear how you can be the CEO of six people!?" she needled him.

"Smart ass." He gave her a kiss, handed her his clipboard, then headed for the door. "Try not to add too many more things to the list. Please!"

She laughed. "Better safe than sorry."

"Safe! You want us to put our toilet paper in baby-proof cosies! I mean, my god! Toilet paper! What possible trouble could a baby get into with toilet paper?"

"He could eat it!" she suggested.

"So? Maybe that would be a good thing. Maybe his stinky crap would come out all pre-wrapped. In fact, I think that might be something to look into."

"I think you should stick to technical shit not baby shit." She beamed, proud of her retort.

"Some days, the line between the two gets very thin."

"And that's why you are the big boss. Sorry—CEO!"

Henry smacked her butt playfully, then exited the house.

Henry pulled his six-month-old Ford F150 carefully out of the garage. It was a big vehicle to store in a space built for two mid-sized cars, but the snug fit alongside Mary's Prius was a small price to pay for the pleasure he got from the truck.

In the chaotic maelstrom that is Los Angeles, driving something high, visible, and loaded with power, is not a bad thing.

Punks who would usually cut in front of a regular car thought twice about doing such an ass-wipe move when faced with, not just a big truck, but one with mean-looking attitude. With its Fab Four black steel custom front bumper, people realised that risking their pride and joy to gain a two-second advantage in traffic just wouldn't be worth the risk.

Henry cranked up 'Rush, Live in Rio', then eased 'the Terminator', as he had affectionately named the truck, out onto Carlton Way and drove his usual circuitous route to Laurel Canyon.

He loved Rush's 'Live in Rio' concert, but it still hurt to listen to it, knowing that Neil Peart, the band's drummer and lyricist, had recently died, way too young. The world would never hear drumming like that again.

*

Henry's bizarre route was necessitated entirely by the need to avoid Sunset Blvd like the plague.

The famous 'Strip' used to be a regular commuter route for those heading east or west against the hills (Beverly and Hollywood). There were few delays, and driving one of the most photographed roads in the world was kinda fun. Besides, it used to be amusing to see what new level of youthful mummification Angelyne had adopted for her pointless pink billboards.

All that changed about fifteen years earlier when the city allowed almost unlimited multi-unit, new construction along Sunset, from Doheny all the way to Fairfax, dumping thousands of additional cars onto the narrow, four-lane road.

Then, as if enough misery hadn't already been inflicted, they, in an effort to protect tourists from meeting horrible ends at the hands of speeding cars, adjusted the traffic lights to intentionally slow the vehicles to a permanent crawl.

What used to take a couple of minutes to go from Doheny to Laurel Canyon, now could take an hour or more. Locals initially knew all the tricky side streets, so they could still get from A to B.

Then the final insult befell LA. Waze! The innocuous GPS driving app that helped everyone navigate away from congested traffic. Initially it was a great thing. Then, as more Angelenos used the app, every side street option became exposed. Like lemmings, drivers were led from one blocked 'short cut' to another. Before long, any driving east of Doheny became nearly impossible.

Henry had been forced to create his complicated, and due to the size of his ride, hair-raising, route to get over the 'hill' and into the San Fernando Valley where his company's headquarters were located.

Though Henry used the term 'headquarters' and 'offices' whenever talking about his work, a degree of artistic licence (or just plain lying) was involved.

His company had a grand total of four full-time employees (including himself) and two part-time interns. They worked out of a 1950s industrial building in North Hollywood, on a part of Magnolia Boulevard that had never seen a magnolia, or indeed, any attempt at beatification whatsoever.

Their thousand-square-foot premises had previously housed a highly unsuccessful video transfer house that had offered the cheapest 8mm to DVD conversion in Los Angeles.

They went out of business when neighbours complained about strange noises coming from the place at odd hours of the night.

It was discovered that the owner, a one-legged, near obese Vietnam vet, was also using his equipment and facility to make porn videos, starring himself and anyone else he could find who wanted to partake.

When the police finally got around to visiting the establishment, they were astonished. Not about the goings-on, but by the fact that the neighbourhood, being made up exclusively of auto repair workshops working twenty-four hours a day, could have been disturbed by sounds coming from the video facility.

They couldn't even begin to imagine what kind of sounds would have trumped the din of auto repair.

Henry's company was called Magic Vision. For the neighbours who remembered the previous tenants of the building, this name brought many a lewd glance or giggle.

On one particular afternoon, a hysterical woman wearing a leopard-patterned Lycra one-piece, a multicoloured tie-dyed wig and a rhinestone encrusted crown, ran into the building. She demanded payment for the two movies she had made on the premises.

She had wielded a plastic prop gun, and refused to leave. It wasn't until Henry convinced her that the movie-making crowd was long gone, that she sashayed back out onto the street.

Henry reluctantly took down his prized, retro pink, neon signage from the building's worn and weathered frontage, and replaced it with a simple black Perspex, 'MV'. He also, at the staff's request, put serious security locks on all the doors, and installed IP cameras at the front and back of the building.

Despite the downmarket neighbourhood, Henry and his team had high hopes for their futures. While just about every phone and tablet manufacturer was trying to create a functional folding screen, Magic Vision was quietly working on creating a device that could project a holographic image that could either be directed above the device's surface, or projected onto another external surface. A little like R2D2's famous holographic projection of Princess Leia's emergency message.

*

Henry had left MIT with a PhD in Particle Physics. He had always been fascinated at the concept of holography, and believed it could be achieved. It wasn't until the later generations of smartphones and ever more powerful lithium batteries, that he began to have an idea on how to make that a reality.

His premise was simple in concept, but almost fantastical in function. The problem with holographic projection had always been down to three simple words: Project against what? For there to exist a true 'free-standing', multi-dimensional projection of an image, the projected light needed to come from multiple sources. That part was easy. But light also had to be stopped, and in a diffused way, reflected back, otherwise the projected light would simply keep travelling and broadening, losing luminosity and focus.

Multiply that by the multiple projection streams needed to make up the full dimensionality, and the problem became exponentially unresolvable.

The good news for MV was that hardly anyone else was devoting the money and time to that technology. The bad news was that progress was slow.

Then again, trying to redefine how the entire world viewed digital images was bound to be a tad complicated.

In the last fourteen months, they had managed to create the multi-projection platform that could deliver sufficient segments of a video image to form the actual holographic illusion. They were also getting close to being able to develop the algorithm to sync all projectors to their unique and individual interfacing focal points.

That was huge. The part that was still completely elusive, and was kinda important, was how to create a way for the multiple streams to terminate against an invisible surface so the image could, in fact, be seen.

So far nothing had worked, and without that part of the puzzle, the whole enchilada was worth less than the cost of an enchilada.

*

Henry sat at his desk and tried to focus on the data that was streaming by on his sixty-inch 4K screen. For the first time in his working life, he was distracted. No matter how hard he concentrated on the calculations in front of him, his mind took him away from physics and software, and back to his being weeks away from becoming a parent.

"Crap!" he mumbled to himself.

"You okay, boss?" David Chen, their resident expert on micro (and even early nano) projection technology, asked.

Chen knew full well what the problem was. They all did. They all loved seeing the great particle physicist squirm under the cloud of doubt and concern, brought on by the new reality of his becoming a parent. This was humour fodder for them all.

Chen had even changed his phone tones and alert sounds to those of various babies crying or screaming.

Yeah. Life was good at Magic Vision.

CHAPTER
NINE

While Henry tried to clear his mind of childrearing terrors, Mary was trying to decide on a colour for the baby's room.

The space had been designated, a year earlier, as her 'studio'. Despite buying canvasses of every size, a massive oil-paint selection box with over 100 colours, a set of ludicrously expensive paint brushes, three easels and four different sized pallets, she had yet to paint a thing.

The problem was that once she actually had the space, the paints, and the equipment, she couldn't seem to get motivated to do what she had always dreamed of doing. She had had this lifelong expectation of being an artist, but once in a position to make that happen, she didn't know if she really could hack it, and, if she were to be honest, wasn't sure she could take the criticism of strangers.

Such was the fragility of her eggshell ego, she came up with the perfect solution. Don't paint anything, then nobody can criticise your talents.

She realised that she was ripe for a good few years of serious therapy to help her navigate through those crazy seas.

*

A few days after returning from Glenwood Springs, Henry had asked what she thought they should do about a) naming the baby and b) where to put the baby. They decided that naming the baby, while he was still in the neonatal ICU, was probably bad juju, so that could wait. As for making space for a child's room, Mary offered up her studio so fast it had caught Henry completely off guard.

She justified that, though it was an incredible hardship for her, other things had become way more important. Henry then offered to convert his little pool-house office to be her studio. Mary had snapped back that they couldn't afford the luxury of another remodel, and that they needed to focus on the needs of their new child.

Hitting him with the 'we can't afford' argument was completely unfair, though a pretty good weapon in the arsenal. They had enough money – in fact they had plenty.

Henry held patents on everything from cyber-encoding software (used by, just to mention one firm, the NSA) to the latest in micro sensors within consumer clothes dryers that, through the detection of humidity in the drum, could stop the cycle at the exact moment that the items inside were dry.

Mary was no slouch either. She was making a killing in the Beverly Hills real estate market, as 'Stager to the Stars'. Her ability to transform a luxurious home into a luxuriously 'inviting' home, was legendary.

So was her fee of one-half percent of the selling price. It may not immediately sound a lot, but then you realised that one house selling for ten million (not remotely unusual in the 90210 zip) would mean fifty thousand to Mary.

Yet sellers were lining up to have her cosify their mini palaces. She did about twenty houses a year, ranging in price from around two mill, to the occasional mega home in excess of twenty.

No. Money wasn't an issue. But Mary, like a top stage magician, used carefully planned misdirection for great results.

Just like her 'selfless' gesture of giving up her studio. Without the misdirection of chastising Henry for his selfish focus on work, and his willingness to waste money on remodelling, she might have got stuck again with a place to paint.

She wasn't having that!

She really didn't like manipulating Henry, but damn, she was just so good at it, and poor Henry fell for it every time.

What was really starting to piss her off was her recent inability to focus. She had always prided herself on being able to zoom in on any issue and devote every brain cell (those that hadn't been washed away by Merlot and the occasional hit of OG Kush) on an issue or project, and work it till it was resolved.

Yet, here she was, three days from having to present her staging drawings to the Weatherlys in Bel Air, and all she could think about was her new baby. She realised that that was probably how it was supposed to be, but having never had a maternal twinge in her life, it felt very disconcerting.

The weirdest thing was that on a number of occasions since returning from Colorado, she had felt the creeping claws of doubt worm their way into her subconscious.

Again, not that surprising. What was surprising was that her razor-sharp mind would suddenly devolve into a mass of random and disconnected thoughts. They were what psychiatrists referred to as 'Monkey Brain Syndrome'.

Mary assumed that this was a normal motherhood 'thing'. After all, she and Henry not only never wanted a child until their trip to Colorado, they downright hated the little things. The screaming, the dribbling, the smells, the neediness. Yuck! They would actually request tables in restaurants as far away from any child as possible.

They decided that their problem was just a simple case of chronic commitment phobia.

Then, a couple of days ago, Sheriff Massey had called. He had advised them that her sister's body would not be released for cremation for another four to six weeks. Apparently, because the accident occurred on a public rail line, the NTSB was now involved. For a group that worked with high speed travel, they sure could slow a process to a crawl.

As the baby was expected to be released from the ICU at roughly the same time, they decided to combine the memorial service and cremation with the collecting of their new baby.

Mary knew that the disruption of her concentration and the call from Colorado were linked. It didn't take a rocket scientist to put those pieces together.

At least there was now a time frame to picking up the baby. No more abstractions. In six weeks, their life as they knew it would change forever.

Mary decided to stop trying to analyse why she was feeling so damn maternal, and instead be thankful that she did feel that way. Bringing a child into a home filled with reluctant obligation would really have sucked.

She smiled to herself as she grabbed her keys. All of a sudden, she felt as if a huge load had been lifted. "Wow!" she said to her reflection in the hallway mirror. "You, young lady, are going to be a mama!!"

She continued to grin the entire drive into Beverly Hills, where, for the second time that week, she felt the urge to peruse the adorable baby stuff at 'Haute Couture for the Less Mature' – the latest outrageously priced baby store to the stars.

CHAPTER
TEN

The weeks passed in a blur. The Weatherlys had loved Mary's drawings for their house-staging and Henry, despite some all-nighters with his team, had yet to make any further headway with the holo problem.

Then, before they knew it, and before they were even close to being physically or mentally ready, it was time to return to Colorado.

*

Doug greeted them with a big smile and wave as they exited the airport terminal. His enthusiasm was clearly contagious, as both of them couldn't help but grin back and even wave.

"Hope you brought your swimsuits!?" Doug asked with wide-eyed sincerity as he grabbed their hand luggage. "This it for bags?"

Henry patted the young man on the back. "Yes to the bags and no to the swimsuits. Sorry, man. We totally forgot."

"No worries." He opened the SUV door for Mary. "They rent them there!"

Mary shot her husband a look of complete panic, which simply cracked him up.

"Where to first?" Doug asked as he climbed behind the wheel, unaware of the reaction to his swimsuit rental remark.

They both responded in unison. "The hospital!"

*

They spent almost two hours in the administration wing, signing one incomprehensible document after another. They had to produce their notarised legal adoption forms which the hospital then had to scan. It all took an inordinate length of time.

The one thing you would expect a hospital to be good at would be scanning, no?

Most of the time had been spent in the company of Simon Paisley, the hospital attorney, who was assigned to walk them through the release process for baby *Daniel*.

*

The name had come to them mid-flight as they tried to eat their brittle, stale, peanut replacement snack.

There had been no real discussion or thought. One moment Henry was gagging on the rock-hard pretzel, the next, he said, "Let's call him Daniel."

Mary had looked over at him and grinned. "Wow! I was thinking the exact same name. Daniel."

And thus, the child had a name.

*

Simon had been patient with the pair, answering every question in as plain English as possible. At one point, as Henry was about to sign yet another form, he glanced over at the lawyer and with a deadpan look, asked if they offered a factory extended warranty, and also, if they could get LoJack installed.

He got the expected glare from Mary and an unexpected titter from Simon. The upbeat mood then took a brief nosedive as Simon produced a copy of the hospital bill.

"You've got to be kidding!" Henry exploded, before Simon could even finish his explanation of the bill and the supporting documents.

"You expect us to pay this? Now? Nobody ever mentioned a bill!"

"Did you believe that hospitals no longer charge for their services?" Simon sat back as he eyed Henry with mild amusement.

"I really can't see what you find amusing. There is nothing funny about this!" Mary joined in.

Simon held up his hands in mock surrender. "Slow down, folks! I haven't asked you for any money—"

Mary grabbed the multi-page bill and waved it at him. "What do you call this?"

Simon gently took it from her hands. "I would call it a receipt and documents that you may need at some point, for Daniel's medical records. If you look at each page, you will see that they are all stamped as having been paid in full."

He laid the paperwork back onto the desk and gestured to the cover page where a black stamp confirmed his words.

"Then who did pay?" Henry asked in a far calmer voice.

"The birth parents had both taken out health insurance that included full maternity care, as well as birth and neonatal costs."

"Wouldn't the insurance have been voided once my sister died?" Mary asked.

"Actually, their policy covered all health costs for the baby, up until hospital discharge, including the eventuality of one or both parents becoming incapacitated or—"

"Dead." Mary finished the sentence for him. "But surely their suicide would have voided the coverage?"

"What suicide?" Simon looked truly shocked.

Mary and Henry looked back at him in complete bewilderment.

"The result of the inquest was accidental death as a result of a mechanical problem with their car," Simon explained as delicately as possible.

Mary was shaking her head. "But we met with the sheriff and—"

"Then perhaps you should talk to the sheriff. If you don't agree with the result, I'm sure the insurance company would love to hear a revised finding that could relieve them from liability."

He gave them a 'If it's not broke, don't fix it' expression.

Mary and Henry looked to each other for any helpful

thoughts. They had nada and looked back at Simon with forced smiles.

Mary finally spoke. "May we see Daniel now?"

A few minutes later, Nurse Carter appeared at the door. After some handshakes and hearty thanks, they said goodbye to Simon and were led back up to the third floor.

They walked past the door to the ICU and continued down a cheerfully decorated hallway to an open-plan nursery.

It was brightly painted in pastel yellow and had painted clouds with rainbows dotted around everywhere. Gentle lullaby music played softly in the background. The feel of the space was one of peace, tranquillity and safety.

Mary and Henry glanced at each other, both knowing that they had found the 'theme' for Daniel's nursery.

Carter walked them to the only occupied cot in the room. Despite being in a hospital surrounding, the bassinet was surprisingly cosy-looking with none of the aluminium and steel one would expect from a hospital bed.

This one was painted white with what looked like a lattice frame. Cocooned within was a sheepskin mattress pad upon which lay their new son.

Daniel was asleep on his back, a light blanket pulled up to his chin. Unlike the last time they had seen him, he now only had one wire coming from his arm. This was to monitor his vital signs. He was a healthy pink colour with rosy cheeks, and the slightest wisp of blonde hair in the middle of his head.

Mary and Henry felt a sudden wave of emotion at seeing their new son. It was the feeling that Mary had been reading about. That first sight of your child. It was a powerful sensation. Henry later described it as a tsunami of love.

"My sister is being cremated tomorrow, so if possible, we would like to pick Daniel up the following morning," Mary explained. "We don't want him having to go through any more discombobulation than is really necessary. We thought he should stay here, unstressed, until we can pick him up and go straight to the airport."

Carter gave an understanding nod. "I completely understand. The flying part will be difficult enough. It would be a pleasure to have him here a little bit longer. As you can see, we're not exactly swamped."

"I noticed that," Henry commented. "Is it always this quiet? Is this like some non-birthing month up here?"

"Actually no. We are usually pretty busy. Not sure why Daniel's all by his lonesome, but it means he's getting all of our attention. He's a lucky kid."

They both turned their focus to the baby.

Henry reached out and touched his foot through the blanket. His touch was hyper gentle, as he had no clue on how to behave with an actual baby.

"You're not going to break him," Mary said. She reached into the bassinet and, seeing Carter give an approving nod, lifted Daniel into her arms. She cradled him facing up at her.

As the two new parents stared at the little face, Daniel opened his eyes. They were a sparkling azure blue. Both parents gasped.

"They are spectacular, aren't they?" Carter whispered. "They may not stay that colour. It's one of nature's little tricks."

Henry moved closer to Mary so he could have better access to the baby.

"Hello, Daniel. I am going to be your daddy if that's all right." His voice cracked with emotion. "My name is Henry. This here is Mary. She will be your mummy."

Daniel's response was a brief gurgle then a toothless smile. They both took this to be an acceptance of the terms.

They spent over an hour, cooing and fawning over the small infant who, for the most part, slept through the entire ordeal. That didn't stop Mary from reading stories from a nursery book she found on a shelf above the bassinet.

Finally, it was time for the two to leave Daniel to his gurgling and dribbling. They needed to check into the Glenwood Plaza Hotel for their last few nights as unburdened adults.

Doug was waiting for them just outside the main entrance. They were relieved, as the temperature seemed to have dropped dramatically while they had been in the hospital. It had been in the sixties when they arrived, now it was in the low forties.

Thankfully, Doug had the heater on high and their heavier coats were where they had left them on the back seats.

During the drive to the hotel, Henry was fascinated by the clouds that were moving in from the north. They were slate gray with streaks of dark charcoal, looking almost like an artist's afterthought.

They stretched from horizon to horizon, dimming daylight below as they approached. Unlike good old Californian clouds which would sneak in among the haze and didn't seem to have a leading edge, these clouds had a razor-sharp line which went from blue to grey to almost purple. The weirdest part, for non-Coloradans, was their speed. It was as if someone was sliding a hatch slowly across the sky.

"Does it usually get this dark this early?" Henry asked.

"Nope," Doug answered. "Only when it's gonna snow."

"Well that's not very likely in September, is it?"

"I can tell you're from California," Doug grinned. "We almost always get a few early blasts in late September. The snow won't last, but the storms can get really hairy."

"Please define hairy." Mary sounded concerned.

"We sometimes get tornado cells. Not like down on the plains. The funnels don't form this high up, but the storms can still get pretty freaky."

"Hairy and freaky! Just what we need," Mary added.

"You folks don't need to worry. The buildings up here are built for big snows and big winds."

"Good to know." Harry gave him a thumbs-up in the rear-view mirror.

"Then again, your hotel lost part of its roof in a September storm once!"

They both looked incredulously back at Doug's reflection.

"No. It's true. Happened in the 1920s, I think. Hit one of the towers."

No one said another word for the rest of the drive.

CHAPTER ELEVEN

"Welcome back Mr and Mrs Trapp." The hotel receptionist sounded completely sincere. "Looks like you just beat the storm. Accuweather says it's gonna be a dilly."

Mary turned to her husband and whispered with a straight face. "Freaky, hairy AND now dilly! What the fuck!"

"I think those were dwarfs eight, nine and ten," he whispered back without looking away from the receptionist.

"We've put you in one of our mini suites," he advised proudly. "Beautiful view. The room is on the top floor."

Mary snorted loudly. "In this storm!? God, man, don't you remember what happened in the twenties?"

Both men looked at her askance.

She glared back. "What?!"

They convinced the young man to give them another room on a lower floor. Though confused at the request, he handed over a pair of plastic RF keys.

"Your deliveries arrived yesterday," he announced almost excitedly. "Shall I have them sent to your room?"

"Yes, please," they both answered in sync.

"I love Amazon too!" he whispered. "They're just so convenient!"

"Yes, they are," Henry whispered back.

The receptionist leaned across the desk. "They say Amazon will end up running the world one day. I don't know if I like that."

"You'll be fine as long as you are a Prime member," Henry deadpanned.

"Thanks for the advice." Again, he seemed completely sincere.

*

In their room, Henry stared out of the window at the otherworldly vista. The sky was now so black it looked like night had fallen, even though it was only 2:45 p.m.

Yet it wasn't completely black. As he watched, he could see blacks and greys swirling and eddying gently above him. It looked like an angry sea at night.

He could hear Mary brushing her teeth in the bathroom.

"Was that guy for real?" Henry asked.

"That's what high-altitude inbreeding will do," she replied through a mouthful of toothpaste.

He continued to stare out into the darkened world. "You think Doug was right about the snow and the storm?"

"Hope not," she replied.

"If it does we might have to—"

He was cut off as the entire outside world erupted blue-white with the intensity of a flash grenade. "What the f—"

He was cut off again, this time by what could only be described as an explosion. The thunder was not only deafening, it was actually concussive. Such was the force of the clap, Henry could actually feel the shock wave through the double-glazed windows.

Mary came charging out of the bathroom in her panties and bra. "What the hell was that?" She looked wide-eyed and terrified. The toothpaste residue around her mouth added to the effect.

She looked almost rabid.

"I believe that was what folks up here in the clouds refer to as 'hairy.'"

They both moved cautiously towards the window.

A loud knock on the door made them both jump! Not metaphorically. They actually got air.

Mary made a dash for the bathroom while Henry opened the door. He tried not to look as shaken as he felt.

"Hi." A young man who could easily have been the receptionist's brother grinned back at Henry. "Got some stuff here for you."

Henry opened the door more fully and saw two baggage carts piled with Amazon boxes. He gestured for the bellhop to wrangle them into the room. As he was leaving, Henry slipped him a twenty.

"Thank you, sir. Need any help unboxing anything?"

"No, I think we will manage." Henry held the door open for him to leave. Once out in the hall the young man stopped. "I love Amazon," he whispered.

Henry closed the door gently but decisively. "Good grief!"

*

They had planned to try somewhere else for dinner, but decided that going outside during the storm was just plain stupid.

They opted for the bar.

Brad wasn't on duty, but a suitable clone, Tony, greeted them like long-lost friends. People really did seem to be friendly in the mountains of Colorado. The place was much busier than when they were previously there; then again, it was prime dinner hour.

"Can we eat at the bar?" Henry asked, after Tony completed a drink order for a six-top.

"Sure. We'll get you folks a couple of menus and set-ups."

The two of them scanned the bar menu and were relieved to see that it was far more basic than the fancy restaurant offering. Not that they hadn't loved the meal, they were just trying to put off gout till at least their fifties.

They settled on bison burgers on sourdough brioche, with honey-baked rosemary fries.

Okay. Maybe gout at forty would be okay.

They washed the meal down with pints of pale lager, that was brewed in Glenwood Springs. Maybe it was the mountain water but the stuff was absolutely delicious. So much so, that seconds were had all round. Mary had to use the super glare to stop Henry from going for thirds!

They sat quietly, in a post gluttonous haze.

"What did you think about what he said today at the hospital?"

"About the eyes changing colour?"

"No, duh! I'm talking about the lawyer. About the inquest verdict being accidental."

"Sounded to me like that was a good thing for our wallets." He shrugged.

"Yeah, but – it wasn't an accident, was it?"

"No, probably not, but what'd be the point of calling it suicide, and upsetting everyone? Sounds to me like Massey decided to make it easy on family and friends. Probably what you have to do in a small town," Henry suggested.

"But it's a lie!" Mary wouldn't back down.

"Maybe it is, but it means Zeke's family don't have to go through life wondering if they could have done something to stop it. Daniel will grow up believing his parents died in an accident, instead of knowing they killed themselves with, one imagines, the expectation for their unborn child to die as well."

Mary's expression softened as she leaned over and kissed him on the cheek. "You're a good man, Charlie Brown."

Later, back in their room, they attacked the Amazon boxes like kids at Christmas.

Mary suddenly burst out laughing.

Henry looked over, and watched as she reached into one particularly massive box and pulled out a piece of brown packing paper. The thing was, it didn't seem to have an end. She just kept pulling and pulling. Finally, with paper surrounding her almost to waist height, she reached into the box one last time. She removed a pink sippy-cup and matching bib, both shrink-wrapped onto a cardboard display backing. The box could have held fifty of them instead of the heavily protected lone unit that was in Mary's hand.

"They better get this wastefulness under control if they're gonna run the world," Mary stated.

"You do realise that they undoubtedly own the cardboard box and paper company?" Henry suggested.

"That would be nuts!"

"Welcome to capitalism," Henry replied, as he struggled to get a baby's pram box out of another, larger Amazon box. "They must have used lubricant to get this in here!"

They spent the next two hours assembling the aforementioned pram and a baby car seat, both of which would be needed in a couple of days for the return trip home.

Also unpacked, but thankfully not having required assembly, were all the other paraphernalia needed to travel with a baby. They had done their best to limit their purchases to the bare minimum. They had already bought enough baby supplies and equipment in LA to stock a good-sized day-care nursery.

Yet, as they surveyed the inventory of baby goods that surrounded them, they realised that it was just possible that they were compensating with volume in place of knowledge.

It hadn't dawned on them yet that the 'What to buy a newborn' shopping lists they found online were actually created by the folks that sold the damn stuff. Almost like they were doing it for profit!

The sky gave one last blast of light, but the following thunder was nearly thirty seconds behind and its gentle rumble was a mere trifle of its earlier self.

*

"Wow!" Henry stood at the window the next morning. "You gotta see this!"

"I've seen daylight before!"

"Not like this you haven't."

Reluctantly, she prised herself out of the warm bedclothes and joined him. "Holy crap! It actually snowed. A lot!"

"Did you doubt our psychic driver? Was this not foretold?" Henry joked.

They both took a moment to fully take in their revamped view. Same one as before, just painted entirely white.

"Ellen used to love the snow. Maybe it's fitting for today."

Henry gave her a comforting hug as he continued to stare outside.

*

The crematorium was on the outskirts of town, nestled up against the base of Flat Iron Mountain. It had been built from the same stone as the mountain, so the effect was a little disconcerting. The building seemed part of the background, and occasionally even seemed to disappear.

"That is so cool. I've never seen anything like that," Mary exclaimed.

"You don't watch enough *Star Trek*. It looks just like the Romulan cloaking device," Henry replied.

"Except this is real, honey!!" She shook her head in mild wonder.

Doug couldn't help snickering from the front seat.

"Don't you start," Mary warned.

"Henry has a point though." Doug sounded amazed. "That is what it looks like. I can't wait to tell everyone. Nobody's ever said that before!"

Mary turned to her husband. "Nice work. You've brought a little extra culture to the Rockies!"

Once inside, they were directed to the chapel. Though small, it was nevertheless striking.

The same rough granite had been used inside, together with highly varnished rough-hewn timber. Most of the chapel light came from a sloping skylight that gave the occupants a view up the side of the mountain. There was something ethereally serene about the building and its setting.

What did surprise the Trapps, was the small size of the congregation. Sheriff Massey was there with someone whom they assumed was his wife. There were about a dozen others dotted around. There was also one middle-aged couple sitting in the back row. There was no sign of Jerry which was kind of sad.

For someone who they believed had a ton of friends, this was a pretty poor showing for the big goodbye.

A non-denominational minister waved to them and gestured to the front row. They must have really looked like out-of-towners to have been recognised immediately as family.

The service was brief and simple, yet somehow personified Ellen. It was what she would have wanted. It ended with John Lennon's 'Imagine' played over the AV system, as the coffin slid silently out of view between parted velvet curtains.

That was it for Mary. Her occasional eye dabs with a tissue turned into a torrent of tears once the song started and the coffin began its journey to the oven. Henry held her tight as the sobs wracked her body.

As the chapel emptied, the older couple from the back of the chapel wandered to their pew, and for a moment, just looked down at them.

"We're sorry to interrupt. We just wanted to say how sorry we are," the man offered in a near whisper.

Henry looked up at them almost indignantly, considering how they were interrupting Mary's grief.

The woman held out her hand. "We are – were – Zeke's parents. We stayed on till today so we could attend Ellen's service. Zeke's was yesterday."

Henry's demeaner changed instantly. Mary's sobbing also stopped. They looked up and momentarily studied the pair. They were both in their early fifties, average height, and average weight. Both had grey highlights in their hair (real ones) and were wearing non-descript, older, yet comfortable-looking clothing. Perfect for a funeral. Central casting could not have done a better job.

"Oh my god! Hello!" Mary sniffled. She and Henry both got to their feet and took the other couple's offered hands.

"We had no idea you were here. We certainly didn't know that Zeke's service was yesterday," Henry said. He suddenly felt terrible that they, at no point in the last few weeks, had given a thought to Ellen's husband's family.

"How did you know Ellen's service was today?" Mary asked.

"We asked!" Zeke's mother replied bluntly. Despite the fact that her answer could have been taken as a rebuke, especially if you were feeling guilty anyway, there was no sign of something so negative in the woman's voice or expression.

"I'm Glenda," she offered with what seemed like a restrained and forced smile.

Mary, completely against type, enveloped Glenda in a hug. "I am so sorry for what happened." She did not notice Glenda tense.

"Just a complete tragedy is what it was." The other man held out his hand again to Henry. "Jed Darnell. We weren't sure you'd remember us. We all met at their wedding."

"Of course, we remember you. How could we forget anything about that day?" Henry reassured him.

*

Even as Henry looked right at the man, he couldn't remember him, or Glenda. Then again, the wedding had been on a misty cliff top, a few miles outside Glenwood Springs, almost eight years ago.

All the guests had been forced to wear white robes and floral headbands, except the bride who wore a bright purple toga thing. Add to that, the hors d'oeuvres had, unbeknown to anybody, included magic mushroom pâté.

By the end of the ceremony they couldn't have remembered their own names.

All that either of them could recall from that day was the intensity of the colours, the random giggling, and how the groom hadn't been wearing anything under his robes. After one strong updraft from the valley below, the entire congregation suddenly got a better idea of why Ellen was marrying the man.

*

Jed smiled back. "We didn't mean to interrupt. We just wanted to—I don't know—talk with you, I guess." There was an almost pleading look in the man's eyes.

The two couples stood at the front of the chapel, both at a loss for words.

"Why don't you come back to our hotel and we can have a nice talk over lunch?" Henry finally suggested.

"We have to catch a plane home unfortunately, but could we just sit here for a minute?" Jed tried to sound casual but there was desperation in his eyes.

"Of course." Mary gestured to their pew.

"Thank you. We won't take much of your time." Glenda tried to force a smile. It came across as more of a sneer.

The pair shuffled into the tight space, then sat next to Mary and Henry.

"When we first heard about the accident, we were obviously devastated," Glenda began. "We couldn't imagine such a thing befalling anyone, especially not our Zeke." She stopped to try and get her emotions in check. "Did you know that he had a law degree from Harvard?"

Her voice had gone suddenly frosty.

The Trapps shook their heads. They were starting to wonder where this little chat was going.

"He was number two in his class. All the big DC and Manhattan law firms wanted him. We were so proud." Glenda had to rummage in her bag for a tissue. After a brief eye-wipe and nose-blow, she continued.

"All that ended when he came out here to Colorado." Glenda looked from Henry to Mary, believing that her statement explained everything.

By their blank expressions, she realised that they weren't on the same page at all.

"He had everything going for him. A great life, a great career, the possibility even of a wonderful family!" She again looked for understanding. Still nada.

"He came here to Vail to ski with some of his law school friends. He never left."

Mary shook her head still not getting it. "I get the feeling you are trying to tell us something but we don't have a clue where this is going."

Glenda turned to face the Trapps full on. Jed, who so far had hardly said a word, put his hand on her arm. "Glen, maybe we should…"

Glenda shook off his hand. "He never left because he met your sister."

The clouds of confusion started to part above the Trapps, though they still didn't understand Glenda's ire.

"I know. They met at The Remedy Bar. Ellen was working there," Mary offered.

"She was a hostess!" The words came out of Glenda's mouth, one at a time. Each filled with more bile.

"Whoa. What the hell is going on here?" Henry jumped in. "They met in Vail at a restaurant where Ellen worked. We all know that. What's the problem?"

"Problem!? Are you dim? Are you one of those California dim people?" Glenda blurted out, spittle and all. Her previous features magically transformed into a mask of pure hatred.

"Our boy! Our beautiful, smart, talented boy, goes away to celebrate passing the bar and instead of coming home and making something of his life, he meets your tramp of a sister, and throws his whole life away. He lost everything! EVERYTHING!!"

"That's enough." Henry rose to his feet and helped Mary to hers. She was so stunned by the other woman's outburst that she could hardly move.

They started for the exit.

The chaplain materialised to check on the raised voices.

"Everything all right here?" he asked.

"She ruined his life!" Glenda shouted after them, not even noticing the chaplain. "Then she let it kill him!" she screamed.

Never let it be said that the Trapps were afraid of battle. They both stopped in their tracks then turned to face her.

The chaplain looked from the Trapps to the Darnells, then quietly slunk back out the way he came in.

"Are you out of your mind?" Henry's voice was low, razor sharp, and cold as ice. He rarely used that tone but when he did, look out.

"We all lost someone. That's the only truth here today. We are all devastated and basically pretty messed up over this, but for you to confront us, screaming that you blame Ellen for your son not coming home like a good boy, and becoming a lawyer or whatever, makes it sound to me like maybe you were the reason he never returned home."

"You have no idea what you are talking about," Glenda said.

Henry continued. "Have you considered that maybe Zeke never wanted to be a damn lawyer? That maybe that was your dream. Perhaps you were hoping for a beach house in the Hamptons you could visit! Well, the Zeke that we knew was very happy and very much in love. Exactly what sane parents should dream of for their children."

Glenda had turned ghostly pale and was trembling in place. Her mouth was open, but no words were forthcoming.

Henry started to lead Mary out of the chapel.

"Didn't you even wonder why we didn't contest custody of the child when your lawyer contacted us?" Glenda's voice was eerily calm. The Trapps stopped but didn't turn around.

"That baby is what killed them. That spawn of her loins took their souls, then took their lives. When your lawyer called, we couldn't sign away our custody rights fast enough. Now he's yours. Just remember what he is. You'll be next when he stops needing you."

Mary started to turn, but Henry stopped her and faced Glenda himself.

"We never realised, until just now, how close it came for that poor child. He could have ended up being raised by someone who should be institutionalised at the earliest possible opportunity.

"Jed, I feel for you, and we are truly sorry for your loss, but I think you should take your psychotic bride back home. You may even want to consider sleeping with a gun under your pillow."

Jed looked back at him with the look of a man who had long ago given away his soul and possibly his testicles.

He simply nodded.

Glenda glared at them as she shook her head. Thankfully, before she could throw any more conspiracy theories at them, they were out the door and into Doug's waiting SUV.

CHAPTER
TWELVE

Doug dropped them back at the Glenwood Plaza then went off in search of lunch. He was to pick them up in two hours so they could visit Daniel at the hospital.

As they entered the hotel lobby, they spotted Sheriff Massey sitting in an overstuffed leather armchair, reading a hunting magazine.

Clearly not a PETA member.

"Sheriff! Waiting for us?" Henry asked. "I didn't want to interrupt you both while you were with Zeke's family at the chapel."

"Thanks a lot for that," Henry replied. "They were a delight. Especially the female."

"Yeah!" Massey looked a little guilty. "Probably should have warned you that she has some – interesting opinions."

"Opinions! She's insane. Do you know what she said to us?"

"Yeah, I got a pretty good idea. She unloaded on me yesterday. Again, sorry about that. Death does some pretty weird stuff to some people."

"Oh, I think the weird stuff has been in that woman for a long time," Henry threw back.

"Can't think of a single way I can argue that point. Anyhow, I just wanted to talk with you both before you headed back, if that's okay. Thought I'd buy you both a coffee."

Mary looked at him with confusion. Massey picked up on the vibe immediately.

"Or maybe something a little stronger, considering what you've been through today. The funeral of your sister would be hard enough without that woman's bizarre baby theories."

They opted to sit in the front lounge. It was far more cheerful than the bar. They needed to de-stress in a happy place. They also needed happy drinks! Mary and Henry both opted for double Bloody Marys. Extra hot, no veggies.

Massey ordered coffee for himself then called the waiter back and ordered the same as the Trapps but regular heat, 'with the salad'.

"Why, Sheriff Massey," Mary teased, "aren't you on duty?"

"Actually, ma'am, I am not. This is my day off. I felt I should explain some things to you before you both leave."

"If it's about the inquest verdict—" Henry lowered his voice. "We know."

"I was pretty sure you would have heard by now. I thought you just might like to hear the reason why it went that way."

Mary patted his hand. "Thank you. We have been wondering about that. We found the result a little strange."

"I told her it was a small-town politics thing," Henry suggested.

Massey laughed. "Not sure what exactly that means, but if you think that I would slant a death inquest result just to keep local folks happy, then you two should lay off that inferior California weed."

He was surprised at the momentary look of surprise that crossed both their faces.

"Guys! This is Colorado. We are the mother ship of legalised pot."

They both relaxed.

"All I'm saying is that trying to not ruffle feathers in this town had nothing to do with the verdict. What did play a part was the beginnings of some pretty weird rumours that started circulating. They weren't that different from the crap Mrs Darnell was spouting."

"What?" Henry was stunned.

"Calm down. Let me finish."

The drinks arrived and the three took mega sips, before putting their frosted glasses down. All eyes were on the sheriff.

"If the findings had come down to them having intentionally died on that railway track, the inquest would have gone down a completely different road. The way the two of them had been acting would have been scrutinised much more deeply than it had been.

"The timing of their behaviour, coupled with the start of the pregnancy, would even have formally come into play. There was already talk of their moods having changed, even before they knew Ellen was pregnant. Some say Zeke even told people that they were only being used until the baby didn't need them."

Mary and Henry glanced at each other.

"That mean something to you?" They had piqued the sheriff's curiosity.

"Just that we were told the same thing," Henry advised.

"See! It was like a weed. If you don't pick it, roots and all, it just keeps coming back. Bigger and bigger. The town council and I spent many a late night over the past few weeks, trying to decide what was right by the law and, by a much lesser degree, for the relatives."

"There was absolutely no concrete evidence that they did what they did intentionally. There were witnesses, but under oath, even they couldn't guarantee exactly what it was that they had actually seen. What they could confirm was that a couple was stuck on the tracks and, at the last moment, looked to each other with love and resignation of what was imminently to come."

"My god!" Mary whispered to herself.

"Then there was the matter of the hospital bills. Time was, we could have convinced the hospital to waive the charges for the obvious reasons. That was before it was bought by the Schneider Medical Corporation. Biggest hospital owners in America. Bunch of heartless assholes."

He looked momentarily embarrassed at his comment, until he saw that both were nodding their agreement.

"So, the decision was made to go the way the law demanded, and we found for a verdict of accidental death. The rumour mill suddenly had nothing to feast on. The crazy stories have already stopped. The hospital got paid by the insurance company, the child will grow up none the wiser, and we had hoped the families would accept the verdict and be able to mourn their loss."

"I don't think you counted on Glenda Darnell when you came up with that supposition," Henry added.

"No shit!" The sheriff raised his eyebrows as he reached for his drink.

"So, that's it? It's done?" Mary didn't seem quite satisfied.

"Yup," Massey replied as he tried to get the stick of celery out of the way of his mouth so he could actually drink his cocktail. "Unless you in any way believe the claptrap that Mrs Darnell was spouting?"

"No!" she replied emphatically. "We certainly do not."

She and Massey both turned to Henry.

"Don't look at me! Of course not. Damien, I mean Daniel, is a wonderful, healthy little boy." He grinned.

"Ouch!" Henry cried as Mary's shoe made perfect contact with her husband's shin.

*

Later that afternoon, as they stood over Daniel's crib, Mary took Henry's arm and pulled him closer to her.

"He is a sweet baby, isn't he?"

Henry laughed. "Of course he is. Look at him."

Mary was looking at him. "I mean ONLY a sweet baby. There's nothing more to it?"

"Wow! That woman really got to you!" Henry nudged her playfully.

"Come on!" She nudged back. "That was pretty creepy!"

"No, honey. **She** was creepy. And do you know why? 'Cause she was completely coocoo for Cocoa Puffs!"

"That's really all it was, wasn't it?" She still sounded concerned.

"You know whose fault this is? That damn chef, Jerry. I bet he's the one that started the rumours in town. I might just have a little word with him when we get back to the hotel."

"After we pick up Ellen's ashes," she reminded him.

They stood smiling down at Daniel as the sun began its descent behind Flat Iron Mountain.

*

Five miles outside of Glenwood Springs, up County Rd 132, a couple of deputies were making their way on foot down an uncomfortably steep hillside. They were there to investigate the sighting of a crashed car.

Hikers had seen what looked like sunlight reflecting off glass, down in the ravine.

The deputies were trying to get down to the spot before losing the light and having to start over again the next day.

Peter Gardiner was the first to reach the flat area where the vehicle had come to rest. The car, a newer model Audi 4, had clearly done some serious rolling as it came off the road.

There wasn't a square inch of bodywork that wasn't dented to hell and back. Most of the windows were shattered, except the rear one which somehow survived. Peter assumed that it was that, that had been seen by the hikers.

He started towards the car when Bradley, the second deputy, stumbled into the clearing.

"Shit. How the fuck are we gonna get back up?" Judging by the dirt and rips on his shirt and trousers, it was pretty obvious that he had had a much harder descent than Peter. Considering that he was two inches shorter, but seventy pounds heavier, it kinda made sense.

"Whoa! You found it! Don't think they'll be driving that out!" Bradley snorted.

The car was almost upright, but had landed squarely on a large boulder. The force had bent the chassis in the middle and given the car what looked like a hump.

As they approached the vehicle from the rear, they could make out two figures still strapped into the front seats.

"You smell that?" Peter asked as they drew near to the wreck.

"Boy, something is ripe!" Bradley said.

They reached the driver's side door and Bradley went for the handle.

"Hold on!" Peter grabbed his arm. "Don't you think we should wait for the techs?"

"No way. They won't come out till morning and we gotta check if they're alive." Bradley tried to justify the fact that he just wanted to see the bodies.

He thought dead bodies were cool.

Peter reluctantly let go of his arm. "Just look. For God's sake don't touch anything!"

"Duh!!" Bradley tried the handle. It didn't budge. He gave it a bigger tug. Still nothing.

"Did you hear something?" Peter sounded a little

creeped out. Then again, he did not like dead bodies at all. Not one darned bit!

"I thought I heard something."

"You probably did! What do you expect from a car that flew five hundred feet down a cliff? The whole thing is broken to shit."

Bradley gave the handle a really big tug. The door flew open with a screech of metal against metal.

"Ta da!" Bradley, proud of his mighty strength, took a bow.

Peter, however, was backing away. His eyes were the size of golf balls and as Bradley wondered what was wrong, a circle of damp formed on his partner's crotch. Peter didn't even seem to notice that he had peed himself.

"Dude! What a freak! You just wet yourself. It's just a couple of bodies."

Suddenly, the air around them started to buzz like hundreds of electric razors played through a PA system. Bradley turned to the open car door.

The two bodies in the car were still sitting rigidly upright, though their heads were both leaning at wholly unnatural angles. Their faces were swollen. Their skin was purplish green and black. Parts of it seemed to be sliding off their skulls, as decomp took over from life.

At first, Bradley was mesmerised by their faces, until he noticed movement in the car. He started to bend forward to see what was going on. Peter grabbed his collar and with surprising strength, pulled him back and away from the vehicle.

"Dude! What the fuck. I just wanted to see—" He gestured to the car.

A single rattlesnake eased across the door sill and slid onto the dry earth. It then coiled and rattled for their benefit.

Bradley was about to make another comment, when a second snake oozed out of the car.

It was then that Bradley finally saw what had freaked Peter out. The entire front seat well of the car was full of diamondbacks. Big ones.

Then the dead guy in the driver's seat moved.

The deputies stumbled backwards. Their eyes were riveted on the open car door.

The corpse's head started to turn towards them in ultra-slow motion. Parts of the man's neck began peeling away, accompanied by a wet, crunching sound.

Just as in the scariest of nightmares, the two couldn't move. They wanted to, more than you could believe. They just couldn't.

All they could do was stare, slack jawed, at the horror in front of them. As if their sleep hadn't already been pretty well fucked up for the rest of their lives, a blood-soaked diamondback started to crawl out of the driver's mouth.

"Fuck that!" Bradley cried as he ran for the base of the hill. He started to claw his way back up.

Peter was about to join him, when he noticed something white moving out of the open car door. Terrified, but curious, he stayed rooted in place as a gore-stained white coat slid onto the ground. An especially large snake slowly appeared from one of the garment's sleeves.

Something in Peter's training kicked in. Though completely terrified, and trying to keep his hyperventilating (and bladder) in check, he picked up a three-foot length of deadwood and carefully, very carefully, snagged the garment and dragged it towards him. The big snake did not seem pleased at sharing the coat, and lashed out at it with amazing speed.

Peter gave the white material one last flick bringing it to within his reach, and away from the reptile's strike zone.

Once he had the coat safely out of rattler's striking distance, he noticed stylised embroidered lettering on the front. Because of the blood and fluid stains, he could only partially make out the words.

EXEC T VE
C EF
JE RY WH T
COLO DO HOTE

He took a firm hold of the coat then followed after Bradley. He could hear him gasping for air as he scrambled up the hillside.

Peter took one last look at the car and saw that, with dusk descending on the hills, the snakes were becoming more animated and active.

He guessed there were, at that point, at least thirty rattlers surrounding the car as dozens of others seemed to be squeezing out of every nook and cranny of the destroyed Audi.

Peter turned away from the macabre sight and started up the hillside. He just wished that his partner could have seen him retrieve the coat from the snakes. It might have partially made up for the peeing incident.

CHAPTER
THIRTEEN

Feeling the need for something less formal than the hotel, the Trapps ventured out into the night in search of local sustenance.

They stumbled across a funky, but fun-looking, micro-brew pub and restaurant. They ate and drank like a couple of teenagers who didn't have to care about their livers or cholesterol.

By the time they staggered back to their hotel, they felt at peace with the world, and also remarkably horny.

After brushing all the baby supplies off their bed and onto the floor, they made love as passionately as you can, with full bellies, bladders and dill pickle breath.

Afterwards, despite both suffering from serious cases of the snoozies, they decided to pack and prep the baby gear for the next day.

They contemplated trying to do it in the morning, but decided that their enthusiasm might be long gone by then.

There is a strange sense of responsibility when unpacking something as simple as a plastic baby bottle or teething ring and realising that it was to become the property of a new life.

Every toy, every sippy cup, would play a part in the development of the child.

Henry shared this 'deep' revelation with Mary who, amused, tossed a box of disposable nappies at him.

"I forgot how philosophical you get after beer."

"I prefer to think of it as becoming poetic." He feigned looking to the heavens for inspiration.

"There once was a girl from St Paul, her vagina was terribly small, but given enough gin, she could let any size in, especially when backed against the—"

"Shakespeare you are not!" She put her hand over his mouth, interrupting the limerick. She then kissed him on the forehead before heading for the bathroom.

"One day my poetry will make us rich!" he called after her.

"Can't wait, honey. No point in counting on the holography then?" she called back through the closing door.

"Mean! Very mean!"

He began sorting which supplies went into which of the colour-coded Panda Bear tote bags.

*

The next day was an exercise in organised chaos. Despite Mary's legendary skills at planning and implementation, adding a baby to the mix humbles even the mighty.

Despite partially packing everything the night before,

it appeared that doing so when filled to the gills with the local IPA, negated any positive outcome.

They couldn't find anything they needed. Baby food was somehow in the same plastic bag as nappy-rash ointment, the nappies themselves, seemed to have vanished completely (though both had a vague recollection of them having had a nappy fight – same rules as a pillow fight – prior to bed).

They finally sorted out what was where, and headed downstairs to check out. This was their first experience with the parental delight of having to carry enough supplies for an army every frigging time you had to leave the house with baby in tow.

The irony was not lost on either of them that, many a time, they had cracked up laughing and watched, as some poor mum, laden like a Tibetan sherpa with a screaming child strapped on her back, tried to bundle everything into her sensible minivan, just to go to the supermarket for something vital, like more nappies.

Now that joke was their reality.

Karma's a bitch.

*

Thankfully, Nurse Carter had prepared a to-go bag for Daniel's departure, and had all of the bits and pieces stowed in one sensible carry-on. Clearly experience only comes with practice, time and dedication!

They said their goodbyes, and with Doug at the wheel and Daniel in his car seat in the back, they drove away from Glenwood for the last time.

Mary was dreading the flight to LA. Nothing upset her

more on a plane than to see a mother board the aircraft with a baby. Even more so, if they sat within twenty-five feet of her.

She had always felt that mothers of infants who chose to fly with their babies were entirely selfish and uncaring of the other passengers' sensitivities. What gave them the right to mess up everyone else's flight? Why couldn't they drive, or better still, leave the baby with somebody?

Now she was to be one of those mums. She was going to feel the eyes of every other person on board, as they glared, angry and disgusted, back at her.

She had no idea what to do when the inevitable happened, and Daniel started to cry. And he would start to cry. All babies do. The altitude change really messes with them. Some babies had a brief cry, then slept. Others, and she just knew Daniel would be in this group, started to wail like a banshee the moment the cabin doors were closed, then would continue screaming till they were reopened upon landing.

She knew she would just die of embarrassment, to say nothing of the fact that she, herself, didn't want to be seated next to something as jarring as an air raid siren for two hours either.

Shit! This was going to be a trip from hell.

She tried getting Henry to feel her pain as they made their way to Vail Airport, but he just kept laughing and telling her not to worry. "It won't be that bad."

"Asshole!"

Meanwhile Doug was trying desperately to keep a straight face, knowing Henry's planned secret for easing his wife's crisis.

As they approached Vail's Eagle County Airport, Doug, instead of turning into the flight departure lane, turned the opposite direction towards what was signposted as 'General Aviation'. Mary didn't start to catch on until they pulled up to an unimposing building with a modest sign that read VAIL VALLEY JET CENTRE.

Doug and Henry both looked to see Mary's reaction.

She was grinning like a demented hyena. "You didn't!?"

"Oh, but I did!" Henry confirmed.

Mary put her hand over her mouth and her eyes moistened with emotional happiness.

Doug looked concerned. "Don't worry, Mrs Trapp. I can still drive you to the regular airport if you want."

Mary and Henry stared at Doug for a moment, then both burst out laughing.

Doug joined in with the laughter, though he wasn't sure exactly why.

*

After presenting themselves to the flight desk, they were asked to sit in a luxurious waiting room for a couple of minutes. It actually took almost four minutes before their flight hostess came in to welcome them and lead them to their aircraft.

They climbed aboard the Citation X, and both let out a sigh of pleasure as they entered the cabin. Even Daniel let out a happy gurgle, though that could have been gas. It was always hard to tell until it was too late.

Though not a big jet, it was plenty for them, especially as it was only for them!

The hostess got them seated, including attaching Daniel's car seat into one of the jet's cream leather armchairs.

The hostess asked them if they needed anything before departure, as she was not flying with them. She showed them the mini fridge and snack basket at the front and the toilet at the rear. She then gave them a short safety briefing.

Her job done, she exited the plane with a cheerful smile and a wave. Immediately the hydraulic steps folded into the door hatch, and sealed them in.

The pilot stepped out of the cockpit and came back to say hello, looking exactly the way one hopes pilots would look; mid-forties, California tan, fit, and with long, wavy chestnut hair.

Captain Audrey introduced herself and gestured to the cockpit where her co-pilot, Greg, gave a brief wave while focusing on pre-flight checks.

She explained the flight time, the approach and the expected weather. She then took a moment to coo over Daniel before heading back to the flight deck.

Henry knew better, but couldn't help glancing at their pilot's firm butt as she retreated. Mary didn't mind Henry's occasional window-shopping, but not when he was stupid enough to get caught doing it.

"You really are a pig in shit at the moment, aren't you?"

"Guilty as charged," he grinned back at her.

"How much of this surprise really was to make the trip bearable for me and how much was about your fantasy about finally flying in a private jet?"

"Why, honey," his eyes held a mischievous twinkle, "one hundred per cent of this is for you! I would have been perfectly happy on a commercial flight. I just hope you remember this day, and the enormous effort I made to ensure your comfort and happiness."

He got the full glare only this one was tinged with a dash of amusement. "You are so full of shit!"

"I know – but look where we are!! On a private jet!"

"You know we have to give it back when we land, right?"

"We'll just see about that." He winked at her then turned to the seat across the narrow aisle and smiled over at Daniel. He was fast asleep.

"How long do you think that will last?" His voice lowered to a whisper.

The engines began to rev up, and within moments the aircraft began taxiing to the active runway. The ride on the ground was much bumpier than on a large commercial jet. They kept their eyes on the baby, waiting for the wailing to begin.

They taxied to the end of the runway, were given immediate clearance, then began to accelerate. It was a completely different experience from a huge passenger jet. The acceleration was more like a Porsche than a plane. They reached rotation speed within seconds, and the nose suddenly lifted off the runway.

They didn't gently climb like an overburdened pelican, as is the usual. The little jet clawed its way up into the sky at a steep angle. The sense of power was extraordinary. Henry was grinning so broadly, he wasn't sure his face would ever return to normal.

Mary, on the other hand, had her fingers well and truly dug into the leather armrests.

Daniel hadn't noticed a thing. He was still happily sleeping the sleep of the innocent.

The flight took less than two hours, and after a delightfully gentle landing at LAX, they taxied to the General Aviation area where their driver was waiting for them just beyond a white slatted security fence.

*

The drive home was the usual Los Angeles cultural experience. The 405 was bumper to bumper, so they opted for La Cienega which was moving, until they crossed under the 10, at which point all bets were off.

Their driver was LA experienced, so knew every side street and alley that could get them a few extra feet closer to home. He was doing a fine job until they crossed Wilshire, at which point it was better for blood pressure just to sit on Doheny, and crawl like lemmings up to Sunset.

The drive from LAX to Sunset is a strange and eye-opening experience. You go from industrial, through low-end commercial, through an oil field, descend into a barrio, then are suddenly in the eastern section of the Beverly Hills commercial district. Then begins the slow climb through BH and West Hollywood until you finally hit Sunset.

You feel like you have travelled through six different countries. On some days it takes almost that long.

It took them the same time to fly from Vail to LAX as it did to drive from LAX to their home. One was nine hundred miles, the other nine miles. Go figure!

The only non-stressed individual was the baby. Partially because he slept the entire way, but also, Henry firmly believed it was because wearing nappies made you feel more prepared for just about anything.

CHAPTER
FOURTEEN

Their next priority was to find a live-in nanny. They had put feelers out before leaving for Colorado, but now the time had come to interview the candidates.

They realised that truly devoted parents would have given up one income and made sure Daniel had a stay-at-home mum or dad. They couldn't manage that. Mary did work from home, but was on call for spoilt home sellers who 'needed' her services at a moment's notice.

Henry wasn't an option either. He was in a race to change the world, or at least some of its technology. So, the decision had been reached that a nanny was the only answer. The moral justification was that Mary would be home a lot, so she really wouldn't be one of those absent working mums.

Planning for the interviews was much harder than expected. Henry had only ever interviewed genius-level technologists where personality came a distant second to talent, so he didn't feel he brought much to the recruitment party.

Mary's history of hiring was for project decorating, furnishing and party planning. Again, not really in the childcare arena.

They came up with the idea, after a couple of designer gins, that Daniel would be made part of the hiring committee.

Their plan was to interview each candidate with Daniel in the room, then find a pretext to leave the unsuspecting individual alone with the baby. Mary and Henry would be watching the interaction from another room, via a nanny-cam in the sitting room. They realised that they were probably on shaky moral, ethical and legal ground, but they just didn't know what else to do. Besides, it was named a nanny-cam and was designed to specifically watch nannies at work when parents were out. They were just following the instructions. Sort of.

They had gone to three agencies that specialised in recruiting nannies. Each of these had submitted three candidates. That gave them nine chances to find the perfect one.

Another issue that was causing them some concern was that they really didn't have a clue what to look for in a perfect nanny. Mary Poppins and Nanny McPhee were fantastic templates but obviously without the magic and cartoon creatures their personalities could get old quickly!

Mrs Doubtfire was another gem but even in West Hollywood cross-dressing and childcare were not always recommended to be paired. Maria from *The Sound of Music* was a perfect example, but the singing might just drive them all a bit loopy.

There was always Jane Eyre for a more classically Gothic alternative, but Mary felt that the predisposition to becoming besotted with the man of the house could, ultimately, become problematic.

The only choice was to find a blend of all the good parts, plus just get a feeling for each person. Then it would be up to Daniel. A bit boring by Hollywood standards, but what can you do? There was another factor to the search requirements which kind of freaked them both out. This person was going to be living in their house. That was a tough one for the Trapps. They liked, no, craved, their privacy. They liked to get frisky. They liked to get silly. They sometimes had screaming fights.

Basically, they liked to be able to be themselves once within the sanctity of their own home.

Sharing their home with a baby was one thing. Sharing their cherished space with a complete stranger, an adult stranger at that, had all the makings of being a complete bummer. They knew this sounded pretty selfish for new parents, but darn it. They felt how they felt.

They did understand that give and take was a part of parenthood. They just hadn't realised yet that the 'give' part was pretty much all on their side for the first eighteen years or so. The 'take' part would be on the child's end, basically forever.

Anyway, all they needed to find was a delightful, nurturing, non-singing nanny who wouldn't fall for Henry, would be devoted to Daniel and would be a houseguest from heaven.

Easy-peasy!

*

The interviews were scheduled to start in two days' time on Wednesday. Three candidates would be seen a day, so they hoped by Friday afternoon to have found the perfect nanny for them and for Daniel.

After basically wasting the next two days on interview rehearsals, rewrites, then for some reason a full dress rehearsal, they were even more confused about what to do than before they started.

This person was going to literally be a life-changer for them. They would have to go from complete stranger, to long-term caregiver and housemate in a matter of days.

"How the hell do you interview for something like that?" Mary suddenly screamed after a particularly bad mock interview. By Tuesday afternoon, they decided that a pitcher of appletinis was the only answer. They reasoned that, if they couldn't work it out on the day, then they had much bigger issues regarding parenting.

*

Wednesday arrived, and, other than a case of butterflies for Mary and Henry, and a spectacular morning poo from Daniel, they were ready to do battle.

Nanny candidate number one arrived exactly on time.

A good start.

Natalie was twenty-seven, was dressed in business casual, and had her blonde hair tied back in a professional manner. All good. She did have a couple of questionable ear piercings, but the Trapps tried to ignore these considering the other plusses.

Natalie handed them her résumé, then introduced herself. At first, they assumed that the poor girl had a speech impediment, till they noticed her oversized tongue piercing. They really wanted to forgive modern trends that weren't in their realm of understanding, but to violate your body to the point of impacting your ability to speak, was beyond their tolerance level.

Still, they were willing to try and not be close-minded, then Natalie took off her jacket.

Though professionally done, and certainly striking, the amount of ink on her arms was mind-boggling. It was as if every single like or dislike in the girl's life ended up as a tattoo on her flesh. They both were scared to imagine how much more 'art' and piercings were hidden from view.

They went through the motions of interviewing Natalie, though her status as a candidate was, at that point, on pretty shaky ground. She answered all their questions well and according to her CV history had been a live-in with two other families. Both had written glowing reviews.

They found an excuse to leave her and Daniel alone, then went to their bedroom to watch and listen to the feed from the nanny-cam.

At first, Natalie stayed seated, then she tiptoed over to Daniel's crib. She smiled down at him and touched the mobile suspended above him, putting it in motion.

Daniel's eyes never left hers. He seemed to be smiling. All was going well until Natalie started to hiccup. At first, they were gentle hics, but within moments they were at defcon 3. Natalie looked completely shocked and embarrassed. Daniel just giggled.

The Trapps decided that their absence was not doing anyone any good, so they returned to the living room. The moment they entered the room, the hiccups stopped.

"Everything okay in here?" Mary asked innocently.

"I don't know." Natalie, red-faced and breathless, responded between gasps.

"You seem a little flustered," Henry added.

"I just had the worst attack of hiccups!" She tried not to look unhinged.

"Allergies?" Mary suggested.

Natalie's breathing had returned to normal. "I don't know. I mean I guess... maybe," she replied.

"Well, we have all your details." Mary shook her hand. "We will be in touch."

"Thank you for your time," Natalie replied defeatedly. She still looked a little out of it.

Henry saw her to the door. As she was about to step outside, she looked to the crib, then to Henry, and was about to speak when, instead, a mighty belch came out. We're talking *Elf*-movie belch. She looked mortified, then turned and ran to her car. Henry couldn't be sure, but it looked to him like she was crying as she drove away.

He closed the door and turned to Mary. "Well! That was a good start!"

The next candidate, Iris, was as lacklustre an individual as could possibly be imagined. She was in her thirties, drably dressed, had greasy, limp hair and seemed not to have one iota of personality. According to her bio, she had lots of experience, but trying to converse with her was almost like going under hypnosis. Her monotonous voice was literally mind-numbing.

At one point, she finished one of her endless speeches and the Trapps were so out of it they just kept staring and smiling at her.

The baby/nanny one-on-one, was just as thrilling. Once they left the room, Iris sat exactly where she was without moving a muscle. She never once looked at Daniel who, to be fair, never once looked at her.

Candidate three got their hopes up immediately. Christy Bellingham was in her thirties. She had been a professional nanny all her life. She had been with five households, none of which had wanted her to leave, even after their children were beyond the need for a nanny.

She had a calming effect on the Trapps the moment she entered their home. She smelled like lavender and cinnamon, and was wearing what looked like an authentic Annie Hall ensemble.

She spoke with just a trace of a southern accent, which both found to be almost melodic. She seemed to have no piercings, tats or nervous reactions to the interview or to Daniel.

Neither wanted to say anything, but both the Trapps were thinking, 'Mary Poppins'.

When they did their subtle exit to spy on her and Daniel, Christy gave Daniel a wink, as if she knew exactly what they were up to.

Huddled in their bedroom, they watched in amazement as she went straight to the crib and carried on a full conversation with Daniel. Though somewhat one-sided, she got a response from him to every question. The replies were mainly burps, gurgles and giggles, but still, it really looked like a conversation.

Suddenly, she gently reached into the crib and lifted him over her head and gave him a gentle spin. He seemed to love it. After planting a gentle kiss on his forehead, she returned him to his bedding.

The Trapps were so moved by what they witnessed that they had to take a moment to compose themselves before returning to the living room.

As they walked back into the room, they were both grinning like trick or treaters after a 'take all you want' house. Their grins diminished slightly when they saw that in the time it had taken them to compose and return, Christy had helped herself to a substantial pour of Bacardi Dark.

Their grins completely withered away and died when, in her lovely southern lilt, she asked if she could trouble them for some ice.

As they showed her to the door, Christy looked utterly puzzled.

"But I don't drink!" She looked both confused and alarmed.

"Neither do we!" Henry replied. "Thanks for coming."

He shut the front door gently in her face.

And so ended Wednesday's interviews.

*

The first two candidates on Thursday were basically okay but just not what they were looking for. They wanted Daniel to have a nanny that went beyond just going through the motions. They wanted someone who could excite and motivate him. Maybe even expand his young mind. The last two candidates gave the impression they'd be glued to their iPhones whenever possible.

Candidate three (for Thursday, number six in total) was a bit of a shock. Teri was a man. A kind-looking man in his mid-forties. He was thin and had receding brown hair. His heavy-rimmed black glasses were thick-lensed and seemed to cause him to squint and blink.

"It really is a pleasure to be here." His voice was a full octave higher than one would have expected.

The Trapps read his résumé and were momentarily stunned.

"You have a PhD from Berkeley in Infant and Early Childhood Development!" Mary sounded a bit dubious.

"Yes, I do. Two to be exact. I have a double doctorate. My second is in Infant Mental Health."

Mary and Henry glanced at each other in amazement.

"I have to ask," Henry tried to find the right words, "why would you want to be a nanny? Aren't you a little overqualified?"

"Not in the least." He puffed out his self-important little chest. "All my education has, to this point, been leading up to what I knew would be a successful academic career. As expected, they have offered me a full professorship when I am ready."

"And you're not ready?" Mary waved his CV to make her point.

Teri looked amused. "From an education standpoint I am." He paused to wipe his glasses with a tiny square of velvet that he produced from his tweed jacket pocket.

"It took me nine years to get my doctorates. They were incredibly difficult years. The amount of study and research was almost crippling. That said, I succeeded. My plan had always been to take a three-year sabbatical after my advanced education to implement my learnings and confirm all my findings. I decided that being a nanny would be the perfect environment for that endeavour."

"You make that sound very clinical," Henry observed.

"It is very clinical. That's how I run my life. That's how I handled my education, that's how I will handle my future pedagogic mission. I promise you, clinical-mindedness will be exactly what I bring to my duties as a nanny."

"Care to elaborate on that a little?" Henry wasn't liking the direction this was going.

"I have found in my studies that one can't simply let an infant brain form its own paths and byways. No, it needs to be given strict direction so that every thought and every brain function is pre-programmed to guarantee an optimal outcome."

"Are you saying you don't believe that a child should develop free thought?" Mary asked.

Teri laughed. Though, in his case, it sounded more like the bark from a small dog. They assumed it pre-programmed.

"Free thought! Good god, no. A baby's mind must be wired at the earliest point. It needs to be in perfect harmony with those of his peers and underlings. Otherwise how is it going to find its place in the world? Free thought is the wrecking ball of clarity and conformity. The young mind must be adapted as soon as possible to a common uniformity."

Mary had gone pale. Henry took a step closer to Teri, causing the other man to blink rapidly. "I've got a couple of questions for you. Firstly, did you repeatedly refer to a child as 'it'? Secondly, are you are aware that you just outlined the hive premise of the Borg, in *Star Trek*?"

Teri smiled at Henry's analogy. "I am delighted you see the parallel. I am not suggesting forced assimilation, obviously, but wiring a child's mind to be part of the collective that is our human race can only be of benefit to all. I'm sure you can see that."

"I think you should leave." Mary's voice practically had ice crystals attached.

"Maybe I didn't explain my premise correctly—" Teri continued unfazed and somehow unaware that he had lost his audience. Big time.

Henry walked over to the fireplace and stood before a standing rack of fire irons. He opted for a long, wrought-iron poker with a bent hook curving up one side.

"I think maybe you didn't understand my wife's premise." Holding the poker with his left hand he smacked the other end against his right hand.

"Let me try to put it in a more pedagogic framework for you. We find your premise, and treatise, to be, not just bullshit, but pedagogically, and socially, insane. Therefore, our collective hive would request that you please get the hell out of our house before my PhD kicks the shit out of your two PhDs."

For a millisecond, Teri thought Henry might have been kidding. The fact that Henry took a step closer to him with the fire iron still in his hand radically changed his viewpoint.

"Fine. I'll go, but this – behaviour of yours is a perfect example of non-conformity." His voice was almost a squeal. "This is what free thinking at an early age can lead to. This is not good hive etiquette."

Henry took another step closer.

It was a good thing that Mary had made her way to the front door and was holding it open. The man ran so fast out of their house that, had the door not been open, he would most likely have run right through it, leaving a cartoon-like cut-out section of himself.

The Trapps collapsed next to each other on the couch. Both of them held their heads in their hands. Long seconds passed until Mary started to laugh. Quietly at first. Then Henry joined in. Within moments they were both howling with laughter, tears flowing down their cheeks.

"Resistance is futile!" Henry's impression of the Borg was perfect.

That sent them into fresh peals of laughter.

Once they got themselves under control, Henry rose to his feet and stretched.

"I need a drink!" he declared. "Interested?"

"What did you have in mind?"

"I thought a Bacardi Dark and grapefruit juice. Oh, wait – did the nanny leave any!?"

This brought on another peal of laughter.

Mary turned on the couch to look over at him. "We do seem to be getting the cream of the crop, don't we?"

"And these are the ones vetted by the agencies," he added.

"Tomorrow will be the day. I can just feel it." Mary got to her feet and went over to Daniel. She lifted him out of the crib and returned to the couch. She lay him on her lap. He looked directly up at her. "Can you try real hard tomorrow to help us find the perfect nanny for you?"

He looked directly up at her and made a goo-goo sound, just before filling his nappy with another special gift for his new parents.

*

Friday dawned grey and rainy. Candidate Myra arrived thirty minutes late, and was completely soaked. Her car had broken down on Sunset and she had run the rest of the way.

Despite the auspicious start, the interview went exceedingly well. She was twenty-three and though new to nannying, came from a big family and loved children.

She was dressed in what looked to be expensive but oversized comfy clothes. She had a small, perfectly symmetrical face, topped by a wild outcrop of naturally curly orange/red hair. She had probably spent hours trying to tame it pre-interview, but a damp day and a half mile sprint will undo the best of coifs.

She was studying for her Masters in Film History entirely online, so felt this job would be the perfect fit. The more they talked with her, the better they felt about her. She was intelligent, bright, enthusiastic, and seemed to be a naturally happy person.

When they snuck off to play their version of candid camera, they were both excited to see Daniel and her interaction. A couple of minutes after they left the room, Myra walked over to the crib and smiled down at Daniel. "You are a beautiful boy, aren't you?" she cooed. "You and I are gonna be great friends."

Daniel held out a hand towards her. She held the tiny hand and Daniel gurgled and smiled. He then let go of

118

her hand, and reached out to her. She leant into the crib, thinking he wanted to touch her face. Instead, he grabbed her by the hair and pulled.

She at first laughed. "No. That's mine." She tried to gently dislodge his hand.

He pulled harder.

"Ouch! Please stop." She tried to sound calm, but it was starting to hurt.

In the other room, Henry and Mary saw what was happening and knew that they would have to break cover to resolve this little bump in the road.

They made a dash for the living room.

By the time they got there, Daniel's tiny hand was holding a substantial clump of freshly harvested red hair.

Myra was in tears and had backed away from the crib. "What the fuck is wrong with you, you little shit!?"

She then sensed that the Trapps had returned. Without another word, and without even acknowledging them, she stomped over to their decorative wrought-iron coat rack, grabbed her wet rain raincoat and left the house.

"Should we have offered her a lift?" Henry tried to make light of the situation. Mary looked into the crib. She was concerned about Daniel, but saw that he was fast asleep, still clutching the wad of orange/red hair.

They spent the next thirty minutes rebooting their frazzled emotions to be ready for the next candidate.

About ten minutes before she was due to arrive, the agency called to let them know that she wouldn't be coming as she had just accepted another position earlier that morning.

That left one.

They were both starting to feel the pressure. Sure, they could contact other agencies, and put up some online postings, but in the past three days, they had supposedly seen the pinnacle of nanny perfection.

They weren't impressed.

They didn't want to feel that all their hopes were pinned on the next and last interview but that was exactly how they did feel.

They were worried that the candidate would sense their desperation the moment they entered the house.

At 2 p.m. exactly, candidate number nine arrived and was ushered into their living room. The Trapps really wanted to like this one, but there was already an issue. Sitting on their couch was a female version of Ozzy Osbourne from the early Black Sabbath period. She couldn't have been more goth had she tried, and there was no question that she really had tried. She probably had a bat in her black leather satchel, in case she needed a snack during the interview.

Sarah Milton formed her thin black lips into a smile. "Hi. So, where's the kid?"

Mary looked over to the crib. Sarah followed her gaze then got to her feet and clomped over. She studied Daniel for a good few seconds.

"Yeah. He'll do," she stated.

"Do for what exactly?" Mary had visions of their child on a sacrificial altar, surrounded by goth clones of Sarah all holding flaming torches as a high priestess approached with a ceremonial dagger in hand.

"The video!" Sarah seemed surprised at the question.

"I'm sorry. There seems to be some confusion here. You do know that this is an interview for the position of full-time nanny?" Henry tried to keep his voice as upbeat as possible.

"What!" Sarah burst out laughing. "No way! That's really funny."

"Funny how?" Mary slowly got to her feet and stood defensively between Sarah and the crib.

"I'm the lead singer for the band Satan's Nannies. We're looking for a baby to be in our video and cover art," Sarah tried to explain. "You thought I was here to look after your kid? Wow. Do I look like what you had in mind?"

"Actually no. How did you get put in touch with us?" Mary asked, still looking concerned.

"Our manager contacted our PR guy in LA to find us a baby we could use. I guess some wires got crossed." Sarah actually seemed disappointed. "You'd be surprised how hard it is to find a baby to do a Satan-themed photo shoot."

"Shocking," Henry answered.

"I don't suppose you would be interested—?" Sarah offered.

"We try to limit him to three satanic projects a month. Sorry," Henry replied.

It took Sarah a moment to realise that Henry was joking.

"Yeah. I get it." Sarah headed for the door. "Good luck with your nanny hunt."

She let herself out.

Mary leant against the closed front door.

"What a nice girl."

*

And then there were none.

121

CHAPTER
FIFTEEN

By six o'clock, they had both consumed a couple of glasses of wine, and had been hashing out all conceivable options they had left. Mary had to be on hand in a few days to manage the Weatherlys' design install, and Henry really needed to get back to the lab.

"I know what we need," Henry suddenly declared.

Mary looked to him hoping for a brilliant solution.

Henry looked her straight in the eye. "Alexa, play Satan's Nannies."

The room suddenly filled with grunge-speed metal music. The opening lyrics pretty much said it all.

"Your nannies all know what Satan needs
What Satan needs
When Satan bleeds
Yeah, your nannies all know what Satan needs
So, fill us please

We're on our knees
One by one with Satan seeds
One by one with Satan seeds
Yeah, one by one with Satan seeds."

They were laughing so hard, they almost missed the Ring doorbell chime on their phones.

"Alexa! Enough!" Henry shouted over the din.

The room went quiet.

Still laughing, Henry answered the front door.

"Who is it?" Mary called from the living room.

Christy Bellingham and an older woman stood on the front porch, both looking exceedingly nervous.

Henry turned and shouted back to Mary, "Hide the rum!"

He then turned back to the surprise guests.

"Well?" he asked bluntly.

"Mr Trapp, this is my mother, Alison," Christy stammered. "May we have a few minutes of your time, please?"

Henry looked them both over and was about to reply when Mary appeared next to him, and took over.

"Of course. Please, come in."

Henry reluctantly stepped aside and let them pass, but not before shooting Mary a WTF expression. She responded with a 'Oh grow up' glare.

It was amazing how communicative they could be without actual speech.

Henry contemplated offering their unexpected guests a drink, but assumed (correctly) that Mary would find fault with that.

Mary led them to the dining area so they could all sit facing each other.

Christy began. "I am sure you are wondering what we are doing here?"

"It had crossed my mind." Mary tried to sound much more casual than she actually felt. "I have to explain something. At least, try to explain it." Christy forged ahead. "I don't drink. I have never had a drink in my life. My father—" She searched for the word. "He had a problem. It impacted all of us – anyway, I vowed to never drink and I never have. This is pretty dumb, but I brought my mum along to tell you that I am telling the truth."

She looked pleadingly at the Trapps.

"Then what was the whole bit with the glass of rum, and you needing ice?" Henry asked.

"I don't know. I was playing with Daniel. I gave him a spin. He seemed to really like it. I remember placing him back in the crib. The next thing, I am standing over there," she pointed to the bar area, "and I have a glass of something in my hand, and I asked you for ice."

"We know," Mary pointed out. "We were there."

"My point is, that I have no memory of moving from the crib and going to the bar, and presumably pouring myself a glass of…"

"Bacardi Dark," Henry added.

"Especially when I don't drink. EVER!" She turned to her mother.

"She really doesn't. If you knew our family history, you would understand. She never will drink."

Mary studied them both for a few seconds. "Okay. Let's say we believe that. I still don't see why you are here?"

"I am here because I really want this job. I thought you guys were great. I thought Daniel was just a dream. You seemed to be impressed with me – weren't you?"

Mary shrugged a reluctant affirmation.

"I can't explain what happened. But why, when I really wanted this job, and we had a great interview, would I go and raid your bar right in front of you?

"I mean, if I had a problem, I am pretty sure I could have waited to get a drink on the way home. Why would I intentionally destroy a perfect opportunity like this?"

Mary and Henry looked to each other then back at the young woman.

"We don't know. But you did."

Alison cleared her throat. All eyes turned to her. "May I offer a theory? You'll have to excuse the psycho-babble, but I think you'll find it fits."

"Please, go on," Mary said.

"My daughter has been a live-in nanny for almost twenty years. She has loved every minute of her career. I believe you have the references from all the families?"

The Trapps nodded.

"The one part she always hated was when the time came to leave each household. Having to say goodbye to a child that you have been instrumental in raising, that you have grown to love, that has become part of your life, was literally heartbreaking. Not just to Christy, but for the child as well.

"Christy left the last family just two weeks ago. She had been with them for almost four years. The day she left, the child cried and cried and wouldn't let go of her. Her mother finally had to forcibly take her away. Christy's last memory was of the little girl screaming in tears as she walked away from the house and got in her car."

Alison took a moment to study the expressions on the faces around the dining table.

"Whether one could call it clinical shock, I don't know. The fact is, that every time she has to leave, part of her is left behind with the family and the child. As I mentioned, the last one was the hardest, and I believe it really had a big impact on Christy.

"I feel that what you saw was some sort of subconscious attempt by her to NOT succeed with the interview and thereby unconsciously avoid finding herself in a position where she would again be hurt. "I know for a fact that she wants to be Daniel's nanny more than words can express. Something inside her, however, just knows that when it comes time to leave him, she will yet again be devastated. That is probably her greatest flaw, but, it's also probably the reason that she is so good at what she does. Honey, what do you think? Is that a possibility?" She turned to face her daughter. Christy was trying desperately to hold back a wave of emotion. She managed a weak nod. A single tear ran down her cheek. She brushed it away just as another one dripped onto the other cheek.

"Sorry. I feel so embarrassed by all this."

Mary, her eyes misted over, reached across the table and held Christy's arm. "I am so sorry too. I had no idea."

The room fell into complete silence.

The only sound was a gentle ticking from a small brass carriage clock on the mantelpiece.

"So, my rum would be safe with you?" Henry as always went for levity.

"Yes, sir. I give you my word," Christy managed through a tearful sniffle.

"Feel like re-introducing yourself to Daniel?" Mary offered.

Christy managed a nod.

Alison smiled at Henry, as Mary led Christy to the newly created nursery.

"He's a very lucky boy to have her."

Henry silently agreed.

CHAPTER
SIXTEEN

Christy moved in the following Monday.

Prior to her start day she had met up with the Trapps at their house a couple of times, and at the famous Terry's on Santa Monica on another occasion.

She had never been to Terry's before, but immediately fell in love with the place. The Trapps were regulars. Henry didn't see how anyone wouldn't love a place that served coffee in cups bigger than soup bowls.

Daniel was in his bassinet, tucked in between Mary and Christy at one of the prized outdoor tables. They noticed early on that Daniel never took his eyes off her. At one point, when she left the table for a couple of minutes, he literally pouted.

They were impressed. They weren't even aware that a pout was in his repertoire yet. They decided that that might have actually been its inaugural unveiling. The moment Christy returned and sat back down, the pout vanished.

In those 'discovery' days, they formed the beginning of a real bond. They found that their interests were similar, with the obvious exceptions of Henry's geeky physics stuff. Their humour was in sync, they seemed to like the same movies, TV and music. Not surprisingly, Satan's Nannies wasn't on any of their top-ten lists.

*

By the time Christy moved into what had originally been built as the 'maid's' room (but had since undergone Mary's magic and had become a cosy bedroom with en-suite), the four were already comfortable with one another.

Mary was able to throw all of her focus back on the Weatherlys' staging and Henry was chomping at the bit to get back to the lab. It wasn't just that he was missing his work. Something happened to him on the previous night and Henry desperately needed to get together with his team.

It is said that scientific breakthroughs are very often the result of a serendipitous event. His revelation came as a result of a new brand of disposable nappies.

It was the last night that he would be doing changing duties. Christy was to take over those responsibilities the following day. The nappies were a brand that Christy had recommended.

They were extra comfy, better at keeping the liquid away from the baby and, most importantly, when the absorbency pad was soaked in urine, it turned purple.

While this was not the greatest scientific breakthrough in history, it resonated with Henry in a big way.

He was changing Daniel just before 2 a.m., following a decent poo (Daniel's), when his son decided to add a little tinkle to the mix. Henry was able to actually watch the nappy pad's colour change from pale yellow to a cheerful lilac the moment the pee hit the material.

"Very cool," he said to no one in particular. He was still grinning when he got back beneath the covers and started to doze off.

His brain had a completely different plan for him. He kept seeing the yellow liquid turn purple. Time and time again.

He recognised that it was clever, but not to the point of his losing sleep.

At three fifteen he finally dozed off.

At three forty-seven he sat bolt upright in bed.

"Holy shit!" he cried.

Mary managed to not wake up, but was still able to smack him in the arm.

"Sorry," he whispered. He tried to go back to sleep, but his scientific brain had just undertaken a quantum leap that was going to change his sleep pattern for a very long time.

The next morning, Henry charged through the kitchen, waved at Christy who was fixing a breakfast bottle for Daniel, and headed out to the truck.

He started the mighty V8 and to celebrate what he was certain would be a big day at Magic Vision, he chose 'The Killers, Live at the Albert Hall'. The first track, 'Human' was one of his favourite sing-alongs for important days.

The sky was clear as bell, which told him a Santa Anna was in residence. The temp was a perfect 72, and he felt every molecule in his body powering him towards a wonderful day.

Brandon Flowers was singing.

Henry was singing.

The Ford was growling.

Nice!

*

There are days, very few of them, when driving to work in LA is actually uplifting. There are three things that make this possible. Flowing traffic, perfect smogless weather, and peace of mind. One can often get number two and three, but the traffic will end up being a shit fest, which in turn negates the peace of mind.

Today the trinity were in line.

Driving up the west side of Laurel without traffic, then down the valley side when you can see almost to infinity, is a wonderful thing.

*

Henry made it to work in almost record time. Even Magic Vision's crappy industrial neighbourhood, couldn't dent his mojo that day.

Henry ran into the facility and shouted for everyone to join him at the conference table. Though puzzled, his team gathered around him with a sense of excited expectation.

David Chen was the last to sit. "If you're going to show us pictures of your new kid, I'm outa here!" he joked.

"Much better than that." Henry mirrored his phone to a 90-inch screen on the wall, then went to his search history and selected one particular video.

The screen came alive with the commercial for the disposable nappies that changed colour.

The team stared blankly at the flat screen, then at Henry.

"Want me to play it again?" he offered.

They looked back at him with growing concern.

"What the fuck, man?" Chen voiced.

Henry waved away his concern. "I showed you that video because I think it might actually be the clue to how we create the receptive and reflective surface for the image."

"You want to project video onto nappies?" One of the interns spoke up.

Henry grinned back at the young man. "Try and keep up!"

He turned to the others around the table.

"The air around us is made up primarily of nitrogen, oxygen, with dashes of argon, carbon dioxide and methane. Right so far?"

His audience mumbled their acknowledgement.

Henry continued. "We need to focus on argon. I believe its molecules could be our answer."

They didn't look exactly overjoyed with the direction Henry was heading.

That didn't stop him.

"Argon is a noble gas. It is inert. It is for the most part unreactive AND it is completely colourless and thus does not react to projected light."

He let this sink in for a moment before continuing.

"So how does that help us?" Chen asked.

"What it does do, and this is where my nappy revelation comes in, is that argon's molecules turn violet when bombarded by an electrical field."

He smiled back at his team, believing them to be on his wavelength.

They were still looking befuddled and concerned until Chen's expression suddenly changed from abject doubter, to fanatical believer.

"Holy shit!" Chen slammed his palm onto the table. "If we can excite the molecules with a consistent reactive to trigger the colour change, we could adapt our image colourimetry to use the violet hue like a blue or green screen."

"Thereby enabling the light from our projected images to be reflected back," Henry finished for him. The others round the room all started to catch on. Their excitement became electric. The supercharged air around the conference table was practically simmering.

Argon molecules must have been changing colour all around them.

Except around the intern, who still hadn't grasped what Henry had just explained. He raised his hand to try and get the attention of the joyously numb technicians around the table. "I still don't get what any of this has to do with nappies?"

CHAPTER
SEVENTEEN

When Henry got home later that day, he was still riding a cloud of euphoria.

Unfortunately, walking into the house put an end to what had been a spectacular day.

Mary was sitting at the dining table, staring fixedly at her laptop screen. She turned to face him and he immediately saw that something was very wrong.

"Honey?" Henry sat beside her. "What's up? What are you looking at?"

"Sheriff Massey sent me this link a few hours ago." She gestured to the screen.

He tilted it for a better view. The screen was filled with a newspaper article about a car accident. The picture showed a wrecked Audi 4, crumpled at the bottom of a ravine. He scrolled the page to see where it was posted. He recognised the header from the local Glenwood Springs paper. The *Post Independent*.

He glanced over at Mary. He wasn't sure what he was supposed to be seeing.

"Read it." Her voice sounded tense.

He started to read.

*

On Friday evening, officers from Glenwood Springs were called to investigate a possible road accident five miles outside of town, on County Rd 132.

The officers located the reported vehicle and discovered that there were two occupants within the car and that both were deceased.

It is believed that the vehicle left the County Rd at excessive speed, and ultimately came to rest at the bottom of a narrow ravine. It is further thought that both occupants died almost immediately from their injuries.

The victims were identified as Jerry White and his son Brad White. Jerry was the executive chef at the Glenwood Plaza Hotel.

Brad was one of the regular bartenders at the same establishment.

As the investigation of the accident is still ongoing, funeral services have not yet been arranged.

*

Henry re-read the article twice before turning to face Mary.

"That really sucks." He took a deep breath and was about to close the screen.

Something dawned on him. "Why did the sheriff send this to you?"

"He sent it to both of us. You probably haven't checked your email in a while."

"Guilty as charged," he agreed. "But the question still stands. Why send this link to us? We hardly knew the man."

"Massey's email asked that we call him once we read this." Mary stared intently at her husband, looking for some sort of reaction.

"What are you looking at me for? I have no idea what he wants."

Mary pushed her phone towards him in response. "Maybe we should find out?"

*

He tried the police station first and learned that the sheriff had left for the day. The duty officer advised that he had been instructed to give them his cell number if they called.

Massey picked up almost immediately.

"Ah, my favourite Californians!" his voice boomed.

"I'm going to put you on speaker, Sheriff?" Henry advised.

"No problem at all. So, I guess this means you read the article?"

Henry looked to Mary to answer, but she mimed for him to carry on.

"Yes, we did. Very sad to hear. We were a little surprised that you thought to send us the link. We weren't exactly that close." There was dead air for a few seconds.

"Sheriff?" Mary prodded.

"Still here. I was just trying to decide how to answer your question."

More dead air.

Henry and Mary exchanged a puzzled look.

"For some reason, I felt that you folks should hear – what wasn't mentioned in that article."

"Go on." Henry felt a sense of dread creep up his spine.

"The last time anybody saw Jerry was about two weeks before you picked up your boy and flew home. Neither he, nor his son, had turned up at work since that time. The hotel manager finally got an answer at his house, and did manage to speak to Jerry. Apparently, all Jerry kept saying was that he was sorry, and had no right."

"No right for what?" Mary interrupted.

"No idea. The GM said that he sounded pretty weird. Out of it, was the expression he used."

"Sheriff, we're sorry about what happened to him, but we still don't get how we're in this loop." Henry tried to sound calmer than he was feeling.

"It's the next couple of things I'm going to tell you that explain your part in the loop, as you put it. Did you know that Jerry visited the hospital about a week before you arrived last time?"

"No. Why would we?" Mary was now starting to get the willies.

"He went to the hospital to visit your son."

137

The dead air came from the Trapps this time.

"It seems he was there close on an hour. No staff member even saw him. We only found out when the hospital security officer did his weekly random check of the cloud interface for the hospital cameras. He saw this guy, just standing there, staring into the crib."

"Okay, Sheriff," Henry broke in. "You have succeeded in creeping us both out."

"Sorry about that. Wasn't really my intention, though I thought you should at least know what I know."

"You said there were a couple of things?" Mary was pretty sure she didn't want to hear number two, but still had to ask.

"The other thing relates to the accident. Our team has studied the site and the car's inboard computer. Jerry was accelerating towards that bend in the road. He never once applied the brakes."

More dead air.

Mary was the first to speak.

"So, it was intentional?"

"Seems that way."

"Like my sister's accident?"

"Now you see why I felt we should speak," Massey stated flatly.

"What the hell does all of this mean?" Henry asked.

"That," Massey continued, "is the part I can't for the life of me put together. Two accidents, same town, both could be intentional, both victims were acting off centre prior to the events, and the only common denominator—"

"Is what?" Mary interrupted. "Come on, Sheriff. What are you saying? I see how there have been a couple of weird

138

accidents in your town recently, but I am pretty sure that there must be a dozen better reasons that don't involve our baby. I mean, do you know for a fact that these cases were related at all? We know that my sister seems to have been depressed, but Jerry's accident could be something else entirely. We know he liked his cocktails. Who's to say he wasn't a pot head as well? That combo could cause you to drive off a cliff any day of the week."

"That's true. No question." Massey was using his patient cop voice.

"So, did he have drugs or alcohol in his system?" Mary used her patient mum voice.

"We are having trouble determining that at the moment."

"Why?" Mary asked.

"I can't go into detail, nor would you want me to, but all I will say is that the toxicology of both bodies had been corrupted."

Henry, ever the scientist, stepped in. "Corrupted by what, Sheriff?"

"By a contaminate."

"Please don't play games. What contaminate?"

Massey could be heard taking a deep breath. "Crotalid venom."

"What!?" Mary had no clue what he was talking about.

"Rattlesnake venom," Henry translated.

"When they went off the road," Massey continued, "the car finally came to rest, smack dab on top of a rattler nest. A big one. It appears they may both have initially survived the crash. They did not however survive the snakes. According to the pathologist, they each had enough venom in them to have killed over a hundred people."

Mary turned deathly pale. "I think I'm gonna—"

"Bathroom! Quick!" Henry commanded.

Mary ran out of the room, her hand over her mouth.

Henry picked up the phone and turned the speaker off. "Sheriff, I am going to hang up now if you don't mind. I'm sure you understand."

Henry disconnected the call. He sat alone in the dining room. The sound of Mary retching in the guest toilet could just be heard above the clock.

Sic, sic, sic.

*

Later that evening, after an unimpressive dinner of canned tomato soup and a wholewheat pitta each, they sat watching the TV with the sound off. They were both in their own worlds. The sound of Daniel burbling while having his evening bottle drifted in from the kitchen.

"It is strange though, isn't it?" Henry broke the spell. "Why would Jerry have visited the hospital?"

"I think we both know that Jerry may have been wrapped just a little too tight. Don't forget his trying to make more out of Ellen's accident. His conspiracy theories had conspiracy theories."

Henry pondered her words for a moment.

"I'm gonna have a beer. Want anything?"

"Holy shit!" Mary exclaimed, slapping herself on the forehead.

"Sorry. It's just a beer!"

"Zeke was impotent! I remember Ellen telling me that when they first met. She said he was the perfect man for her. Hung like a horse and snipped like a rescue dog!"

"She always was a classy gal," Henry quipped.

"Yes, she was! She was also the founding member of the Colorado Anti-Monogamist Society."

Realisation of where Mary was heading finally started to creep into his grey matter.

"Oh my god! Zeke wasn't the father. That would explain Jerry's preoccupation with the baby."

"Me thinks Jerry's rump roast wasn't the only meat Ellen was working with during those cooking classes!" Mary grinned at her own raunchiness.

"You really are a genteel little flower, aren't you?" Henry shook his head in wonder.

"You know the good part of all this?" Mary was totally psyched. "This explains everything. Ellen was depressed about having another man's baby. Zeke was angry, and depressed for the same reason. Jerry was obviously simply screwed up over the whole mess."

"You seem bizarrely happy over a pretty sordid situation," Henry observed.

"I know, but it's great. I mean it's not great for Ellen and everyone, but don't you see? There is nothing creepy going on!"

"You don't think that four suicides within a matter of days warrants being considered just a little creepy?"

"Not any more!" Mary was on a roll. "The funny thing is, we were getting kinda creeped out at the way all this seemed to involve Daniel. Now we know it absolutely involved him! But not in the way we thought! This was just love triangle shit!"

"As opposed to pentangle shit?"

Mary laughed. "Clever! But yeah. I guess so."

- "So, we're agreed. He's just an ordinary baby!?"

"Boring, but yeah, ordinary."

*

Daniel had finished his feeding and Christy had just succeeded in easing a burp out of the little man. She gave his face a quick wipe then brought him into the living room.

"Hey, big guy!" Henry called out.

"Who's had his din-dins then!?" Mary cooed.

*

Daniel recognised the two people in the room. He was way too young to understand that they were family. He somehow knew they were good for him. People who were good for him had a blue fog surrounding them. People who were not, had a red fog. People who played no part in his existence had no colour. Henry and Mary had a bright blue fog.

When he first saw Christy, she had had no colour at all. Then she grabbed him out of his bed which he didn't like. Her fog turned red.

When people went red, he didn't want them around so they stopped being 'around'. There was no conscious or deliberate action. It just happened. It's just the way it was.

When Christy came back the second time she was colourless. Now that she was feeding him and taking care of

142

him, she had colour. Her fog was blue. Very light blue, but still blue. He hoped it would stay that way.

At least while she was important to him.
The blues gathered around him and made a big fuss.
He liked that.

PART II
THE LEARNING

CHAPTER
ONE

The next few years passed in a daze.

Daniel went from a poor defenceless baby requiring constant care and attention, to a two-and-a-half-year-old defenceless toddler, requiring constant care and attention.

There is a reason it is called the terrible twos.

Henry and Mary had been under the completely misguided notion that once out of the baby stage things start to calm down slightly.

No one knows where this horrendous fallacy came from. Probably 'Fake News'.

The reality was, as everyone but the Trapps knew, it just keeps getting harder and harder. When Daniel was snuggled in his crib, he was pretty much at the mercy of those around him. He could be lifted out and delivered wherever and whenever the holder wished.

Sure, there were the night feeds, the incessant crying,

the random but frequent pooping and peeing, yet one still felt in some control of one's life.

If you needed a break, you'd plop the little treasure into his crib, turn on the baby monitor, then relax in another room.

Just before they turn one, a momentous yet horrifying event takes place.

The damn things learn how to walk.

The first steps are cause for great celebration. The first few weeks fall into the 'still adorable' category. After that, forget it.

There's nowhere to hide. The child becomes omnipresent.

You might have an extra six months while the physical act of his getting out of the crib is still too cerebral to manage. But after that, they are basically on the loose.

Daniel stuck to that timetable like he was reading from the manual. The only saving grace for the Trapps was Christy. She was a godsend from the moment she first arrived, and was now, well, holding more than enough credit to justify sainthood.

The thing that the Trapps couldn't get over was that she seemed to love every minute of it.

Every nappy change was a joy.

Every battle to get him to eat his food was an exciting challenge. She even found it worthy of laughter and mirth when Daniel changed from processed veggies to processed meat, resulting in the smelliest shit in the world.

Christy must have got in line twice when God was passing out the nanny gene.

Henry and Mary frequently looked on with relief, a little guilt and still more relief, as Christy performed her nannying miracles. They just knew they could never do what she did. Ever!

Christy realised early on that the Trapps only had so much blood, tears and parenting to give, and even that was from the sidelines. She sat them down one morning and requested that her job (and pay) increase, to include general cleaning and cooking so as to better help out.

Mary and Henry were stunned by her offer and took almost twenty seconds to deliberate the plusses and minuses. Okay, there were no minuses.

Christy had, from that point on, single-handedly managed to make parenting a viable, and survivable, part of their lives.

It wasn't that they didn't love Daniel with all their hearts, it's just you're either born to live in puke-stained sweats or you're not. The other priceless aspect that Christy brought into their lives was that both of them could carry on their businesses as before.

Mary's real estate staging had become so successful that she had had to increase her staff, and even rent grown-up office and warehouse space to handle her blossoming business.

*

Magic Vision was also moving up in the world.

They had perfected the molecular colour tinting and, through some seriously complex software development, had created a mobile demonstration unit to display actual, live, holographic video. Their demo unit was still substantially bigger than a handheld smartphone, but it clearly showed the application. The unit was built to scale and designed to look just like a high-end smartphone. Just four times bigger.

They had had a few in-house demos for friends and families to ensure they could make the presentation both robust and repeatable. Despite being friends and family, they were still all required to sign heavy-duty non-disclosure agreements.

This was business after all.

The demo was only thirty seconds long, but was beyond groundbreaking.

The 'phone' was placed on a custom (if you consider Ikea to be custom) black cube in the centre of the room. Chen would then push the 'play' button on the screen app.

Emerson, Lake and Palmer's 'Fanfare for the Common Man' started in clear, rich audio. The air above the screen took on a slight violet hue, at which point a 'virtual' trapdoor opened upwards from the screen.

Henry's 'holo' then walked up through the trapdoor opening, seemingly from inside the phone, then stood facing his audience. Because of the holographic matrix, the observers could be sitting in a complete circle, and the effect was the same.

Henry's 'holo' self reached back down into the opening and retrieved a chair. He placed it on the surface of the screen, then sat on it.

"Ladies and gentlemen," he announced with deep gravitas. "I bring you the next generation of media viewing. The first 4D, 360-degree experience."

At that point, a massive T-Rex head dropped into the holo-field from above. It roared loudly at the audience, then grabbed Henry in its maw-like jaws. It chewed once then swallowed him whole, roared again at the audience, only now with blood oozing from its teeth. The T-Rex rose back out of view. The music faded, and the violet light vanished into the phone.

That was the entire demo. The thing was, it was like nothing anyone, anywhere, had ever seen.

The clarity, the definition, the contrast, the colourimetry, the holo effect, everything was seamless, to the point that at first viewing, your brain couldn't quite grasp what you had just seen and heard.

Henry and the others at MV had all decided early on not to show or even tease the industry with each stage of what they had developed. Too many high-potential innovations had died because of poorly presented, premature demos that should never have taken place.

Theirs, however, was ready.

They were going to launch their demo at 'ground zero' of consumer technology.

CES in Las Vegas.

They expected to make waves.

They didn't expect the tsunami.

*

CES is held every year in the second week of January. The convention is spread across the almost two million square feet of exhibition and meeting-room space within the Las Vegas Convention Center.

There are approximately four thousand exhibitors and two hundred thousand attendees. The giants, Panasonic, Sony, Samsung, etc. hog the biggest floor space, with display stands the size (and cost) of a luxury home.

The little guys, selling concepts, support and parts are usually banished to the back walls of the event halls, with tiny show stands made up of as little as a hundred square feet.

Magic Vision had no intention of being anywhere near a back wall, or indeed, squashed under the shadow of one of the giants, showing off their new two-hundred and fifty inch, 6K, curved screen, ultra-smart TV.

Their plan was not to try to get thousands of people squashed onto a stand, rather to get the top hundred people who matter to attend a lavish 'unveiling' party. It was to be held in a private convention suite at the ultra-trendy Cosmo Hotel on the Strip.

To make it even more enticing, the MV party was scheduled after most of the giants' events were winding down. The cherry on the cake, and a personal fantasy of Henry's, The Killers had agreed to play a small set (at a huge price).

As Vegas was their home base, the buzz went viral.

The launch was not cheap. Okay, it was obscenely expensive, but Henry and the team felt it was their one shot, and it needed to be the biggest bang in town.

It was.

People tried to buy tickets for thousands of dollars apiece, but couldn't. MV's strategy was to keep out everyone who couldn't make a difference to their potential product.

It was so exclusive that each invite required that the invitee use smartphone biometrics to accept. Their eye or fingerprint would be verified at the door so scalping was impossible. Even the Vegas convention ritual, of turning up with a bunch of friends hoping to get in on the one ticket, was to be a no-go for this event!

Such was the mystique garnered by the exclusivity of the event, almost every invitee accepted just to see what all the fuss was about.

What was even more amazing was that every single invited guest actually turned up.

Champagne and martinis were poured like the night before prohibition. Trays of canapés, catered by Gordon Ramsay, were plentiful and were passed around freely to the delight of the crowd.

In the centre of the room was a large circular roped-off area, in the middle of which sat MV's 'custom' display stand.

At the far end of the space, a stage had been set up with serious amplification and speakers. A drum kit was off to one side.

When Henry felt that most folks were nicely buzzed on his hooch, yet still of sound (if a little mellow) mind, he signalled for the room to darken. Not to black, just to a moody dusk.

David Chen, in purple dinner jacket and paisley waistcoat, walked into the middle of the roped-off circle and reverently placed the smartphone mock-up on the stand, directly under a single spotlight. With a huge grin, he pressed play. The spotlight dimmed, and the experience began.

At first people were slow to gather around the velvet-roped circle, until Henry's holo appeared to walk up, out of the demo smartphone screen. People then began to move almost hypnotically towards the viewing circle.

When the T-Rex appeared, people gasped and actually cheered. When Henry got eaten, they screamed even louder and laughed almost maniacally.

They couldn't comprehend what they had just seen.

Henry (the real one) walked into the centre of the circle and asked if they wanted to see it again.

The crowd basically went ape shit.

Henry pressed play, then walked out of their view.

The crowd reaction the second time was even more enthusiastic than the first go-round.

This time the audience, as one, applauded and cheered Henry as he again stepped into the centre of the circle after the demo.

"Thank you, all. It's not bad, is it?" he asked with feigned modesty. "We will be moving the unit to our suite upstairs for those of you who would like a private viewing over the next few days. You have all just been sent an invite to your phones. To set up a time to swing by, just put your name in any of the vacant time slots. Then come on by and have a closer look. In the meantime, we found this little local band we thought you might like."

The stage lights at the other end of the hall came on, revealing The Killers already in place.

"Well, hello there!" Brandon Flowers called to the crowd. "We are The Killers."

They opened with 'This is your Life'.

CHAPTER
TWO

Magic Vision never looked back.

By week's end, they had met with just about every major entertainment and phone hardware manufacturer on the globe. They had so many future meetings booked, most of which required long-distance travel, it was going to take months to complete the tour.

They decided almost immediately upon their return to LA that the first thing on their agenda was to get some serious legal representation.

People were talking about money, and IPO shares, and participation, and other board-level stuff that was simply beyond their experience level.

They needed someone to actually look after their interests. Though they felt it both unprofessional and a possible jinx, they on one occasion sat at the conference table and did some hypothetical fantasising regarding money.

They felt that if they were indeed able to produce the miniaturised phone-compatible version, which was still going to be at least a year away, they could easily each make somewhere in the seven-figure range.

They decided never to have such a discussion again. It was just too dizzying and distracting to even contemplate!

*

Over the next few months Henry and Chen spent more time on planes, many of them private, than they did at home. Preliminary proposals started coming in almost immediately.

Some of them were big.

It was time for the lawyers to earn their retainer.

*

The MV team met in Century City with their new legal team who reviewed every last one of the proposals. They explained in dumbed-down legal what each was offering and what their expectations were regarding deliverable timelines.

The complexity and detail of the proposals was mind-numbing.

They were holed up in their conference room for three days and still had more to review.

In the middle of the fourth day's session, Arnie Lowe entered the conference room. Everyone went quiet. Arnie was the senior partner at Lowe and Price, and was considered one of the most powerful business lawyers in America.

He was dressed in his usual dark grey pinstriped Savile Row suit, custom silk white and blue shirt and Hermès tie.

"Hope you don't mind if I stop in for a moment?" Arnie wasn't really asking. "I've been on the phone with some folks from up north who, it seems, would like to stick their oar in the water as well."

"Are we still taking any other proposals?" Henry sounded concerned. They had all exerted so much effort already to review the existing bids.

"Have we met with these people before?"

Arnie sat opposite Henry. "No, son. I think you would remember if you had."

"Okay," Henry said. "What do these 'folks up north' think they can add to the pot that isn't already there?"

"If you don't mind, Henry, I'd like to first have a quick sidebar with you. Just the two of us, if that's all right with everybody?" Again, it wasn't a question.

Henry was about to argue.

"Just you." Arnie must have read his mind.

Arnie led Henry down the plushest hallway he had ever seen, and into the man's office, which made the hallway look like a New York tenement. Henry immediately decided that it was the most beautiful room he had ever stepped into in his life.

The cream carpets were so soft and giving it was like someone else was doing the walking for you. The woods were exquisite, the light tan leather chairs, though modern, looked to be of a level of comfort that mere mortal men rarely experience.

Arnie pushed a button on his desk, and the twin twelve-foot mahogany doors closed silently behind them. Even the doors latching sounded more expensive than normal locks.

"Sorry to cut you from the herd back there, but these people want to talk to the company owner, not a committee."

Henry was about to push back again.

"These boys understand that your team all get a vote" Arnie mind-read again. "But for this conversation to start, they want to talk to you. Only you."

"So, who are these big shots from up north?"

Arnie gestured to the far left wall of his office. A massive flat screen was in videoconference mode. Two men were sitting at an unremarkable conference table, smiling back at Arnie and Henry. Both were casually dressed and both were in their late twenties.

"Hi, Mr Trapp. Nice to finally meet you," the man on the left began.

"Sorry about the cloak and dagger stuff, but I'm sure you understand," the other man added.

Henry was at a complete loss. He didn't understand. He turned to Arnie who just gave him a pat on the back and gestured for him to sit in one of a pair of chairs positioned perfectly in front of the videoconferencing screen and cameras.

Henry did as he was told. As he waited for the conversation to continue, he noticed the Ident bug in the top right of the picture.

It read simply:

VC Rm 2
G-Plex
Mountain View
Ca.
11:32am

The two young guys on the screen turned out to be the Sr Vice President of New Technologies, and the Sr Vice President of New Acquisitions.

Their little operation 'up north' was known by the name GOOGLE.

The two didn't talk in legalese, or in any other lexicon. Just straightforward English.

Google wanted to buy Magic Vision.

They wanted it structured so that they would have an ironclad option to proceed with the purchase for two years.

During that period, they would fund all costs needed for MV to get the functionality of the holo system down to standard smartphone size, without any loss of image quality.

MV would create a software app that would function on any phone. Plus, firmware and hardware that could be implementable within any future, next gen phones, two years out.

At that time, with all conditions met, the option would be exercised and the purchase would take place.

The two made it clear that MV would remain almost entirely autonomous. All current employees would stay on. Minimum interference from HQ.

There were a few immediate requirements for the deal to proceed.

MV had to move out of its current facility, and move into Google's Playa Vista campus, for, as they put it, obvious security reasons. Apparently, the boys were not impressed with their North Hollywood dump.

They stressed that during the two-year development, testing and implementation phases, complete and utter secrecy would be required. NDAs would be created with enforcement clauses that made waterboarding sound fun.

They explained to Henry that other companies were spending small fortunes trying to catch up to MV's demo level in Las Vegas. None, however, were even close to a prototype stage, let alone scaling and production.

Henry kept looking to Arnie, expecting him to be phased by the simplicity of the proposal.

Arnie knew that the actual contract and supporting documentation would not be so simple. There would be literally thousands of billable hours for Arnie and his company as well as massive time commitments for the Google legal team before any ink would ever touch the contract.

Arnie was used to big deals, especially tech and IPO creation. He could see no red flags in what the two men in Mountain View were, in principle, proposing.

"May I ask a couple of simple questions?" Henry looked to the screen and to Arnie.

"When you say, fund all costs for two years. What exactly does that mean?"

The SVP on the left smiled. "What would you like it to mean?"

Henry pondered a moment. "The problem is we don't even know what the hardware and firmware miniaturisation will entail yet, to say nothing of creating the universal implementation template for the new phones. The costs could add up pretty quickly."

"How about an initial limit of ten million a year with the ability of accessing more if justified?" the second SVP suggested.

Henry stared at the screen, completely dumbfounded. "What was your other question?"

Henry shook off that shock. He tried to sound casual, as if he had that type of conversation every day.

"Not wanting to sound crass but what sort of figure did you have in mind for the actual purchase?"

"We will work out exact figures as we draw up the final paperwork, but we and Mr Lowe, we're in agreement that the purchase monies, once the option is exercised, would probably be in the region of around twelve to fifteen," SVP Two answered casually.

Henry couldn't hide his disappointment. He had hoped they would be substantially more than fifteen million. Then again, that was millions he never had before.

Arnie sensed Henry's deflated mood.

"Henry. That's just the sale money." Arnie tried to comfort him. "I informed these gentlemen that you would not give up this technology without a licensing fee on top of the purchase price.

"That means that every single phone, or any other piece of hardware using your technology will have to pay a fee. The percentage still has to be worked out, but it'll add up. Same goes for the software. You get a cut from every purchase."

"I'm sorry, but what does that even mean to us?" Henry asked half-heartedly.

SVP One leant further into the camera. "Last year one point five billion smartphones were sold worldwide. This technology of yours will probably be adopted by ninety-five percent of the global providers. Off the top of my head, I would guesstimate that the licence fee would probably be around a dollar, maybe a dollar fifty."

"So," Arnie explained, "on top of the twelve to fifteen BILLION initial purchase amount, Magic Vision should take in an additional one and a half to two billion a year, at least for the first five years of launch, just from licensing. After the five-year mark, the numbers get a little vague as new technologies come into play."

Henry had always said that when the time came that Magic Vision finally made money, he would remain cool and aloof. He didn't want to act like some amateur and end up woohoo-ing or high-fiving everyone. He just wanted to stay totally chill.

Arnie patted Henry on the back. "You all right?"

Henry couldn't answer with his head between his knees. Plus, it would have been hard to speak through his loud, joyous sobbing.

He managed to at least nod!

Yeah! Very chill.

CHAPTER
THREE

It took a surprisingly short time for the details to be ironed out, and for the purchase option agreement and contract to be finalised and signed.

The final amount, once the option was exercised, was just a smidge over fourteen and a half billion.

After paying the lawyers, and the partners taking their split, Henry expected to see, after tax, around four big ones. Then there was the licensing which he reckoned would bring him an additional four to five hundred million a year.

*

Once over the initial shock, Henry and Mary were then in a unique form of limbo.

They had two years to wait until they were stinking rich. In the meantime, Henry was being paid just under four hundred thousand per year, for the two option years.

Nice money, but a mere piss in the ocean compared to what was coming. The strange thing was that even with the increased cash flow, and the potential to soon be able to buy countries, their lifestyle hadn't changed.

It was as if the entire thing wasn't even real. If they did, in fact, land the crazy payday, they decided that they would just have to find a way to muddle through.

In the meantime, they stayed in the same house. Henry was happy to keep his Ford. Mary did go a little off the rails, and traded in her old Prius for a new one. Other than that, everything was status quo.

*

Because of the unspeakably long commute time to get to Playa Vista, the team decided after only one week to start work at 6 a.m. and finish (when possible) at three. As they didn't have to coexist with other support entities during 'normal' working hours, why not?

Henry was a little nervous about running it by the Google boys, but their response was that it was his company. They didn't care what time they worked, so long as they produced the product at the end of the two years.

The new hours were life changing. Henry's drive took less that twenty-five minutes. The guys in the valley, forty minutes. Plus, they found they could focus better, without having had their brains fried during a three-hour commute.

Home life was a little trickier.

Leaving the house at four-thirty, without disturbing its occupants, was a whole new skill set that Henry had to learn.

He started showering at night. He laid his next-day clothes out before bed, and ate breakfast at work.

He did sneak into Daniel's room just before leaving each day and gave him a non-awakening kiss on the head. Daniel never woke up, but did sometimes smile in his sleep.

He couldn't offer Mary the same goodbye, as she was a light sleeper, who, if touched in any way, woke with a jerk, involving arm and leg twitchings in all directions.

Henry only tried once to give her a gentle goodbye kiss. The result was a hard left elbow to the nose.

The evenings were interesting under the new schedule. Mary would get home, usually at around seven, and expect her extra dry Henderson Martini to be ready and waiting. Once consumed, she was ready for a nice family evening.

The problem was that Henry's evening now ended at nine. Counting his shower time and clothes prep, that gave them about forty-five minutes to share their day, eat dinner, have the obligatory fifteen minutes with Daniel, and discuss worldly issues.

They did however manage to make up for it at the weekends.

The MV team found it initially hard to come to terms with basically unlimited funds. For the first time ever, they were able to buy exactly what was needed, when it was needed. This was a totally new concept.

Like real troopers, they found a way to cope, and before long, had equipped their new three-thousand-square-foot space with everything they could possibly need to bring their dream to market.

They also got to hire three additional full-time staff just to cope with the frenetic level of work that was now required. After a brief meeting to discuss these new positions, it was agreed that they should first offer the jobs to the two interns. They had been with them for a while, and had basically become part of the family. They were also both highly productive workers, which didn't hurt.

Once approached with the good news, Henry was surprised that they were both a little leery of taking on full-time employment. They felt that it would interfere with their non-specific, long-range goals.

When they heard what their two-year bonus could be, they decided that goals were very passé.

The third hire was probably the most important one. They needed an office manager. Someone to keep track of orders, manage the phones, and create an inventory system just so they could find the stuff they'd just bought.

But most importantly, this person had to fill out the monthly status report that went to Mountain View.

This was no one-liner, saying all's well down here in LA!

The form was an online horror, created by Google HQ to keep track of every single aspect, of every project, on their books.

MV may have been autonomous, but that didn't stop the big G from wanting to know the status of every layer, of every facet, of every project. Nobody wanted to fill out the damn form. It took hours, and that was if you had all the data to hand.

No. They decided that their time was better spent making miracles.

Some other schmuck could document them!

Another urgent task was for them to come up with an acceptable name for the product. They'd been calling it the 'Holo' forever, but G felt it was too generic. It would be like calling a new vacuum cleaner 'VAC'.

Naming their child proved to be one of the hardest tasks they had so far encountered.

They weren't marketing guys. They were tech geeks.

They knew they could hand over the naming assignment to the boys up north, but they really wanted to be able to name their baby themselves.

Mary suggested 'Purple Nappy'. Henry actually loved it, but was pretty sure that a technology that was about to go global needed a more grown-up and professional handle.

Plus, less reference to excrement.

They couldn't use holo in the name at all, as the sci-fi movies and TV shows had pretty much grabbed all the good ones. There was also the problem that shows like *Star Trek* had used the term so frequently and for so long, that it actually made the technology sound dated.

Andy, the oldest of the two new employees (ex-interns), came up with the name 'Purple Haze'. They all loved the idea but thought their baby shouldn't have the same name as a particularly righteous strain of California weed.

They must have considered over a hundred names without something clicking. It was getting frustrating.

Despite knowing the negatives, Henry couldn't get Purple Haze out of his head. He thought Andy was on to something. He just couldn't quite get there.

A few mornings later, Henry was waiting for his morning instant porridge to microwave, when Andy stumbled in heading for the industrial-sized Keurig.

"I can't stop thinking about Purple Haze as a name. I really like it. It's just got to be a name that's impactful," Henry said as he watched the guy hack the Keurig into letting him use three pods for one mug.

"I had a vape full of Purple Haze last week," Andy mumbled. "Trust me. It's impactful."

Once Andy had had his first gulp of the hi-octane Jo, he looked pensively at Henry for a few moments, then, just as he started for the door, he stopped, and without even facing Henry, said,"Hendrix. Call it Hendrix."

He then exited the kitchen, leaving Henry in a complete stupor.

The kid had nailed it.

Purple haze——Hendrix——Duh!

As Henry tried to eat his microwaved mush (with raisins and toasted almonds), he realised that the shaggy-headed kid, who weeks ago was no more than an intern with very non-specific life goals, had just come up with the perfect name for a multibillion-dollar technology. To give him his due, he had devoted approximately fifteen seconds to the task.

Henry was always fascinated by how abstract the human thought process could be.

After all, the solution to Hendrix's entire display functionality had come to him after a nappy-changing incident with Daniel.

That extra bit of tinkle was one hell of a stroke of luck.

Talk about a golden shower!

CHAPTER
FOUR

Within nine months, they had a working Hendrix prototype, sized to be within spec for smartphone adaptation.

Usually such an achievement would have necessitated a summons to give a demo up at the Mountain View compound. Because the project's progress was still closely under wraps, it was decided that the Google elite would come to Playa Vista.

The demo didn't have any of the pizazz of the Vegas unveiling. These guys just wanted to see that it worked.

With zero fanfare, a spread of Domino's Pizza and a selection of soft drinks, it was definitely a low-key kinda thing.

Henry and the guys had created different holo media for this crowd. No fanfare, just a selection of different image sources and uses.

They showed how you could call a fellow Hendrix user and have that person seemingly stand on your screen, talking to you. You could even have a shared call with multiple people, all within the holo field. That one, though, still needed work, as it was hard to get everyone seeming to face the right way.

The way the phone chat app would work was that each user had to set up their Avatar 'shell'. That was easy. They just took a video of their face and the software's interpolation filled in the rest. The one vital thing that Hendrix needed during each call was a full-on front view of the 'client's' face for mouth movement and expression.

The problem was to shoot the user's face during a call while the phone was held flat so that the holo effect could mount on the screen.

That was when Chen hit one, not just out of the park, but out of the galaxy.

The edge of the phone needed to be curved. The entire bevel became what Chen referred to as the Living Digital Membrane. It was made up of hundreds of micro cameras and projectors.

The phone could be placed flat on a table and the user could open Hendrix then choose their phone avatar. With the help of refined facial recognition software, the cameras in the phone's LDM would locate and be able to capture the user's face, even at an extreme angle from the phone. The software would realign the image geometry, and the avatar would appear dimensionally correct and lifelike.

Far easier was the holo display for TV or movies. Though, like 3D, everything had to be custom shot during production at the same time as the regular cinematography. To do this, they would use the newly developed Hendrix 360 matrix camera array.

Once that media was available for download, you basically could watch a movie with a bunch of friends sitting in a circle and the action would occur in the centre of that circle, almost like live theatre in the round.

This still needed work for the bigger 'tent-pole' pictures that filled the screen, frame to frame, with action. Their intent was to expand the holo field into more of a reverse cone shape to permit a much wider holo-phonic aspect ratio.

In addition, they created all sorts of much simpler apps, such as holo chess where the pieces were actually animated. A bit like the holo battle game on the *Maltese Falcon*.

There were educational apps, where instructors could teach a circular class full of students.

Basically, there was no end to how this new medium could develop.

The execs from Google HQ were amazed. They understood that what they had seen was just one milestone out of many, but still, it was beyond 'next gen'!

The final key was to create a platform whereby the technology could be adapted into different-sized phones and tablets and be seamlessly incorporated into the manufacturing process.

That was going to be the real bitch. They would have to start working with the leading phone and tablet manufacturers, and create both universal and customisable solutions.

The software and the app were child's play at this point. Integrating the micro cameras and projectors into other corporations' design platforms was going to require a Herculean effort in cooperative tact.

These mega corps were at the top of the food chain. They took no prisoners. The Chinese and South Korean boys played for keeps. They had quietly entered the marketplace with little to offer and now, pretty much dictated design, function and manufacturing protocols for the world.

They wanted Hendrix, but fitting it into their stringent design parameters was gonna get interesting. They would have to re-jiggle their entire manufacturing protocol. This was not something these people did. Thankfully most of the battles would be waged way above the heads of the MV team. However, as in any war, there can always be collateral damage. Hopefully Google would cover their asses whenever possible.

It was going to be legendary.

*

Within a couple of weeks, highly detailed design specs from the big players started arriving. Not, as MV had expected, by dedicated encrypted data lines direct to Google.

No way! This stuff was so sensitive, they arrived with design escort teams from each manufacturer. They each had their own proprietary Cad-like software which could only be viewed on their own computers.

It was unheard of for these companies to share advanced prototype specs, years before market.

They were not going to make it easy.

Security within the MV hangar became intense. Each company ended up with their own fully isolated, built out, and fully enclosed, work area.

Each provided their own security, including guards.

It was the first time that all key players were going to integrate a technology not designed by them. It was also the first time that these mega corps were working towards the same goal, in the same location, trying to integrate the same technology.

The playbook was literally being written as they went.

The MV team had to add five more technologists, just so each manufacturer had their own rep, that would not be shared with anyone else.

Despite the bizarre workflow that the security necessitated, progress was made.

Fifteen months later, and three months shy of the option period deadline, the MV lab was devoid of all but their own crew. Every manufacturer had departed. Each had formally advised Google that they were ready for production.

That final milestone, plus MV's own project completion reporting, triggered the Magic Vision purchase.

The original four were about to become very wealthy individuals.

*

Over the next few months, while the purchase contract kicked in fully, the team came up with new and different applications for the Hendrix software.

The best of which was a way of using a nano-sized camera array, at the end of a spreadable filament bundle, to allow doctors, and especially surgeons, to view a 360 holo-image of any area within the human body.

Even though MV was now owned by Google, these new potential products would still fall within the shared licensing revenue portion of the contract. In other words, even more money for the boys down south.

*

Once the initial monies were paid, the Trapps had a huge decision to make. Stay in the home they loved, or live anywhere else they pleased?

One of the criteria for a new home, one that they had never even imagined, was that it had to have serious security.

It seems that once you become a billionaire you also become a target for everyone.

Charities, criminals, distant family; you name it.

Everyone wanted a piece.

Mary and Henry had made initial plans for the funds, soon after learning of their possible upcoming wealth. They created trust funds for themselves and Daniel. They didn't feel that even they should have access to that kind of money right off the bat.

There were too many stories of people and families that had been destroyed by sudden wealth. They felt they would never be in that demographic. They also realised that having never actually had billions of dollars, they had no idea what kind of whack-jobs they could turn into.

Deciding where to live was tough. They really loved West Hollywood, but realised that it wasn't the easiest area to live securely. They considered Malibu but decided that the fires, landslides and coastal flooding were all just a bit too biblical for a cosy life.

They discussed doing some serious travelling, but felt the time wasn't right for long-term trekking until Daniel was a little older. Besides, Henry was still having to travel extensively for Hendrix.

Mary made the decision for them. Though stupid rich, she wanted to keep busy. She proposed that instead of her just staging multi-million-dollar properties for their owners, she would get much more satisfaction and a heck of a lot more profit, if she owned the homes she staged.

Her plan was to buy the right mega properties, one at a time. Then move the whole family in, and basically remodel them, turning each into her special style of spectacular home.

She didn't intend for them to live in construction sites. These were homes that would be transformed slowly, and where possible, graciously, room by room. She felt each would take eighteen months to two years.

Henry agreed wholeheartedly, so long as he had a suitable workspace and had room for the car collection he was pondering.

She didn't bite. She knew him too well to worry that he would fill garages with dozens of half million-dollar monstrosities.

Though, to be fair, he did go out and buy a brand-new Ford truck the same week the funds were released.

Ya see. You never know what wealth can do to a person.

It was decided that Mary's business would incorporate, then she could start the search for her first project home. She also kept the staging company and folded it into the same corporation.

They also reached a consensus that they could never sell their Hollywood Hills home. They decided to let their closest friend, Joshua, live in it rent free, in exchange for upkeep.

Henry's dance card was completely full. Hendrix had given him unwanted though enjoyable fame. He became a talk-show favourite. He lectured around the world. At the same time, he and Chen continued to tinker with new concepts for media presentation.

The other two original staff of MV had taken their money and dived head first into the trough of gluttony. They went for the super yachts, the super cars, the super models.

All very superficial.

*

Daniel did not seem remotely phased by the new wealth. He was too busy getting into mischief. Running, potty-training, making Christy chase him everywhere!

He was also learning that just by thinking bad things about someone, they would get the red fog. If he thought nice things, they got blue. It was fun but he was learning that if he gave someone the red fog, they changed. Sometimes he never got to see them again.

CHAPTER
FIVE

One depressingly grey afternoon, Mary came bounding into the house, almost unable to speak. She was giddy with excitement. Henry couldn't understand how anyone could be enthusiastic about anything during the annual Los Angeles festival of June Gloom.

Everyone, except those living in southern California, considers its weather to consist of nothing but endless sunshine. Though partially true, each spring, a phenomenon called a marine layer would slide along the south California coast, then creep inland a couple of miles, every morning. The result was a low altitude grey fog bank that arrived around May and could stay as long as September. The fog layer rarely reached the ground. It just sat about a thousand or so feet above it, blocking all sunshine, and dropping the temperature by twenty degrees.

Its other delightful characteristic was that it wasn't intermittent. You didn't have a sunny day then a gloomy day. No, when this mother moved in, it stayed for months.

Despite the gloom outside and the gloomies within Henry, Mary was so bubbly, she was effervescent.

"I found it!" she exclaimed.

"What? Sunshine?" Henry's mood really was piss poor.

"No, dummy. The house. I found the house." She looked for him to share her excitement. His reaction was lacklustre at best.

"Come on. Get off your ass. We're going there now. In fact, we'll all go."

She ran off towards the kitchen.

"Christy. Get Daniel ready, we're going to see a house!"

Turning it into a full family road trip did nothing to improve Henry's enthusiasm level.

Mary drove them in her brand-new Hybrid Volvo SUV. Despite its safety record and perfect size for a family, she still felt guilty about buying it. She was having trouble adapting to being a billionaire.

As one does!

Determined not to lose her positive buzz by attempting to drive (or rather not drive) along Sunset, she opted for the scenic route along Mulholland.

For nine months of the year, the winding road at the crest of the hills dividing LA from the Valley offered outstanding views. On a really clear day, you could see to Catalina Island on one side and the Sierra Mountains on the other.

Not that day. They were literally in the cloud. All they saw was watery grey mist.

It didn't deter Mary one single bit. She was too busy describing every nook and cranny of the house they were about to see.

Henry was actually quite grateful for the diminished visibility on the mountain road. Something about Mulholland usually turned Mary into an F1 driver.

She would suddenly take the vehicle out of automatic and paddle-shifted her way from one terrifying dead-drop corner to the next.

Thanks to the June Gloom and the resulting fog, she was having to drive calmly and sedately.

She made a hard left at Beverly Glen, then started the descent back down towards the LA side. Before reaching Sunset, she turned right onto a side road that snaked into the Bel Air estates.

This was where the super-rich lived. Some of the most expensive real estate in the world is tucked away up its narrow hillside roads.

Mary turned onto St Cloud Road then turned into a gated drive that curved graciously up to what looked like a transplanted English country manor house. It looked that way because the silent film star who built it, had bought an actual English country manor then disassembled it, and shipped it back to California where it was put back together.

It was nestled within twelve acres of manicured lawns and mature trees.

It was stunning. What added to the first impression was that the clouds above the house seemed, just for a few moments, to part, sending a shaft of spectacular sunlight directly onto the property. It was as if the house wanted to show the visitors what it could look like on a more typical LA day.

They pulled up next to a bright-white Cadillac Escalade. The driver's door opened and a tiny woman stepped out. It turned out she really wasn't that small, it was just the effect of alighting from an SUV the size of a house.

"Henry, this is Margie. She is the broker for this house." Mary did the intros. "Margie, this is my husband." They shook hands.

"This is our son, Daniel, and this is our constant saviour, Christy."

Christy shook hands, as Daniel play-hid behind her.

Margie stepped over and smiled down at him. "Aren't you a big boy!?" She reached out and ruffled his hair before turning away and leading the pack into the house.

Christy and Daniel brought up the rear.

When Daniel first saw Margie, she had no fog at all, but after the hair ruffling, which he didn't like, he could see that a faint red haze had started to develop around her. At the same time, her cheerful realtor patter lost some of its vivacity. In fact, she seemed to have almost lost interest in showing the home.

*

Luckily for her, Mary was doing enough hard selling for them both. She dragged the group through every room, on every floor.

It was almost a beautiful home.

The problem was that over the life of the house, each owner had put their mark on it. Whether through a remodel, or through redecoration, none of them seemed to have ever stepped back and looked at the interior as a whole. They had just done what they felt was needed to suit them.

Sure, it had a fantastic chef's kitchen with white marble floors and ultra-modern matt black cabinets. But then, the dining room was done in 'elegant Manhattan chic', with creams and gilt from the late nineties. Plus, it was in the wrong place.

That was the case throughout the house. The feel and vibe changed from room to room, and although each was tasteful, the effect was jarring. Not the emotion you wanted within your home. After spending over an hour on the interior, they stopped for a brief glass of water in the kitchen. Mary, once refreshed, led the troop outside so they could see the gardens, pool area and tennis court.

Margie didn't join them for the garden tour. She felt a little out of it and hoped that the grey weather and lowered temperature hadn't brought on one of her sinus conditions.

With Margie resting in the kitchen, Mary could talk freely about the property.

"Isn't it fantastic!" She actually pirouetted on the back lawn. Not quite a full Julie Andrews, but close.

Henry looked at her with real concern, wondering what on God's earth she could like about the monstrosity they had just toured.

"Honey! It's a mess. It's like someone put twenty years of *Architectural Digest* into a blender!"

"I know, isn't that great? This is the perfect first house!"

"I'm sorry, babe. I'm not getting it. It just looks like a complete shambles to me." Henry shook his head.

"That's 'cause you're a left-brainer! You just see the house that exists in front of you! I see what it could become."

"Please, at least tell me you're stealing it."

"That's the great part. The owners are in deep financial trouble, and want to move it quickly. For almost nothing!"

"How very *Schadenfreude* of you!" Henry mocked. "So how much is 'almost nothing'?"

"Margie thinks, for an all-cash, quick sale, we could get it for eight to ten million."

"You have got to be fu—"

Mary and Christy both cleared their throats loudly. It had the desired effect. Henry turned and smiled apologetically at Daniel then looked back to Mary.

"You must be fudging kidding! Ten million – for a house?"

Mary smiled at him as if he was a tad simple. "A six-thousand-square-foot house with twelve acres, in the best part of Bel Air! For crying out loud, the land's worth almost that!"

Christy and Daniel had been closely watching the argument with growing amusement.

Mary noticed and turned to Daniel. "Honey, would you like to live here?"

Daniel looked back towards the house. "Yes. Booful hus!"

"How about you, Christy? Could you manage to live here?" Mary joked.

"Well, I don't know." Christy kept a straight face. "I prefer a south-facing tennis court, but one occasionally has to make do."

Henry looked back at the others with complete incredulity.

"Well, looks like I am outvoted. When do we move?"

The four of them headed back to the house to tell Margie the good news.

CHAPTER
SIX

Mary had found her first mega mansion to flip.

Despite all the best intention, it got off to a terrible start. At least from a P & L perspective.

It took almost two years to fully redo number 12, St Cloud Rd.

She did such a breathtakingly magnificent job, they decided not to sell it. They learned to love the house so much as they watched it transform into a dream home, they just didn't want to leave it.

Thankfully, they were fiscally able to tweak Mary's business plan so that they could live in the St Cloud house, while she worked on the next flip.

Back before the work had started in earnest on St Cloud, they decided it would be best to start Daniel at a pre-school. They felt that it would be a good 'constant' in his life, especially while work was being carried out on the house.

Plus, they realised it was time for him to start learning social skills from people other than his self-centred, and often tipsy, parents.

They enrolled him at a highly-rated pre-school located just west of Bel Air. It was known to foster mindfulness, kindness, and excelled at early childhood socialisation.

All they had to do was to tell Daniel the good news.

That didn't go well.

*

By the age of three, Daniel had mastered the art of the tantrum. When not getting his way, or was just overtired and cranky, he would suddenly stamp his feet, turn his face almost purple, cry, scream, and to complete the performance, roll on the ground while slapping the floor.

Any mention of the pre-school resulted in the full, long-version performance.

So, they tried to gradually hint at the idea.

Tantrum.

They sat him down, and tried an adult conversation.

Tantrum.

Finally, they decided on a more radical option. They took him to see the school, telling him it would be his choice if he wanted to go or not.

This struck Mary and Henry as very forward-thinking on their part. In reality, it was a completely normal process for the school. In fact, they offered all prospective children a half-day 'visit'.

A few days later, Christy, her eyes moist with tears, waved goodbye to the Trapps as they drove the short distance to the All-Friends Pre-School. As they pulled up to its ivy-covered frontage, all occupants of the car went very quiet, and very pale.

This 'visit' was a big deal.

Though tightly scripted, the whole thing appeared casual and spontaneous to the kids. It was almost like the school knew what they were doing.

Mary and Henry walked Daniel into the pre-school just after lunch on yet another grey day. He was introduced to some staff members and to some other children. Daniel was then shown into one of the 'classrooms'.

These were not really classrooms as such. These were playrooms with so many different choices of fun things to do, it was almost exhausting just looking at them.

The Trapps watched in amazement as Daniel joined in with the other kids.

At first, he kept glancing over at them to make sure they were still there, but after a while they were entirely forgotten.

The head teacher suggested they leave him for a couple of hours.

Mary looked close to tears. Henry had to convince her that the nice teacher had not actually suggested abandoning their child.

Reluctantly, they left the school grounds and tried to think of something besides Daniel for the next few hours.

That, of course, resulted in them thinking of nothing but Daniel.

*

When they got back at the appointed time, they expected their distraught son to be in tears, anxiously awaiting their return.

What they got instead, was Daniel, their little blonde, blue-eyed baby, sitting in the middle of one of the classrooms with eighteen other kids sitting in a circle around him. At first, they were devastated, thinking they were picking on him. Then as they kept looking, they realised that Daniel was actually leading the group in play.

It was bizarre to watch. He would grab a toy from a pile next to him. The other kids would dash around to find an equivalent. They then returned to the circle and watched in awe, as Daniel showed them how to play with the item. Or, at least gave his version of how to play with it.

All but one followed his lead. The loner seemed to be on a whole different plane than everyone else.

As they kept watching, they realised that the young boy was actually Down's syndrome. He was having a whale of a time, just not in the same way as any of the others.

*

Daniel found out almost immediately that once he was left with the other kids, he seemed to be able to make them do what he was doing. He wasn't trying to make them do it, they just seemed to want to. All except the strange boy.

While all the other kids had fogs in the blue spectrum, his fog was like nothing Daniel had seen before. It was filled with colour. Not just one, but countless colours, all shimmering around him.

At first, Daniel had tried to change the boy's colour, to get him to do what the others were doing, but it didn't work.

The boy simply did what he wanted to do, even if it wasn't the way anyone else was doing it.

At first this really bothered Daniel, but as the playtime progressed, he decided the boy was okay in his own world. He decided that he didn't need to control him.

*

As the Trapps watched, unseen from the hallway, the head teacher joined them.

"Is that normal?" Mary whispered.

"At that age, normal is a relative term," the woman answered. "I will say though, a lot of playgroups end up with an alpha, but I've never seen anything quite like this."

"Is it a problem?" Henry tried to sound casual.

"What? That a new child seems to be able to make an entire room full of other kids behave and play calmly together? I would like that sort of trouble on a daily basis, please!"

She gave them a reassuring smile then left them to their spying.

*

On the drive home, Daniel wouldn't talk about his school visit at all. It wasn't as if he was sullen, he just wouldn't talk about it. Unfortunately, what he did do was sing a new song he learned. 'Five Little Monkeys'. He sang it over and over and over.

It was cute the first few times.

Then it wasn't.

The fact that Daniel really didn't remember most of the words, was also initially cute.

Then it wasn't.

Each time he finished his botched rendition he clapped his hands, and screamed, "Yeah!"

Okay, that kept being cute. In fact, it got to the point that each time he came to the end and did his thing, Mary and Henry both laughed. Every time!

As they made their way up the drive to the St Cloud house, they saw that Christy was waiting anxiously for the return of her charge.

As soon as Daniel was out of the car, he grabbed her hand and started to lead her inside.

"I wuz at skule taday," he announced.

"Will you tell me all about it?" She honestly sounded like she wanted to hear everything.

Daniel nodded enthusiastically. "We pwayd games." He practically dragged her into the house.

"Tell Christy about your new song!" Henry called after them.

Mary slapped his arm.

*

Over the next four years, Mary restored three more homes, netting just under eight million for her trouble.

Not living in the project houses enabled her to turn each around almost thirty percent faster.

During that time, Daniel thrived at pre-school and was actually excited about the next adventure.

School!

Real school was a whole different experience for Daniel. There were far fewer games, you had to listen to the teachers, and you had to actually remember what they were saying.

*

Daniel's was a private school on the Valley side, just south of Ventura Blvd, between Coldwater and Beverly Glen.

It was named simply, the Valley School, and if there were a Stamford for K-12, this would be it. If you've ever wondered where the kids of celebrity parents go to school, wonder no more.

Tucked in the foothills of Sherman Oaks, the place reeked of money. That's a good thing in LA. If, however, you would like your offspring to mix with gang members, drug dealers and generally disenfranchised youth, there are a number of schools to choose from within the LA school system.

*

Once Daniel was accepted, the school sent them a huge list of the clothing they needed to buy. Along with grey shorts and shirts, there was also the formal outfit which included a blazer and tie. This stuff wasn't cheap either.

The first time Daniel tried on the whole outfit, he looked very uncomfortable. Especially with the tie. Even though it was a clip-on, he kept fiddling with it, trying to adjust the length. For some reason he never seemed to think it was long enough.

Strangely, other than the uniform, Daniel took the whole prospect of the transition, from pre-school to 'big boy' school in his stride. He was tall for his age and was big enough to not be immediately viewed as a target by the school bullies.

Yup, even the elite schools have them!

*

The next four years passed in the blink of an eye.

Daniel survived school without incident. However, his report cards consistently showed him to not be trying very hard. He seemed to be more interested in teasing the girls than focusing on the lessons.

Mary and Henry both felt that some of that blame fell onto the school. After all, over the course of the four years, eight of his teachers had upped and left the school with no notice.

Everyone agreed that the real shame was that the teachers that left were some of the tougher ones. The ones who really tried to push their students to do their best. Including Daniel.

Daniel's homeroom teacher in the third grade really went out of her way to get him to buckle down and to take an interest in the subjects.

Sadly, she never came back from a weekend trip to Catalina Island. She somehow fell off the ferry on the return trip. Her body was never recovered. It was never determined whether she fell intentionally or by accident.

Her untimely death cast a pall over the entire school.

Everyone in her homeroom class signed a beautiful condolence card for her family.

Daniel's signature was by far the biggest.

CHAPTER
SEVEN

Henry, meanwhile, was pretty much done with celebrity, Los Angeles and above all, Hendrix.

The Hendrix trend boom was over. Everyone in the world had partaken of that technology. The new 'it' thing that was revving up the market was 'LID' (limitless interaction device). It was a completely clear rectangle of what looked like thin glass, but was actually super-lightweight transparent carbon fibre.

By waving your hand over it, or just by saying 'open', it transformed into an edge-to-edge screen that did absolutely anything you could imagine. The fact that the design and function seemed identical to data screens used, yet again, on *Star Trek* didn't seem to faze anyone.

Thankfully, Henry had made more money during the Hendrix 'years' than he could ever spend. Now it was the turn of someone else to take the techno-geek celebrity reins.

And the burden.

The boys from the north had known what they were talking about. They gave Hendrix about five years of being on top of the market after initial penetration. They actually got six.

Nobody was complaining.

The fact that the software licensing was still bringing in multi millions didn't hurt.

The problem was, Henry desperately needed a change. He certainly didn't have to work. Their money, by that time, was making close to a billion a year just in interest from their investment portfolio.

He wanted a complete, emotional blank slate. That included their location.

*

About a week before Daniel's fourth grade graduation, Mary came home, and after angrily dumping her coat and bag on the floor of the entry foyer, she headed straight for the bar.

Not that unusual after a hard day at work, but on this occasion, it was only eleven in the morning.

"If I have to deal with one more Russian oligarch asshole, I will go fucking crazy!"

Henry tried to suppress a grin. "So how was your day?"

"I spent the last two years making the Brentwood house into the most beautiful, subtle and gracious home, and now this ass-clown basically wants me to redecorate it from scratch. He wants it to look like a Cossack brothel; everything has to be black, gold or red. Plus zebra skins, leopard skins. Jesus!"

"So not great then?" Henry observed.

She glared at him from the adjoining room. "You know what!? I've had it with this town. It was bad enough when I had to deal with simple gazillionaires, now, every big buyer seems to be a friggin' Russian. Those people are pigs!"

"The entire population?"

Mary couldn't help but smile. "No, just the super-rich ones."

Henry watched his wife gulp a sizeable Bombay Sapphire Martini.

"Honey, just how serious are you about being fed up with the whole place?"

"Completely!" She downed the last drop.

Henry grinned over at her. "I think we should talk."

*

It took almost a month before they had formulated a plan.

They would move to Europe.

It then took another month to get up the nerve to broach the subject with Daniel. They needn't have worried. He loved the idea. In fact, he had been doing research online about Europe for over a month.

They thought that was odd as that was before they had mentioned it to him. They assumed they just both sucked at secrecy.

The plan was simple. They were going to move to London. Henry had spent a few months there in the early days of the Hendrix unveiling, and had fallen in love with the place.

*

Prior to the big move, Mary and Henry made a number of quick trips, to check out where they would live, and also, where Daniel would go to school.

Finding the house was tough. Especially after living on twelve acres in Bel Air. Then they decided that if they were going to really enjoy London, they needed to actually live in central London so they could walk to everything.

After an exhaustive search, they found a gorgeous end-of terrace house, at the Sloane Square end of Eaton Square in the heart of Belgravia. Though impossible to see from the outside, it was almost as big as the St Cloud House, and had a pool. An indoor pool but still!

They checked out a number of the best London schools for Daniel but found them all to be a bit depressing and a tad Gothic.

During one of their return visits to LA, they showed Daniel the various prospectuses from the schools.

He didn't like any of them. He asked if they had checked out Swiss schools?

They were shocked. Not just because he had knowledge of Swiss schools, but also that he had any wish whatsoever to go to a boarding school.

Apparently, two fellow students from the Valley School had gone off to the same place, located just twenty miles outside Geneva.

Known informally as the School of Kings, it was considered one of the best boarding schools in the world. The autumn and spring term took place at their main facility on Lac Leman, the winter term, at their alpine compound in Chateau D'Oex, high in the alps.

Daniel studied up on all the school stats.

He was strangely excited at the prospect of studying with the children of the world's political and business leaders.

He felt it would be a great foundation for his future endeavours.

"What endeavours?" Henry blurted out during one of Daniel's sales pitches. "You're ten!"

Daniel looked him straight in the eye. "First of all, I will be eleven in three weeks, secondly, I see myself one day being involved in a business that would benefit from having international contacts. I feel this would be the right place for me to start making those contacts."

"Who are you?" Henry laughed.

"It's never too soon to plan for one's future!" Daniel added.

"May I ask what future business you are planning for?" Henry tried to keep a straight face.

"I want to do what mummy does!"

Henry's first thought was 'drink and swear' but he managed to keep that to himself.

"I want to buy and sell houses and maybe one day even – buildings." Daniel nodded to himself, then turned away and trotted towards the library.

Mary couldn't stop laughing when Henry told her what happened.

"It's not the worst choice of careers. He'll certainly have the funds to get started."

"Not till he's twenty-one," Henry reminded her. "He sounded like he wanted to start tomorrow."

"Well maybe he should. I didn't know he was interested at all. Maybe I can start teaching him a little about real estate."

"What about this Swiss school he wants to go to?"

She pondered for a moment. "Let him go to Le Lac if he really wants to." She shrugged.

"But that means he'd live at school. When will we ever get to see him?"

Mary gave him a knowing look. "We'll see him during the holidays, at half-terms and on most weekends."

Henry looked puzzled.

"Did I forget to mention the little pied-à-terre we're going to find for ourselves in Geneva?" She gave him a big wink. "In fact, Daniel can help me find it. That will be lesson one."

"My little Machiavelli!"

"You bet your ass!"

"And pray tell, what will I be doing, while you two are off being Swiss property moguls?"

"I would have thought that you would've wanted to spend the time playing with your old cronies at CERN. The Hadron Collider is just outside Geneva, isn't it?"

Henry stood, utterly stunned, with his mouth hanging open.

"And they call you the brains of the family!" she teased.

Henry was almost emotional. "That's the most wonderful idea I've ever heard. Carl is still there. So is Jullien. Oh my god. I wonder if they'd actually need any help while I'm there?"

Mary kissed him on the cheek. "When I spoke to Carl on Friday he said they'd love to see you. He said something about there being an opening for a visiting researcher – or something like that."

"But—" Henry had lost his words.

Mary had not. "Well don't just stand there, get me a Sauvignon!"

Henry, still dazed, wandered out of the room.

Mary called after him. "Better make it a big one."

She grinned to herself.

CHAPTER
EIGHT

They moved to England just in time to enjoy a British summer. They flew into London City Airport in a chartered Gulfstream.

Long gone were the days since Henry's first fantasy flight on a private jet.

They landed in a heavy drizzle, which is London's way of welcoming summer visitors.

They had decided not to go straight to their new house. Instead they stayed a full week at the Devonshire Hotel in Mayfair so they could 'adjust' to London before tackling the million and one things that needed doing in Eaton Square.

Their first night, exhausted, jet-lagged and generally discombobulated, they ate in the historic and lauded Devonshire Grill. It had recently been given a complete facelift, including removing all of its renowned dark wooden panelling.

Initially, this had been considered a sacrilege, until it was announced that they were being replaced by custom wood panels created by the Nakashima Woodworkers.

Mary had always fancied herself a gourmand of sorts, and was obsessive about researching the best restaurants, and especially what to eat, once there.

Once presented with the menus, she took the lead in ordering for the four of them. The Grill was considered one of the last few places where some of Britain's finest classic fare was prepared to perfection.

She chose a selection of 'starters' for them all to sample. Everything was delicious and elegantly presented, however the jury was still out on the star attraction, the infamous (and what many feel is an 'acquired' taste) potted shrimp.

Baby shrimp are encased in chilled, set, clarified butter. It comes in a small ramekin, and is served with toast triangles. It was a favourite of British aristocracy for hundreds of years.

After his first taste, Henry felt they may well have been served some from the original batch.

Mary however, loved it. Daniel was undecided, though he did help Henry with his.

Christy tried to pick out just the minuscule shrimp and avoided the clarified (Henry referred to it as rancid) butter altogether.

Instead of their usual habit of ordering something different for each of them, Mary insisted they all have the Dover sole as their main course.

This had sounded like a good plan, until their soles arrived. They were about eighteen inches long and fully intact. Head, tail, bones, everything.

Their waiter offered to remove the fillets for them, but out of some misguided obstinance, they insisted on doing the work themselves.

Mary and Christy did a careful and thorough job of deboning their soles. The waiter even gave them an appreciative nod.

Henry made a complete mess of the process. It was doubtful he had one bite without a mouthful of bones.

Daniel, on the other hand, did a relatively good job. He only lost points by covering the fish's head with his serviette.

He said eating the fish while it's looking at you was just gross!

The next day was devoted to touring London. Despite their financial ability to probably hire a member of the royal family to give them the tour, they wanted to do it like real tourists.

They made their way down Mount Street to Park Lane where they bought tickets for the hop-on/hop-off bus tour. This allowed you to either stay on the double-decker bus for the entire three-hour guided tour, or get off anywhere that caught your fancy. You could then get back on another bus whenever you wanted to.

In a strange, and almost unheard-of freak of nature, the London day was sparklingly bright, the sky was blue, and the weather was actually warm.

Thanks to this bizarre phenomenon, they were able to sit on the open-top deck, and see the city from a 360-degree perspective.

They had a blast. They saw just about every notable cathedral, statue, government building and abbey. Even

Big Ben. They took full advantage of the hop-on/hop-off policy and did so countless times.

They had lunch at the Hard Rock Cafe, which was actually a noted part of the tour.

Though most consider it just another branch of the notable American chain, the London restaurant was in fact the very first of the Hard Rock Cafes.

Their three-hour tour (no relation to Gilligan's) clocked in at almost eight hours. They were wiped out by the end, but had all fallen for London.

*

The rest of their intro week was spent checking out the huge department stores, Harrods and Selfridges being their favourites. Just perusing those two took almost a whole day.

They also found time to look in at some furniture shops and auction houses. Mary was trying to get some inspiration as to how to tackle the Eaton Square house.

She had arranged some basic furnishings and stuff, so they could live there without too much hardship, but the place was going to need some creative magic to make it their home.

They had earlier decided to wait until they were in the UK to start work on the house. They wanted it to be a group effort.

Daniel was especially excited as this would be the first time he would be at his mother's side throughout the entire process. Or at least until school started in September.

*

They moved out of the Devonshire and into Eaton Square, one week to the day after arriving in London.

It was the first time Daniel actually saw the house. He was speechless. It was nothing like any home he'd ever seen. Built at the end of a row of famously prestigious (and unspeakably expensive) Georgian terraced homes, theirs was the jewel in the crown.

It looked like a miniature White House. Columns and all. Because it was at the end of the terrace row, it actually faced away from the square itself, but had room for an imposing entry portico.

Once inside, Daniel immediately saw the scope of work that was needed. It was understatedly grand, but had no personality at all. Like their St Cloud home, lots of changes had been made over the years, but none had thought to highlight the beauty of the original fittings, fixtures and architectural touches.

Mary pointed out one of the best examples. The entryway led to a sweeping curved staircase, that rose to the next level. The banister and railing were painted bright white. Mary used a key and scratched off some paint from the railing revealing the original wrought iron underneath. She then did the same to the banister, revealing solid mahogany.

"Imagine what this will be like when the staircase goes back to how it must have looked when it was built." Mary sounded almost emotional.

Daniel nodded, feeling her love for the property.

He couldn't wait to get started.

Mary had bought some neutral but attractive furniture for the upstairs sitting room, dining room and the bedrooms on the floor above.

That only covered about a third of the house. Mary included Daniel in all the meetings with the contractors, and various custom vendors. She took him to Bonhams' auction house, opposite Harrods, three times so she could bid on specific pieces of furniture that she wanted for the home.

He was in heaven. More than ever, he wanted to follow his mother's lead, and devote himself to real estate.

Quite a decision for an eleven-year-old.

*

The work started in earnest at the end of July, and by the end of August had barely scratched the surface. Daniel was devastated that he would have to head off to Switzerland without being able to see all the changes and improvements actually take shape.

*

There was one other important task to be tackled before Daniel's start day in Switzerland. The boy was eleven. He was about to mix with over a hundred and fifty boys and seventy-two girls, all at some stage of budding puberty.

It was time for the talk.

Having not been around kids, or even couples with kids, they were utterly unprepared for this parental duty.

They went online to get what they hoped would be some sage advice. When they entered 'Sex Education' into Alibaba search, they ended up on a number of sites that certainly taught them a thing or two, but did not address the immediate pressing issue. At least not in a suitable format for an eleven-year-old.

Henry did however take note of the URLs.

Once they found the right wording for the search, they became completely overwhelmed by the sheer volume of advice that was available online. They focused on the professional sex education teachers and a few parent-sponsored sites.

The consensus ranged from telling your child nothing and letting nature take its course, to sitting your child in front of *PornHub* for a few hours.

They even asked Christy for her advice.

She laughed.

"Do you two still have sex?" she smirked.

"Of course we do," Henry replied.

"Do you both know how babies are made?" Christy continued.

"We're not idiots," Mary replied.

"Then have a glass of wine, sit him down and tell him."

They both looked at her with new respect.

"Just the basics at this point, though!" she winked.

*

They decided to follow her suggestion, and asked him to sit with them for a moment before dinner.

It was amazingly hard to get the topic started. They talked about just about everything else on the planet, before finally diving in.

"So, Daniel," Henry began, his voice a full octave lower than usual. "Let's talk about girls for a moment. You may have noticed that their bodies are different from boys' bodies."

For some inane reason, he chose to gesture to Mary at that point.

Mary simply shook her head. "Look, honey. There are differences in men's and women's bodies. There is a reason for that. It's all about procreation."

"Not just procreation!" Daniel looked amused. "I mean, sex is also kinda fun too, right?"

They both tried not to look too dumbfounded. They failed.

"This is really great for you to sit me down like this—" Daniel interrupted, clearly enjoying himself, "—but you do know that we all had to take sex education at the Valley School, right?"

They both tried to cover the fact that they had no such knowledge.

"And did they teach you all the basics?" Mary attempted to save face.

"Yeah. They covered all the basic stuff."

"That's good." Henry relaxed.

"The rest we learned online. Ever since Hendrix, and the porn sites going 360-holo, we've pretty much been able to fill in all the blanks!"

"You've watched holo-porn!?" Mary asked.

"Damn right. Dad's invention changed everything. Now you can see when…"

"Whoa!" Mary held up both hands in surrender. "I think we got the gist."

"Don't you guys watch it?"

"Go to your room," Mary said, shaking her head.

Daniel grinned and headed out of the room.

"Keep your door open," she called after him.

"Little pervert," she mumbled to herself.

"I heard that," Daniel called from the upper landing.

Mary turned to Henry. "Did you know that kids are watching holographic porn?"

Henry got to his feet. "Kids!? Everybody's watching it. I think that when the porn companies went holo, it helped Hendrix's penetration. If you'll excuse the pun."

Mary gave him the full force of the super glare.

"Does it really work in holo?" she asked casually.

"Where's the HPad?" Henry smiled.

"In the den," Mary answered.

"Then go get it."

*

Henry, Mary and Daniel flew to Geneva a few days later. They stayed at the Grand Hotel, overlooking Lac Leman (or Lake Geneva as many refer to it).

The following day they were picked up by a huge Mercedes that was a cross between an SUV and a minivan. They headed along the lakeside towards the town of Dully.

Henry attempted to make small talk with the driver who simply nodded without saying a word. Very Swiss.

After about thirty minutes, they turned onto a long treelined drive that took them alongside the original chateau, around which the school had been built. Parents were encouraged, where possible, to personally bring their children to the school on 'drop-off' day, and even hang around for a while.

A short while.

Once Mary and Henry had seen the room he would share with another boy, and toured some other parts of the school, they heard the chateau bell ring.

That was the signal for all parents to say their goodbyes and leave their children in the care of those who actually knew what they were doing.

Before long, all the parents, the Trapps included, were gone.

The farewell had been pretty unemotional, at least from Daniel's side. Mary had let a few tears roll down her cheek, and Henry seemed to have to blow his nose more than usual.

Daniel, however, remained stoic.

Though not quite twelve years old, he was close to six feet tall. His shoulders had broadened and he had already learned how to give off a passable 'don't mess with me' vibe.

*

Daniel would have been a good-looking kid if it weren't for the one thing he had inherited from Zeke. He had a slightly chubby face. He had hoped it would tighten with age. But so far, there was no sign of that happening.

This trait also resulted in his eyes appearing to be set further back than they actually were. This made them seem, just a tad, beady. He made up for that with his hair. He had inherited his birth mother's thick, naturally lustrous blonde mane. He usually kept it long, but Le Lac required all boys to keep their coifs to a strict, short, maximum length.

Most new kids, upon arrival at Le Lac, sensed that their entire time there would depend on the level of dispassion they displayed while saying their goodbyes to their parents.

Any sign of *tristesse*, and you were screwed. Any sign of over devotion to your mother, and you were screwed. If you actually cried during the farewell process, you were basically ostracised for the duration.

Kids think high school is tough. Try it somewhere where you don't get to go home at the end of the day. There is nowhere to hide. Nowhere to recover.

The social protocols at boarding school are not that different from prison. Minus the guards and guns.

Attitude is everything.

*

One poor boy was clearly not going to score too many popularity points. He was sitting on a circular bench under a huge elm tree, just in front of the chateau and annex building. His parents had just left. He was weeping openly and was clearly in great distress.

As if intentionally wanting to end any future chance of social potential within the school, he suddenly screamed, "Won't anybody be my friend?"

*

Daniel looked at him and saw that his colours were like those of the strange boy at pre-school. They were all over the place. Unlike the other boy, however, this one's colours didn't shimmer. They just kind of melted together, like spilled paint, then separated, then mixed again. It was kind of disturbing. Also, none of the colours was bright. They were all darker, muted shades. It was depressing just to look at.

This kid wasn't right. Even Daniel, at only eleven, knew the kid shouldn't be there.

He wouldn't survive. Kids can be cruel at the best of times. Let them get a whiff of insecurity and vulnerability, without family around to protect you, and you just become prey.

*

The kids were left pretty much to their own devices until the dinner bell rang.

The majority of the children were returning so knew the ropes. They found friends and fellow students from the previous year and formed into small cliques. Soon the only ones wandering alone were the newbies.

It suddenly dawned on Daniel that the other kids were boys.

The school advertised itself as being co-educational.

So, where the hell were the girls! WTF.

Daniel approached another newbie, who looked to be about the same age.

"Hey, I'm Daniel."

"Hi. I'm Giles." He held out his hand.

They shook.

"Aren't there supposed to be girls at this school?" Daniel got right to the point.

Giles laughed. "I thought the same thing. I asked an older kid. He said they stay miles away, in a whole other town. But they get bussed here every day for classes. They don't even eat here. Pretty weird, huh?"

"Why would they do that?"

"The older kid said it was to stop them getting pregnant."

Daniel had no idea how to respond, though both boys smirked knowingly.

A bell rang in the chateau tower and suddenly staff and students appeared from everywhere, all heading towards the dining room.

Dinner time.

CHAPTER
NINE

The Trapps didn't say a word on the drive back to Geneva. They were both mentally questioning the whole concept of leaving their eleven-year-old son in the care, not just of complete strangers, but in a foreign country.

They felt like crap. They tried justifying what they had done by reminding themselves that the school was considered to be the best in the world.

That didn't really help. He was still only eleven!

This self-tormenting lasted until they reached the hotel bar. The self-recriminations remained into the evening, but were held at bay, just, under a layer of delightfully chilled, and mind-numbingly yummy gin.

They ate a sombre and silent meal in the hotel dining room. After a while, they realised that almost all the tables were occupied by other miserable-looking couples, all eating in silence. They also looked remorseful about some recent act of unspeakable cruelty.

Obviously, this was the place to eat after abandoning your child in Switzerland.

*

The next morning, they felt a little less like actual criminals, but were still questioning their decision. Actually, Daniel's decision. Whatever! They were at fault for going along with it.

"You know we could drive right back there and take him home?" Henry suggested.

"Then what?" Mary countered. "Send him to one of the English schools he hated?"

"We have to do something!" Henry argued.

"No, you don't," a gentle English voice advised.

They looked up and thought they were dreaming. Standing next to their table was Gail Chambers. *The* Gail Chambers. Four Oscars, two Tonys, three husbands, and she was still considered one of the best actresses to ever come out of England.

She must have been in her mid-forties, but still looked thirty. She wore her signature pageboy hairdo, and her green eyes really did sparkle as they did on the screen.

Mary and Henry looked up at her with stupefied and confused expressions.

"May I sit down?"

Mary practically shoved a chair out to her.

"May I assume that you have just left your – son, is it?"

They both nodded.

"At boarding school?"

More nods.

"First time?"

More nods.

"Eleven?"

"How do you know all this?" Mary patted the empty chair.

Gail sat. "I have just left my youngest child, Giles, also eleven, at Le Lac. I assume yours is at Le Lac?"

They nodded again.

"This will be my third one attending Le Lac. Not that it's of any consolation, but this feeling of guilt, reproach and abject misery, happens every time."

"Then why do you do it?" Henry asked

Gail smiled at his bluntness. "While we are sitting here, weeping into our overpriced breakfasts, they are at this minute gathering for their first general assembly.

"They have had a healthy and tasty breakfast with the most astonishingly delicious hot chocolate. They are about to be introduced formally to the school staff and programme. The new children all have butterflies. They don't know if they will fit in. They don't know what's in store for them. In about an hour from now, the buses from Bonsol, the girls' school, will be arriving and they will join the boys in the assembly room."

"But what about—" Mary tried to speak.

Gail held up a silencing hand.

"The one thing that our children are not thinking of, and believe it or not, will continue to not think of, is us. Their poor forlorn parents. Their days and evenings will be packed with work, play, sport and thoughts of girls, or in the case of the girls, thoughts of boys. We will hardly get even the briefest of consideration, except perhaps at phone time. At that moment, they will profess great misery, longing and may even voice a wish to be removed. The second they get off the phone, however, they will resume their new school lives, not realising the impact that their little phone performance has had on the parents. Thankfully, after the first half-term, the pretence of misery is usually dropped entirely and they will actually confess to enjoying the experience, and will regale us with tales of their exploits. By that time of course, we will all be wrung out like an unwanted tea towel."

She smiled over at the Trapps, who had listened, enraptured by every word.

"Oh fuck!" Gail suddenly gushed. "I never even introduced myself. Gail Chambers."

She held out her hand to Mary. "And you are?"

"Sorry. This is all a bit surreal. I'm Mary Trapp, this is Henry. My husband."

They all shook hands.

"I hope you don't mind my butting in and boring you with my little discourse. It's just I hate to see people going through all this without understanding that it's all just part of the game."

"Game?" Henry asked.

"Why, Henry! It's all a game." She glanced at her watch. "I must dash. I left my better half in the gift shop. He always buys me something to cheer me up after we drop off another one. You see. Just a game."

She started to get up. "Wouldn't it be nice if my Giles ends up friends with—?"

"Daniel." Mary nodded "Yes. That would be nice and thank you. Really! You've literally made our day, and most likely stopped us from doing something stupid like planning a break-out."

"Marvellous! Hope we meet again. Ciao."

And she was gone. Leaving the Trapps feeling as if their emotions had been on a trampoline for the past twenty-four hours.

Daniel did, in fact, settle into the routine of the school, and did become friends with Giles. They were almost inseparable and became each other's sounding boards for just about everything.

*

Giles' aura was bright blue, and became denser as their friendship grew. Daniel had learned that what he used to think of as fog hanging over people, was actually their aura. Or at least the aura he could see. Most of their schoolmates remained colourless, but a few were starting to have blue tinges to their outlines. Others had earned differing shades of red. These were the bullies. Their auras had colour, even before Daniel knew anything about them.

He could see their auras during the first general assembly. He could also tell that they, on the first day of school, were already targeting those destined for their brand of rebellion.

Daniel had realised at the Valley School that his abilities weren't changing, he was just gaining the skill to use them with better control. He also appreciated the need to use them sparingly, so as not to attract attention.

By the time he left America for the UK, Daniel knew that what he had was something very different from everyone else. It was something that had to be kept in the dark. People wouldn't like what he could do. He also understood that these traits needed to be carefully controlled. But, just like any muscle, they needed exercise and practice. He soon found that, just by focusing negatively and deeply on a person, he could give them the red colour, which in turn gave them an overwhelming melancholy, that would grow over time, and ultimately lead to intolerable depression.

He had learned that the hard way back at the Valley School. One day, his homeroom teacher kept him after class and told him that she was going to recommend his being kept back a year because of his grades and unwillingness to 'buckle down'. As he looked at her with growing disdain, he could see her colour change from blue to red. The more she went on about his lack of effort, the darker her aura became.

He focused hard on that.

She never acted on the threat to hold him back. Instead, almost overnight, she became despondent and before long, required treatment for chronic depression. Unable to cope with her endless dolefulness, she ultimately chose to throw herself over the side of the Catalina Island Express.

By practising his techniques 'under the radar', mainly on people he met on the street, he found that he could, instead of focusing deeply, just 'tap' the person very lightly.

Rather than have a long-term depressive reaction, the individual would immediately come over confused and sad. They were usually unable to continue with what they had been about to do. Daniel found he could intensify this reaction, just by thinking of hate. The more hate, the better the reaction.

At least for Daniel.

One week before leaving the Valley School, a much older kid cornered him by one of the playing fields. He wanted the candy bar in Daniel's hand. Daniel tapped hatred at the bigger boy. A red aura immediately surrounded him. There had been no conscious action from Daniel at all. It just happened.

The kid's expression lost all sign of aggression, and instead he started to cry. He dropped to his knees and veritably howled. Other kids walking by, saw who it was, and that he was bawling like a two-year-old.

They scurried off, laughing joyously.

The other side to his ability was how, when faced with those with strong blue auras, he could get them to follow his lead, just by thinking about it.

This was what had happened at the pre-school, during his first visit, only back then he had no idea that he was controlling the situation.

This ability was far more limited than his power over the 'reds'. While he could guide the blues, he could not actually change them or give them a physical reaction. They had to, somewhere inside themselves, already be willing in some way to do what Daniel was suggesting.

It wasn't anywhere near as fun as his red power.

At least at that point in his life.

CHAPTER
TEN

During his first half-term break, Daniel helped Mary look at suitable properties in Geneva for the Trapps' pied-à-terre.

They found the perfect place. The building was only a block from the Grand Hotel, and fronted the lake. The penthouse apartment was available. Though the building itself was shabby chic on the outside, the previous owner of the penthouse had remodelled every inch of its four thousand square feet.

Amazingly, he had done so with taste, and restraint. The other bonus was that the place was for sale completely furnished. Again, in such a way that Mary felt that nothing needed changing.

*

While they were buying the penthouse, Henry was meeting with the academic director of CERN. He was the gatekeeper of who could be invited to join their Hadron research teams.

Though Henry had been given the green light by almost the entire team at the collider, he still had to sit through the interview.

Herr Frankle was deeply in love with his own voice. The interview had been going on for twenty-five minutes, and Frankle had yet to permit Henry to get a word in.

The man just droned on in a heavy German accent, outlining his achievements (which were few and inconsequential) and those of CERN (which were vast and scientifically earth-shattering).

What made matters worse, was that he spoke in a loud and monotonous baritone. He had no regard for oral punctuation. He just talked, and talked and talked.

Henry at one point wondered if Herr Frankle, even remembered that it was an interview.

After checking his watch at the forty-five-minute mark, Frankle suddenly stood up, shook Henry's hand, and left the room.

Henry sat there for a full ten minutes before realisation set in that the other man wasn't coming back.

As Henry and his driver started to leave the compound, Henry's phone rang. It was his friend Carl.

"Wow! I don't know what you said to Frankle, but you passed with flying colours."

Henry looked at the phone as if not trusting the technology.

"You're kidding, right? I never said a word!"

Carl laughed. "This is no time for modesty. The guy won't stop talking about you. Come to the collider site tomorrow mid-morning, and ask for me. I'll walk you through all the security crap. Bring your passport and any other ID you have."

Henry thanked him and hung up. He was confused.

At the Hadron Collider site, Carl and a couple of his colleagues were in tears, they were laughing so hard.

Henry's interview had been a complete set-up. Henry Trapp didn't need to interview for any position in the physics sciences. Carl, who had always been a prankster, asked Herr Frankle, the most narcissistic, verbose, and generally boring physicist at the facility, to do them a huge favour.

They asked him to sit down with Henry and outline the CERN achievements and of course his own. Carl knew Frankle would jump at the chance and also knew Henry would fall hook, line and sinker for it being an 'interview'. He loved putting one over on Henry.

*

The family settled into a steady routine, living between London and Switzerland.

Mary had found a decrepit house north of Regent's Park. It had been on the market for years, and was deemed unsalvageable. Empty for over four years before it even went on the market, it had become a squatters' nest. They had pretty much trashed any redeeming features the home may have once held.

The roof had leaked in numerous places damaging much of the upper two floors. Rising damp had taken hold of the basement and ground floor.

Normally an investor would have snapped it up and levelled it immediately, before building a modern mega mansion, making a huge profit along the way.

The issue was that the property was held in a trust that would only permit a conditional purchase. The condition was that the home could not be demolished. Apparently, the previous owner had cherished the home. Illness and diminishing funds however, had forced her into a retirement home.

Before she passed, she had her solicitors create the codicil that ensured that her once proud and stately home would never be demolished. She also ensured that her executors would only accept an offer of no less than two and a half million pounds. In addition, the buyer had to be legally bound to fully restore the home. Also, it could only be used as a single home. No subdividing, no VRBO, just a single-use house.

Nobody would touch it. Nobody until Mary Trapp came along.

When she walked into the damp and smelly mansion house, she immediately saw it in its past glory.

She placed an offer but advised the estate agent that her son had to see it before the deal could proceed.

As per their agreement, Mary now included Daniel in every step of her investing process.

The following Friday evening, after classes, Daniel was driven to a private airfield outside Geneva. He was in London just over an hour later.

The following morning, they met the estate agent at the house first thing. In the morning.

The rain was tipping down, both inside and out.

The electricity was off and there was minimal light from outside.

The estate agent wouldn't shut up and was trying to give them the 'big' pitch.

Daniel asked to be allowed to walk through by himself. Mary was delighted. The agent, not so much. He couldn't understand why she had flown her eleven-year-old brat, all the way from Switzerland, just to see the place. He was just some snotty-nosed child.

He tried to hide his disdain from his clients, but didn't do a very good job. He clearly felt himself too superior to have to show Americans, one a child even, around that dump of a house.

Daniel could see the beginnings of a red haze around the older man.

He decided to give him the slightest of *taps*.

Firstly, the man shut up. Then he started apologising for the condition of the house. Then, for the weather. Then, he actually sniffled, then apologised for that.

From then on, he became the perfect estate agent. Informative, helpful, but maybe just a smidge too subservient.

*

Daniel was really getting to like the reactions from the little taps.

*

Mary bought the house, though the process of purchasing property in England dates back to the earliest days of land acquisition, when a plot could be bought/exchanged for anything tangible. Gold, livestock, a wife!

It took forever. Mary's solicitor would only ever talk to the trust's solicitor. No one else. Every question or concern was sent by mail. MAIL. Like with a stamp!

It took over six months.

The only good part was that the sale's completion coincided with Daniel's summer break.

*

The two worked tirelessly throughout the summer. They had the various trades lined up in order, so each could step in as the previous one finished their task.

Everything that was rotten or unsalvageable was hauled away immediately. Next came a team of damp proofers. They replaced the damp course around every exterior wall, then, injected damp-resistant chemicals into every wall cavity.

More than half of the roof joists were removed, and replaced. Those that remained were treated for both damp and woodworm. None of the existing tile roofing was salvageable, so once the joists were all sturdy and new, cross-braces were cut in, then, thousands of new, curved terracotta tiles were carefully installed.

Next came the windows and doors. Almost all were rotten. These were removed and replaced with triple-glazed PVC windows, and solid oak doors throughout.

Suddenly, after the last window was put in place, the house was, for the first time in many years, weatherproof. Now that the interior was no longer open to the elements, dozens of industrial dehumidifiers and corresponding generators went to work to fully dry out the interior, permitting Mary, Daniel and the contractors to see what could be salvaged.

Much to Mary's delight, the solid oak floors upstairs, and the tile and walnut floors downstairs, were mostly salvageable. Master carpenters would need to restore some sections, especially where intricate wood inlay work had been severely damaged.

*

Daniel returned to school at the end of the summer, but spent every break, and long weekend, by his mother's side. The home slowly morphed back into the grand old mansion she had once been.

Mary had to scour the British Isles for the skilled craftsmen needed to restore or replace carved wooden bannisters, inlayed wood flooring, mosaic bathroom floor – the list went on and on.

It took almost three years to complete. The end result was nothing short of spectacular. The house looked as it had when newly built, only now with every modern improvement imaginable.

Her cost: twelve million pounds or around sixteen million dollars.

Mary staged the entire home, then listed it with Sotheby's International. The list price was thirty-two million pounds or approximately forty million dollars. One of the highest asking prices ever for a property in that part of London.

Her estate agents pleaded with her to lower the price as it was never going to get a showing, let alone an offer at that price.

Less than one week later, it was shown and sold with a full price offer, contingent on all Mary's staging furnishings being included.

Mary had never felt so proud of a project in her life. She was about to call Daniel to give him the news when her phone rang.

It was Henry.

Daniel had been expelled from Le Lac.

CHAPTER
ELEVEN

They flew out immediately and were sitting in front of the headmaster by early dusk the same day.

Jacques Allette had run Le Lac for over thirty years. He looked just a little like the classic horror actor, Vincent Price, which made the whole vibe even stranger. Jacques advised that, in his time at Le Lac, he had seen it all.

Until Daniel.

There was no preamble, or offer of beverages. As soon as Mary and Henry were seated, he began.

"Your son is currently confined to his room. He will be released into your care after we have spoken and you have agreed to certain terms. Is that clear?" His gravitas was intense.

"No! It is not clear!" Mary launched into him. "That's our son you're talking about. How can anything be remotely clear when you haven't told us what he is supposed to have done."

"It's drugs, isn't it?" Henry asked. "You know, we understand how serious that is for an institution like yours. But, doesn't the school have to shoulder some of the blame. After all, he is in your care and—"

"Enough!" Allette held up a hand, palm out.

His words hung in the air for what seemed like an eternity.

Mary and Henry stared blankly back at him, then at each other, then back at him.

Suddenly Henry had a thought. "What do you mean, may have?"

The headmaster took a long breath, rose from his chair and walked to his office window.

"First of all, I want you to know that the police have not been contacted." He spoke while still staring out of the window. "In addition, the parents of the girls have also not been advised."

He turned to face them. "We only learned of this unique situation, because a teacher overheard a couple of girls talking about it."

"Talking about what?" Mary kept her voice calm.

"It would seem that your son has spent some of his time this term taking young ladies out to the pool house, then – touching them inappropriately."

"Against their will?" Mary sounded doubtful.

"Yes and no – maybe." He saw that neither parent was going to buy that answer for a second.

"Please. Let me try to explain. Each young lady went to the pool house with your son, willingly. Your son seemed to have a key for the storage area. They hid in there and kissed, which in turn led to fondling. Before you ask, yes,

229

they were all willing participants, even to the point that the fondling of their parts was – mutual."

He let this sink in.

"What makes this situation so unusual is that afterwards, the girls could clearly remember every second of the event, but couldn't understand how they ended up in that position. Each girl—"

"How many were there?" Henry interrupted.

"There were seven in total. Roughly one a week. As I was saying, each girl clearly remembered Daniel asking them to come to the pool house with him. I should mention that 'going to the pool house' is synonymous with – well, you know.

"All seven clearly remember saying yes, and agreeing to go there. And they did. They also remember..." he cleared his throat, "quite enjoying the experience."

"I'm not sure I'm quite getting—"

"Please, Monsieur Trapp. Let me finish. The girls, each of them, felt no attraction, or interest in your son. They had never considered him as – a candidate for romance, shall we say. Yet they, against type, immediately dropped what they were doing, and snuck off to a somewhat squalid, windowless shed, and basically had sexual foreplay with a boy to whom they were not attracted. I should state that there are a few girls at the school to whom such behaviour would not come as much of a surprise. But not these seven girls."

"May I ask a quick legal question? How old were these girls?" Henry was dead serious.

"Five of them were sixteen, the other two, seventeen."

Henry nodded. "And Daniel is—?"

"Sixteen," the headmaster replied, clearly seeing where Henry was headed.

"And the age of consent in Switzerland?"

"Sixteen."

Henry slapped his palm on the headmaster's desk. "Aha!"

"Before you continue in that direction, Monsieur Trapp, we all agree that there was no legal transgression in regards to age. The area in question, is that of consent."

"But you just told us that all the girls said they acted willingly," Mary pointed out.

Allette walked back to the desk and, with a sigh, sat behind it.

"They gave their consent, but don't know why. That is the problem."

"Are you suggesting he drugged them?"

"*Mon dieu*, no! They were asked the same question, and all stated that they felt no drug effect whatsoever. Nor did they ingest anything prior to the incidents. They were fully cognisant of their actions. In fact, they laughed with your son as they walked to the pool house. They even laughed and enjoyed the kissing and touching. There is no evidence whatsoever that they were drugged."

Mary leaned forward towards Allette. "Did they regret what happened?"

"*Voila, Madame*! That is the strangest part of all. No. They do not. They all actually enjoyed it. They just don't know why they did it."

"Could this be a guilt reaction?" Mary asked.

"The exact same reaction, from seven different young ladies! *Je ne crois pas*! I don't think so. The fact is, we don't know what happened. Each girl snuck off with the same boy. None found him attractive. They fooled around, enjoyed it, then can't remember why they did it. None of them, even though the incident seemed to be worth mentioning to school staff. It is very strange. I'm sure you can see that."

"We do see that," Mary agreed. "However, as this seems to be the case of some kids, consensually fooling around behind the shed, so to speak, please explain why Daniel is in so much trouble? You're expelling him."

"Yes, we are. The rules at Le Lac are very clear when it comes to sexual fraternisation between the boys and the girls. It is forbidden. I am relatively certain that parents do not send their daughters here, for *that* kind of further education."

Henry was on his feet. "Are you telling us that you believe that your rules actually mean diddlysquat when it comes to keeping girls and boys apart?"

"Sit down, Monsieur Trapp. There's only three of us here. There is no need for grandstanding. Of course, we know that there is occasional mischief."

Henry sat and snorted.

"But you would be surprised how aware we are of these occurrences, and how we ensure that they are brief, and not repeated."

"Then why is Daniel being singled out?" Mary asked bluntly.

"Because, Madame Trapp, in the first seven weeks of this term, your son has had relations with seven girls, who all feel on reflection, discomfort about the manner in which their liaison transpired."

"So, you're expelling him for being a horn dog?" Henry jumped in.

"Firstly, Monsieur Trapp, in this day and age, your son would be considered more a predator, than a 'horn dog'. Secondly, your son is failing seventy-five percent of his classes. In the last two terms, he has been insolent towards many of his teachers and seems to consider himself superior to almost everyone here at Le Lac. Those reasons alone merit expulsion.

"We would have waited until the end of this term to notify you that his presence here is no longer an option, however this new situation with the young ladies required immediate action."

It was amazing how loud silence could actually be.

*

As his parents waited in the car, Daniel was in his room, packing his final bag. Giles suddenly came running in.

"I just heard! What a load of bollocks!"

"It's not really though, is it?" Daniel smiled sheepishly at his friend.

Giles grinned wickedly. "I suppose not. At least you proved your *tapping* could do some good!"

"Remember. Not a soul! Never!"

Giles laughed. "I know. Never! I have to say, though, you really are the luckiest bugger I've ever known."

"I got expelled!"

"Exactly!"

They both laughed."See you in London?" Giles asked, as he headed back out of the room.

"Absolutely! Good luck on your finals."

"Fuck!" Giles spat out. "You've wangled a way out of those too!"

"As you said, I'm just a lucky guy!"

CHAPTER
TWELVE

Before they even got home, Mary and Henry realised that their son had changed. Outwardly he was the same, but they could both feel that something inside was different.

After dinner in the Eaton Square house, they had a family meeting. It was a first. Henry wanted to lead it, but Mary convinced him they might actually want to accomplish something.

He conceded.

They first asked him about the girls.

"The whole thing was bullshit!" Daniel began. "Lots of guys took girls to the pool house. I just got luckier than they did."

"Seven girls in seven weeks!" Mary countered.

"What can I say? They love me," Daniel replied.

"Let's put the 'loving you' part on hold for a while, and focus on why you felt you had to do that with seven girls."

"It would have been ten if I'd got to stay till the end of term."

"You are being a real dick at the moment," Henry chimed in.

"Oh, please. What's the big deal?"

Mary leant over and took his hand. "The big deal is that there's something very wrong with trying to score with as many girls as you can. It's vulgar, and it's not how we raised you. Were you trying to prove something? Was there a bet?"

Daniel didn't seem quite so cocky. "No. I just, I don't know – like girls."

"That's good, but don't you think it would be more special if you found the right one and focused your attentions on her?" Mary offered.

"Don't you get it? That's what I was doing. I was trying to see which one I wanted to keep as my girlfriend."

Mary had no reply.

Henry did. "Jesus Christ, man! These are young ladies. You're not buying a car. You can't test drive every single one on the lot."

"Why not? That's what they used to do on *The Bachelor* on TV!"

Now they were both at a loss for words.

"Let's change the subject for a minute," Mary said, still trying to get her head around the *Bachelor* comment. "What's with the grades and the attitude at school?"

Daniel stared down at his feet. "You wouldn't understand."

"Try us," Henry offered.

"I can't focus on that stuff. I don't care about what the King of Timbuctoo did seven hundred years ago. I don't want to read some old book about a mockingbird. None of that stuff is going to help me later on."

"You can't know that. What they teach you is a foundation. You don't know it now, but in the future, you'll build on everything you learn at school." Mary tried to sound reassuring.

"Are you telling me that in twenty years, in a business meeting about a building I'm renovating, my ability to dissect a frog will suddenly give me an edge? Or maybe knowing the atomic weight for lithium will help with the choice of flooring? And I'm absolutely certain that knowing the names of all of Henry VIII's wives, will help me get planning permission to extend the front entry."

Mary looked at him with concern and sympathy. Henry was actually trying his best to not smile.

"Look at the classes I did well in. Physics," he nodded to Henry. "Maths, economics, even art. All of those are going to help me. The other stuff just isn't."

Mary studied him closely. "I am not saying I agree with you. And I am certainly not condoning you being rude to the teachers at Le Lac, but I have a suggestion."

Both Henry and Daniel were both surprised and intrigued by her statement.

"I'm listening." Daniel sat back in his chair, waiting to hear the idea.

"So am I." Henry wasn't kidding.

"You will spend the next nine months at a tutorial college in London. They call them crammers. They will work with you on physics, maths and economics. You already took the GCSEs last year in those subjects. You didn't exactly pass with flying colours. So, we are going to let you prove to us that you are willing to actually study. Only this time, you're going for A levels. If you pass all three, you will have a partnership share of my company."

Daniel looked stunned. "What about university?"

"That will be your choice. If you are still as dedicated to working in real estate, I believe the A levels will be enough to see you through. I would have loved for you to go to a really great university, but frankly, with your grade transcripts, we'd be lucky to get you into Santa Monica Community College! So, your undergrad workload will just have to come from me."

Henry was staring at his wife like she was a complete stranger. "When did you come up with this?"

"About ten minutes ago!" she replied.

"There's one other thing. If you pass your A levels, and do formally join my company, we will open a bank account for you. It will be solely for the purpose of real estate transactions, with an initial deposit of one million dollars."

Daniel looked concerned. "There's not much I can get for a million dollars."

"That's the point. We will move back to California for a while, and you will be one hundred percent responsible for finding, negotiating and buying a property. You will then flip it yourself. Should you make a decent profit, we will review the stake."

Daniel was nodding and smiling.

"Okay. I like it. It's a deal."

Mary grabbed both his hands, and looked directly into his eyes.

"You haven't heard the final condition."

"I thought the A levels were the condition?"

"No. Those were to prove you actually want to do the work. The condition is, that if at any time while you are a member of my company I hear that you've disrespected another woman in the manner you did at Le Lac, you will be out."

"Out?" Daniel actually looked concerned. "What? You'd fire me?"

"In a split second. But that's completely hypothetical, right? Because it's not going to happen. Correct?"

He took a big swallow, and looked to both his parents.

*

It was obvious that Mum meant every word, His dad, though, was still trying to catch up.

It didn't matter.

He could study hard for a few months and pass the stupid exams. He could even try to respect women. Or at least pretend to. After all, his parents were basically funding his start-up. He didn't want to screw that up.

It was simple. He just had to tone things down for a while, and learn everything he could about making money from real estate.

Maybe he'd even find a nice girlfriend. One that he could fool around with without having to give her the tap.

Perhaps that was asking a bit much.

Maybe just a little tap.

Then, maybe she would let him fuck her.

CHAPTER
THIRTEEN

Daniel passed all three A levels. Not spectacularly, but with a decent enough score, to show that he had at least been trying. During the nine months, he had focused almost entirely on the studies.

He went out a few times with Giles, mainly just to mess around. Being sixteen didn't really offer too many options for getting into big trouble. You couldn't drink yet, and couldn't get into the clubs.

Plus, his mum had put him on a curfew. Home by nine.

So, they goofed off in Hyde Park. Ogled some girls. Sometimes grabbed a pizza. Basically, kids' stuff.

His parents were getting their way. He was being the perfect son. Respectful and gentlemanly to a fault.

He was outwardly behaving like every other well-mannered teen.

Except maybe the one time in the park. But that was Giles' fault.

They'd gone to Speakers' Corner in Hyde Park, which was one of Daniel's favourite places in all of London. It's a paved corner of the park, right next to Marble Arch, where anyone could stand and speak publicly. About almost anything. On weekends the crowds could be huge.

It was an amazing example of a functioning democracy. There'd be twenty different people, some on soapboxes, some with actual risers, all rambling on about stuff that bothered them.

It could be the government, conspiracy theories, censorship (for or against). There are not many places in the world where an individual can voice his opinions openly, without fear of reprisal.

That said, if someone tried to rally for violence or racism or anything blatantly illegal, they would be none-too-gently removed from the public venue.

*

Giles and Daniel stood there watching these people ranting for over an hour. They were loving every minute of it.

Giles then nudged him.

"Why don't you give it a try?"

Daniel looked at his friend, like he'd suggested raping livestock.

"I can't do that."

"Yes, you can. I've seen you do it at school," Giles insisted.

"That was to girls."

241

"So, let's see what happens if you try it to a bigger audience."

"What's the point?" Daniel shook his head.

"I want to see if you can pull that shit with a crowd." Giles nodded encouragement.

Daniel walked around the area considering whether to try or not.

He then suddenly stopped, spread his arms in greeting, and began to orate.

"Ladies and gentlemen, I need to talk to you about a problem we all have. We don't want to admit it, or even talk about it, but we all suffer from it."

Nobody paid him any attention. They just walked by, ignoring him entirely.

"We have been told that as males, we have been disrespecting the opposite sex. We have considered women merely as sex objects. We are now told we have to change our ways of thinking—"

Still nobody was listening. Daniel glanced at Giles who gestured for him to give them a little push, as he called it.

Daniel began *tapping* individuals in the crowd. Just enough to give them just a hint of blue.

"Yet how are we supposed to look at a woman, and not think of her sexually when she's chosen to wear a skirt that's so short, her only intent had to have been to catch our eyes? But it's not just our eyes, is it? If we see someone sexually attractive, it catches way more than our eyes. Our minds want to see more. Our very loins react to such stimuli. We have been led into lust!"

A couple of people stopped to listen.

242

"I say to you, that if we are being forced to rewire our very brains so that we will no longer look at a woman and find her attractive, or sexy, then they have to share the burden of this change and no longer dress in such a way as to elicit exactly that reaction."

The crowd had grown to about twenty. They were nodding in full agreement. Including three women. One was clearly trying to pull her T-shirt down to cover her exposed midriff.

"So, I ask you, one and all, to listen to my words and spread them among your friends and acquaintances. We will respect all women, so long as they respect our efforts and start dressing accordingly."

There were now over fifty people. Some were clapping, a few were even cheering.

"This does not just relate to short skirts, or tight tops. If you don't want us to be drawn to your sexuality, then perfume also has to go. Covering yourself in pheromones designed specifically to lead our senses into lust and longing can only achieve just that!"

There were now over a hundred people of all sexes, and they were all cheering him on.

"In closing, we will not look at you as sexual objects, if you promise to not display yourselves in that manner." Daniel looked over the crowd which was still growing.

"Can I hear agreement on that, please!?" Daniel bellowed.

The crowed went crazy.

They loved him. They felt his words were life changing. They wanted to follow him.

Giles, sensing that things were getting a little too real,

grabbed his arm and they both ran across Park Lane and down into the Marble Arch Underground station.

Once they reached their platform, completely out of breath, Giles smacked him on the arm.

"What the fuck was that? I've never seen or heard anything like that in my life."

"I know. That was – epic!"

"How did you even come up with that shit?"

"I've heard my dad using that argument with my mum, whenever he tries to defend male values."

"Did he ever win?" Giles sounded hopeful.

"You mean did he ever win any of the hundreds of arguments?"

"Yeah."

"Nope. Not one." Daniel smirked. "Haven't you learned yet? We are always in the wrong."

"I forgot. Thank you for reminding me." Giles' expression changed to a look of concern. "You don't actually want women to stop dressing skanky, do you?"

"Fuck no. The skankier the better!"

They watched as their train emerged, almost phallically, from the tunnel.

A detached voice filled the platform.

"Please mind the gap."

"Please mind the gap."

CHAPTER
FOURTEEN

It felt really strange being back in Los Angeles. They'd all become used to the culture and vibe of Europe.

LA certainly had vibe, lots of it actually, but culture – not so much.

*

They settled back into the St Cloud house and Mary, true to her word, brought Daniel into her company. Being months shy of eighteen, he still had a few legal impediments to juggle in order to negotiate and buy property.

He couldn't get a full driver's licence yet, but that's why UBER Ground and UBER Air existed. He loved UBER Air but considering his budget, the places he was going to see were unlikely to have the space, even for VTL (Vertical Take-off & Landing).

The other age issue was that being under eighteen, he

couldn't legally enter into a contract to buy a property. Actually, he could, but there was this whole legal thing where the contract could be voided by *him*, because of his age, making it basically unenforceable. Weird, huh!

Obviously, nobody was going to get into that situation, so until the big one eight, his mum would have to be the signatory.

Big whoop. It would still be his project.

*

LA is probably one of the most diversely overpriced real estate markets in the world. Houses have gone for over one hundred million in the best areas. Yet less than five miles away from those elite neighbourhoods is the other extreme. These were the war zones, but to buy a three-bedroom, seven hundred square feet dump, with bars on the windows and bullet holes in the front wall, it could still cost close to half a million.

The mantra of US realtors is location, location, location. People think this is some kind of gag or hype. It's not. It is the basis upon which any budding investor needs to live by.

Buying a piece of shit, in a war-torn neighbourhood, then trying to spruce it up for a big profit – well, to quote one of America's more interesting politicians – 'Would be like putting lipstick on a pig!'. The fact is, unless your business plan is to become a slum lord (amazingly, some people do strive for that), you need to know where to buy.

The rule in LA to play it safe (literally) is keep north of Wilshire and west of Fairfax. That's not to say that there aren't some other nice bits dotted around elsewhere, but in most of those border areas, you just won't feel comfortable being out after dark.

Mary spent almost a full week driving Daniel through every neighbourhood, giving him the positives and negatives of each. She knew the median price ranges, the demographics, even which individual streets cost more, which ones less, and why.

Daniel was really impressed by just how much his mum actually knew. Funny how that can work.

She also showed him how to use her realtor ID (against every rule imaginable) to access the MLS (multiple listing service). This was the bible for buying or selling property. The public did not have access to this resource as the info contained about each property was so detailed, it could be just a smidge too helpful for burglars, etc.

Mary felt that at that point, he had the tools to fend for himself. Daniel agreed.

She didn't throw him completely to the wolves. She hooked him up with a friend, Evelyne Peten, who was a licensed real estate broker, who had basically made so much money in the business that she, at that point in her life, preferred to spend her time trying to write poetry.

It was terrible poetry. No, that's not strong enough. It was pure shit.

Let's just say that she was in a close tie with the Vogons for some of the worst poetry ever written (thank you *Hitchhiker's Guide*).

Some of Evelyne's wealth had been earned as the direct result of Mary's dealings with her, so when asked if she would mind acting as Daniel's realtor, she jumped at the chance. Besides, it gave her the opportunity to play Daniel some audio recording of her best works.

The one ground rule imposed by Daniel and Mary was that he would pick which properties to see.

Daniel wanted to be in complete control.

Daniel spent every minute glued to his LID, looking at home after home. He finally realised that with his budget he wouldn't get much in the way of an actual house, then, add on all the remodel expenses specific to a detached property, and he would be upside down in five minutes flat.

He decided to switch his search to condos, or as referred to in England, flats!

Even then, his budget was still sorely inadequate for certain areas. Beverly Hills, Westwood, Brentwood, these were all the higher-priced condo areas. Studios (basically one-room condos) could go for half a million.

Daniel decided on West Hollywood. Though some parts were way out of his budget, the great thing about WH was that tucked away next to a five million per unit condo tower, could be a 1940s funky character building, where a two-bed condo could be had for six to seven hundred thousand.

And the kicker was that these would, for that price, need some serious TLC and a creative mind. Just the target for a flipper!

Daniel looked and looked and looked. He kept finding ones with the right bones, but they were just too far neglected or had some serious structural issues.

If you were going to basically have to rebuild a unit almost from scratch, the chance of a decent profit was about as likely as Kim Kardashian developing modesty.

He was starting to grow disillusioned with the whole thing, when Evelyne asked if he would consider breaking their 'no helping' rule, and let her show him what she felt was an interesting prospect. It had been on the market for a while but could, at the right price, be his perfect cherry breaker.

By that point, he was more than happy to be thrown a life jacket.

Evelyne first made a couple of phone calls to make sure they could see the unit. She then drove along Fountain, turned north up Orange, and pulled into an off-street entry, lined with individual garages.

Daniel still couldn't see the actual property. It was surrounded on almost all sides by incredibly tall, mature ficus trees. You would never know the building was even there.

They walked through a beautifully maintained used brick lanai surrounded by large copper planters. Giant palms towered over them, shading the entire entry.

The building was a 1930s Mediterranean, that oozed charm. It was a little shabby chic, but was still delightful. Each unit was cleverly separated from the next, giving each a sense of individuality.

Every four units had their own foyer entrance. Evelyn made for the last one.

There were four entry buttons. Evelyne pushed one. An elderly voice crackled back at her.

"Who is it? I don't talk to strangers!"

Evelyne tried to hide her amusement. Daniel wondered what the hell they were doing there.

"Hi, Mrs Bellows. It's Evelyne Peten. I'm here to show your home."

Her words were met with dead silence.

"You better not be trying to sell me anything. I don't buy from strangers," she finally announced.

The door buzzed, and they entered one of the complex's three entry lobbies. Heavily glazed terracotta tiles greeted them. They looked original and added to the unique feel of the place.

A studded oak door opened on their right. Mrs Bellows' head poked out to check out the potential trespassers. She was old. Very old. And as cantankerous as they come.

"Hi, Mrs Bellows," Evelyne chimed cheerfully.

"I know you," Mrs Bellows replied uncheerfully. "I've shown your lovely condo before, but not for a while."

"Maybe that's where I know you from." She sounded unconvinced.

"This is Daniel Trapp. He's looking to buy a condo, and I immediately thought of yours."

"He doesn't look old enough to have pubic hair! How the hell can he buy a house?" She suddenly turned to Daniel. "You got pubes yet?"

"Actually, yes, I do." He was shocked at the old woman's vulgarity.

"Well I'm too fucking old to want to see proof, so I guess I'll just have to trust you."

"That's a relief, ma'am," he managed.

"Then what the hell are you both doing standing out in the hall. I'm not selling the fucking hall!"

She swung the door open, and stepped aside.

They entered.

Daniel's breath was taken away the moment he saw the place.

Not in a good way.

Mrs Bellows was a hoarder.

A serious one.

The entry, the living room and both bedrooms were filled with a mix of old newspaper, magazines, food packaging, discarded cardboard and, even more oddly, brand-new clothing still in its bags.

The collection was piled against every wall to a height of over seven feet. There was only just enough space to move through the condo, if one turned sideways.

Despite the detritus, Daniel could see beyond that, and realised that the place actually seemed in great condition (considering). The bathroom and kitchen were uncluttered and pristine. The bathroom suite looked brand new. Unfortunately, it was the trendy colour of the bygone era when the place had been built. Avocado.

*

Of all retro looks, the one that will never come back (one hopes) is that bile-green shade of avocado. For some inexplicable reason, this colour, that looks more like a bodily discharge, was the rage for a whopping twenty-five years. The stuff is still everywhere.

*

Despite that, the original and gorgeous tiling was done in dark green and black. There wasn't a crack or blemish. It was museum quality.

The kitchen was equally impeccable, except for the

antique appliances. All of which looked showroom new, despite being older than Mrs Bellows.

Daniel could see that the whole place would need modernising and cosmetic updating, but no construction was needed. A flipper's fantasy.

After touring every nook and cranny, unescorted by Mrs B, Daniel looked over at Evelyne and nodded excitedly. She gestured for him to calm down.

"Let's put in an offer right now," he whispered.

Evelyne gave him a concerned look followed by a rolling of the eyes.

"What does that mean?"

She led Daniel back to the entry where Mrs Bellows was seated on a pile of faded newsprint.

"Mr Trapp is somewhat interested. I have convinced him that despite the condition, it could be quite a nice place with enough work. I have suggested that he makes what he feels would be a fair offer."

The elderly woman looked shocked. "Oh, I don't know about that. This is my home, you see. I mean where would I go?"

Evelyne smiled knowingly. "I believe your son has already bought you a beautiful retirement home, just outside San Diego. That's why you are selling."

Mrs B looked at her as if this was the first she had heard of it.

"I just don't know. If I were to sell, it would have to be for the right price."

"We completely understand. We know that other units here have sold, but they were fully modernised and move-in-ready."

"Like mine then!" Mrs B replied.

"I believe my client was thinking in the six hundred thousand range."

The old woman guffawed. Daniel had read about them, but had never actually witnessed a guffaw.

"Oh my! I know for a fact that my kitchen is the nicest of all the units here. Why should I get less?"

Evelyne did her best to be diplomatic. "With all due respect, Mrs Bellows, most people want new kitchens and bathrooms. At least new fittings and appliances."

"Why? Mine all work perfectly. In fact, the fridge is still under warranty."

Daniel snorted before he could stop himself.

"When you say under warranty—" Evelyne asked gently.

"Absolutely. When we bought that fridge in 1957, the Kelvinator Company gave us a lifetime warranty."

"I think you'll find that Kelvinator hasn't been around for a while." Evelyne tried to be gentle.

"What poppycock! Lifetime is lifetime! Anyway. It's never needed fixing."

Evelyne shot Daniel a look that clearly said 'Now do you see the problem?'.

"What price do you think is fair?" Daniel decided to join Evelyne in the Twilight Zone.

Mrs Bellows looked at him, then at her, then back at him, as if she couldn't understand why they even had to ask.

"I think as this is the nicest unit, nine hundred thousand. Yup, nine hundred thousand would be very fair."

The three stared at one another. Each waiting for someone else to say something deeply poignant.

Evelyne was the first to cave. "What if we went to seven?"

She checked Daniel to make sure he was on board.

He gave her what he thought was a shrewd nod. It looked more like an uncontrolled tic.

"I don't think I need to be insulted in my own beautiful home." Mrs Bellows slowly and creakily got to her feet then opened the front door so they could leave.

"Mrs Bellows." Daniel stood directly in front of her and offered a warm and sincere smile. "May I suggest that you and I sit for a few minutes and see if we can't come to some mutual agreement about your lovely home?"

Evelyne looked aghast. She had promised to keep him under her wing. Daniel gave her a reassuring nod.

The older woman took his arm. "Let's talk in the lounge."

She then looked at Evelyne. "You can wait outside."

They had to crab walk through the piles of crap, but once in the lounge, there was a tiny section of uncluttered space where Mrs B could sit in her recliner and Daniel could balance on a pile of debris.

"So, what do you think you can bring to this party, Mr Trapp!?"

Daniel looked closely at her face, with its lines and wrinkles that can only be carved by time and a full life.

He then gave her a very slight *tap*.

A faint and weak blue haze slowly wrapped itself around her head.

"Let me tell you why I think seven hundred thousand is a fantastic offer," he began.

*

When he stepped out of the building, Evelyne was waiting with a sympathetic expression.

"Don't feel too bad. Just about every agent and developer in LA has tried. She just won't budge."

Daniel nodded his acceptance of her statement as they walked back towards the car.

"Funny thing, though."

"What?" Evelyne was distracted as she searched for her car keys.

"She just agreed to seven."

Evelyne looked at him with stunned confusion. "Seven what?"

"Seven hundred thousand. Thirty-day escrow. All cash." He looked over at her with a cheeky grin. "I was kinda hoping you could write it up for me."

"Are you serious?"

"I am always serious when it comes to making a deal."

She stared at him with wonder and a huge grin. "You cocky son of a bitch."

*

When Daniel got home and told his mother, she couldn't stop laughing. Mostly because of his managing to buy the property that Evelyne had been pushing for years.

They immediately Skyped Henry, who was back in Switzerland working on another project for CERN. Such was their excitement, they totally forgot the time difference and woke him up.

When they told him the reason, he couldn't have been happier for the interruption.

Mary and Daniel went back the next day and viewed the property. She was as taken with the place as he was. She started to outline what needed doing, who to contact and how to schedule the trades.

Daniel just stood there smiling at her.

"What?" she asked.

"We had a deal, remember. My property, my project."

She was about to argue.

"A deal is a deal," he chided.

"I was just trying to—"

"I know, but let me do this. I know I might screw up, but that's how I'll learn. I'll tell you what. If it starts to go pear-shaped, I'll bring you in."

"Promise?" she laughed.

"Promise."

*

He never did need to bring her in.

Much to Mary's delight, but also annoyance (pride basically), he seemed to be able to get the contractor to move at twice the speed he ever did for her, and what was worse, he got everything discounted by at least twenty-five percent.

That was unheard of in the flipping business.

Mary happened by the condo one day. Daniel was in the middle of executing a change order on the kitchen cabinetry.

Daniel had decided that he wanted hand-finished natural maple, instead of the laminate the contractor had quoted for.

The contractor told him it would be at least five thousand dollars more. Her son smiled and stared at him.

"Let's meet in the middle and call it twenty-five hundred?"

Mary waited for the builder to laugh. Instead the man nodded happily and shook Daniel's hand. Mary could only imagine that Daniel must have had photos of the guy humping barn animals. There was no other explanation for a contractor in LA to suddenly discount their work.

*

Daniel netted over one hundred and thirty thousand on that first flip. Just over two hundred on the second and close to four hundred thousand on his third.

Not bad for a kid about to turn nineteen.

But those were nothing in comparison to profits he was soon to bring in.

And those were nothing compared to the interest on the trust fund that he began accessing on his twenty-first birthday. It's amazing how well one can live off the interest on five hundred million dollars.

The trust was very specific.

Five hundred million at twenty-one.

Another five hundred at twenty-five.

The same at thirty.

He could only access interest on the monies until he reached forty. At that point, the entire one and half billion, his share of the trust, was his to do with as he pleased.

In the eventuality of both parents being deceased, he still would only have access to the interest till forty, but the interest would be on close to seven billion dollars.

PART III
THE POWER

CHAPTER
ONE

Daniel got better and better at 'negotiating', and thus made bigger and bigger profits from his projects.

Having access to around forty million dollars a year interest didn't hurt, though he still liked the thrill of the deal-making and widening the profit margin.

His biggest coup to date was buying a dilapidated twelve-storey (fourteen if you counted the two underground parking levels), once grand, art deco monstrosity, just off Wilshire on Bundy. It had managed to survive the wrecking ball because of its historic architecture, even though by then, it just looked seedy and blighted.

It had been a landmark for so long that nobody seemed to realise what a dump it had become.

The interior had been luxurious, with three-thousand-square-foot, three-bedroom apartments, that each took up an entire floor. Even once the place had lost its original lustre, the apartments had still rented for over three thousand a month.

Finally, the complete lack of preventative, and even emergency, maintenance, took its toll. Plumbing failed. The antique boiler packed up, then the elevator failed its safety certificate.

The city finally refused occupancy until the place was back up to code.

So, with the renters gone and the owners broke, it went on the market.

Because its footprint wasn't that large, and the cost to demo alone would have been in the millions, developers just weren't that excited about it. Even if you brought it back to its former glory, which wouldn't be cheap, you would have had to either sell the building as a whole, or go condo and sell the units. No matter how one crunched the numbers, there was no way to do the work, and still make a profit on the sale of twelve condos.

Daniel, now twenty-three, looked at it from a completely different viewpoint.

The location was prime. It was also relatively close to UCLA. The University of California had a student population of over forty thousand. All of them needing housing. Many, preferring to buy rather than rent student 'digs'.

Daniel worked with his regular architect (who only charged him half the going rate), and drew up plans that gave each floor an elevator lobby and four one-bedroom, six-hundred-square-foot condos. Each was ultra-luxurious, with all-natural fibres, woods and granites, floor-to-ceiling windows, and even an underground parking space. They were small, but extraordinary.

The perfect condo for the upwardly mobile student, or one whose parents were already rolling in it.

After carefully studying the small condo market, he realised that just a short distance up Wilshire, in Westwood, his units would sell for over seven fifty.

He knew his location was prime but not 'as' prime as the Wilshire corridor, so he priced them starting at six fifty for the first four floors, six seventy-five for the next four, and seven hundred thousand for the final floors. The variation was entirely view driven. The higher you went, the better the view.

He sold the last unit three and a half months after putting them on the market. As he had taken the time to become a licensed broker, he was able to sell without a realtor, saving a whopping three million in sales commission.

After all was said and done, he netted close to twelve million dollars.

From that point on, house flipping was out. Building development was where to make the real coin.

*

Daniel left his mother's company and formed Trapp Development Inc.

TDI expanded at lightning speed. Daniel couldn't seem to put a foot wrong. His company was in profit, big profit, on every single project.

The industry couldn't believe the luck Daniel kept having.

His contractors and vendors stayed irrationally loyal to him, despite being paid less by TDI than by any other company in town.

By the time he reached the grand old age of twenty-eight, he was no longer doing projects one at a time. TDI had at least three large-scale buildings on the go at any given time.

He also had a growing staff, who were fanatically protective of their boss, and worked crazy hours for very average pay.

The one part of the business that he never left to anyone but himself was the negotiating. He had to be the one to meet the sellers, the builders, contractors, even the supply vendors.

He explained to those who asked that looking someone in the eye when negotiating was the only way to keep it real.

*

Daniel's other area of interest was women.

He had perfected the super light *tap*, and found that it was just enough to get a girl to go out with him. Once he took them to the best restaurants or VIP events, it didn't take long for them to warm to him.

He prided himself that he could usually get the girl 'stripped down for business' as he liked to refer to it, by the second date. The fact was, that if they weren't willing by then, he gave them another little *tap*.

That was guaranteed to get their panties hanging from the bedpost.

*

Word spread in Los Angeles about the miracle 'kid', his development company and his dazzling social life. The *LA Times* got wind of the story, and ran a two-page article in the Sunday *Real Estate* section.

That got the attention of the local broadcasters.

Suddenly, Daniel was always on TV, on some local magazine show or other.

Daniel was as surprised as everyone else when TV stations wanted him for their shitty, off-prime, news magazines shows.

At first, he was reluctant to go on the air. He felt nervous, and even when he gave the hosts a little *tap*, which resulted in them becoming much friendlier, he still didn't like the feeling of being interviewed. He felt like they were prying.

He was about to give up on the whole TV personality thing when he was invited to be a guest on *The Nick Chavez Show*, one of the bigger local programmes. He almost declined the invite, until he heard that they had a live audience.

The moment applause greeted his walking on set, Daniel felt completely different. There was a buzz to hearing a crowd welcome you.

The interview itself was the same boring crap, with the same stupid questions about how he made his money, how he picked which building to work on, etc.

Daniel decided that he was going to take it up a notch, and try something a little different.

After the obligatory mini tap to Nick Chavez, Daniel then tapped the entire audience.

He could feel the audience lean forward in their seats, almost as if they wanted to be closer to him.

He liked the feeling. He stopped answering the questions by rote, and instead added a little sarcasm, a little humour. He even went for some pathos, as he recounted the story of his days at the boarding school.

The crowd reacted to his every nuance, as if they were watching a one-man show on Broadway.

He felt power. He felt he could actually control the audience.

It was like a drug. It was addictive. He wanted more.

He looked directly into camera 2, and tapped the home audience as well.

*

The reaction to the show caught the producers completely off guard. Here was this, not particularly attractive guy, who was doing pretty well in the LA real estate market, telling weak-ass jokes and stories to the audience and for some reason, they seemed to love it. To love him.

While they were scratching their heads, trying to work out what the hell people were seeing in the dude, their phones started ringing. The station phones, the production office phones, the control booth phones, even their cells, all started ringing at once.

The viewers at home loved the guy.

They all wanted more.

*

Daniel had become a mini celebrity overnight. People wanted to hear more about him. More about his lifestyle. More about his beliefs. More about his women.

He was shocked, but also kinda chuffed to find out that he had even become a trending topic on TMZ. Especially the dating part.

As his persona grew, so did the celebrity level of his 'girlfriends'. Suddenly he was seeing starlets, and models. He was having a ball.

*

The Nick Chavez Show producers contacted him a few days later, and basically begged him to come back onto the show.

Daniel played hard to get, just to mess with them a little. After all, he wanted to be back in front of a live audience as much as they wanted him back.

What the producers weren't expecting was that Daniel demanded that he be given a full fifteen minutes of air time.

Alone!

Nick Chavez could introduce him, but then the time was his. He would choose the topics.

They tried to explain to him that that just wasn't how it was done.

Daniel disconnected the call.

The producers sat, hunkered down in their conference room, trying to avoid the incessant calls, emails, texts and even attempted drop-ins, all of whom wanted more of Daniel.

They decided that they really had little to lose. The fact that he wanted to be on set alone, without the host of the show, removed a lot of their liability if the guy screwed up badly.

Despite a continuing gnawing at their collective guts, they called him back and agreed to his conditions.

They booked him for the Friday show. Two days away.

Daniel was delighted. He wanted the audience to meet the real man. Not just the golden child of real estate.

He had views, and thoughts, and opinions that people needed to hear about.

His phone's ringtone sounded Megadeth's 'Family Tree'.

"Hi, Mum!" he answered.

CHAPTER
TWO

It was rare to get summoned to St Cloud. Ever since he moved into the top unit of one of his restored buildings, home visits had become a rarity.

He was just too busy.

The moment he walked into the living room, he knew it was a trap.

Mary, Christy and Henry were already seated, clearly awaiting his arrival.

"Gee, guys, do I have to get another tutor?" he quipped.

Mary gestured to one of the plush coral armchairs that had been strategically placed so that they would all be facing him.

"Oh, oh! Daniel's been a baaad boy!" His Elmer Fudd impression wasn't half bad.

"Please sit with us. We're all on your side," Henry said. "We just want to have a little talk."

Daniel shrugged, then plopped down in the interrogation chair.

"So, what's up?"

"That's what we want to ask you," Mary replied using her 'nurturing' voice. "We watched you on TV yesterday and – we all felt very concerned about it – about you."

"What the hell! I was great! The show wants me back on Friday to do a full fifteen minutes."

Henry leaned forward on his hands. "We're not sure what you were trying to do. You were—"

"Crass!" Mary interrupted. "The way you talked about women – it was almost – sociopathic!"

"It wasn't you!" Christy blurted out, then immediately started crying.

Daniel looked at her like she was crazy.

"She's right," Henry agreed. "It wasn't you. You came across like some arrogant deviant."

Daniel cracked up laughing. "Fuck, man. What century are you guys from? I came across exactly as the audience wanted me to come across. I didn't do the show for you. I did it for them – for me. What I wanted was to get the audience on my side, and for them to want more of me. And guess what, it worked."

"But, honey, we don't understand why you suddenly care what other people think of you. You were never like that," Mary pleaded.

"Well I am now. And do you know why? Because the more people love you, the more power you have over them."

"But *we* love you," Mary exclaimed. "Does that mean you want power over us."

"That's different. You guys 'really' love me. The others just think they love me. That's the trick!"

He suddenly got to his feet.

"Anyway, this was a real blast." He rolled his eyes. "Please, just let me do what I'm doing. I have a plan. I'm not an idiot!"

He headed for the door.

"You're not going anywhere!" Henry shouted. "You are going to sit back down, and we are going to talk about this. We did not raise you to be – whoever, whatever, the hell that was on TV yesterday."

Daniel stopped. He slowly turned to face Henry. It was obvious that his father was furious.

"We raised you with decent values. We taught you right and wrong," Henry continued. He hadn't noticed the mood change in Daniel.

"If you think that we are just gonna sit on our backsides while you fuck every model and actress in Los Angeles, then you have another thing coming. You will not carry on like this any longer. Am I clear? Don't think for one second that we can't undo the trust we set up for you."

"I don't need your fucking money, in case you haven't noticed."

"Well you sure as hell need the help of the planning commission, and the licensing board, don't you? May I remind you that Mayor Starling is a close friend of your mother's. One word from her, and just maybe your planning permits might start taking longer, and your occupancy inspections, just might start getting delayed. How about that? You might not need our fucking money, but you still need our contacts, don't you, big man!?"

Daniel couldn't remember feeling such anger before.

His own parents were trying to hold him back.

And his dad was being a complete douche.

Before he realised, what he was doing, he tapped him.

His own father.

It was a big one too.

He immediately saw the light in Henry's eyes lose its sparkle. His aura, that had always been bright blue, was now a dull red.

Henry's face sagged, and his lower jaw hung loose, leaving his mouth agape.

Daniel couldn't believe what he had just done. He turned and ran from the house.

Daniel had hardly ever cried his entire life.

Now he couldn't stop.

He knew what was going to happen to Henry.

Once the tap was delivered, there was no way to retract it or change the outcome.

This wasn't the post office.

There was no return-to-sender.

*

Henry was rushed to the UCLA Emergency and Trauma centre. The doctors first thought it was a stroke. They ran every test imaginable. But couldn't find anything physically wrong with him.

What was even stranger was that during the time it took to carry out all the tests, he seemed to recover somewhat.

His facial features returned to normal. His speech, though a little hesitant, showed no sign of impairment.

Mary tried to explain to them that something had changed. You could see it in his eyes.

They finally determined that he must have had a mini stroke. They explained that these can happen, almost without symptoms, and usually the patient recovered completely. They described it as a slight blip to the system.

Maybe, it had been a stress reaction to the confrontation with Daniel.

After almost eight hours in the ICU, Henry was moved to one of the top floors. The VIP rooms. The part of a hospital that mere mortals never get to see.

These VIP floors were where the celebrities, the rich and the politicians stay when in hospital. Each patient suite is more like a living room, with a comfortable seating area for guests, a convertible sofa for sleepovers, even a mini kitchen.

In these rooms, the patients and guests do not eat 'hospital' food. Their menu reads like a four-star restaurant. Sure, there are dietary restrictions, depending on each patient's condition, but the 'menu consultant' is always happy to work out which of the gourmet choices best fits the patient's desire and digestive ability.

*

Once they were alone, and the doctors had signed off on his condition, Mary sat holding his hand as he dozed.

Henry opened his eyes and looked over at his wife.

Mary smiled lovingly. "Well look who's back from the dead! You certainly gave us a scare."

He just continued to stare at her.

"Can I get you something?" Mary patted his hand.

Henry tried to talk but could only whisper.

"I couldn't quite hear that, my darling."

He tried to talk, but his throat was too dry after all the tests. Mary grabbed the paper cup with ice chips, and gently placed some between his lips.

After a few more helpings of chips, Henry weakly cleared his throat a few times

"Try to speak again," Mary urged gently.

She sat on the edge of his bed and leant against him so her ear was near his mouth.

Henry managed a croaky and weak whisper. "There's no point. I'm not part of the plan."

At first Mary didn't think she had heard him correctly. It made no sense.

Then a distant memory fought its way to the surface.

She had heard that before.

Ellen.

Colorado.

Zeke.

Mary's screaming was so loud it was heard on the floor below. A floor without private rooms, special menus and mini kitchens.

CHAPTER
THREE

Daniel spent Thursday alone in his condo. He had stopped all the pointless self-recrimination and had convinced himself that it had been entirely Henry's fault. He had no right talking to him like that. He wasn't some kid that had been caught shoplifting bubble-gum.

He was Daniel Trapp. Real estate mogul.

Nobody could talk to him that way.

Besides, Henry wasn't even his real dad.

Fuck him!

*

The following day, when Daniel walked onto the set of *The Nick Chavez Show*, he was stunned by the audience reaction. They were on their feet, cheering and clapping.

Maybe his idea of leaking the fact that his dad was in hospital hadn't been a bad play at all. The crowd seemed to really appreciate the fact that he had managed to break away from his vigil at his father's bedside, just to be there for them.

Or, it could just have been the extra spin he'd put on their *tap*.

It took almost three minutes for the crowd to settle down. Daniel wiped an emotional tear from his face, and nodded his heartfelt thanks to them all.

"You guys are too much. Thank you all. You've given me strength."

He watched as the audience themselves became emotional.

"I felt that my personal issues were not the most important thing here today. It felt that maybe by my being here with you, my friends, whether in person or for you watching at home, we could discuss some things that are – well, I don't know if I can even say it on TV, but, things that are really starting to piss me off."

The audience cheered. Daniel could have sworn he even heard a few hallelujahs and amens.

"We live in one of the richest cities, in one of the richest states, in one of the richest countries in the whole goddamned world. But you know what I see every day on the street? I see men and women whose fortunes have turned. Who no longer have a home, or even a roof to shelter beneath. These once proud souls are lucky if they can find a big enough cardboard box in which to lay their heads. Do you know why these poor individuals have fallen soooo very far from grace? Do you?

"Well I do! Drugs!

"This once clean, proud, honest and true country of

ours, has been invaded. Our borders are as porous as a sponge. Drugs enter our country with as much ease as water running through a colander.

"Our population has been infected. Not by some virus or bacteria, but by pills, and crystal and powder! This infection isn't gonna go away with a couple of aspirin and a day in bed. This infection is only gonna go away when the leaders of our states and our country get off their fat asses, and for once in their miserable careers, do something for the people. Something revolutionary. Something fantastic. Let's not forget – that was how this great land was founded.

"Do you think, while our Founding Fathers were forming the greatest nation this planet has ever seen, they were ever hesitant to act in case they lost votes back home? Of course not. I will guarantee you that our Founding Fathers acted solely for what was best for America, and best for those who lived in America.

"Do you honestly believe that our forefathers would have made sure that they had guaranteed lifetime health insurance, but did not ensure the rest of the population had the same?

"I don't think so!

"These timid, sycophantic, self-serving excuses for lawmakers that fill our state and federal offices of government have had their time. They have shown us that they don't care for the people. They care only for the people's vote.

"Well I am sick of it."

Daniel got to his feet and stood at the front of the set.

"This indomitable and proud country once revolted against what it felt were oppressive and unfair leaders just so it could bring fairness and equality to all.

"Do you believe our congressmen and senators spend their days trying to create that equality? That fairness – for us?

"The next time a man is shot by a policeman in front of his family, solely because of the crime of driving while black, ask yourself how hard you think your representatives are really working to make sure that that travesty never happens again.

"Are you happy that our schools have regularly become the sites of mass murder? That farmers can no longer plant the seeds they can afford, only those that are forced on them by one mega corporation? That the role models for our children today are gangsters and reality TV stars posting nude photos of themselves on the Internet?

"I have a question.

"Are you really, deep down, happy with how this country is being run?

"I have another question. When did everything start to go so wrong, and when the hell did the government stop caring about it?"

For a moment the audience remained in shocked awe.

Then they exploded into cheering, applause, amens, you name it.

Daniel held up both hands. The audience slowly silenced.

"There's one more thing I need from all of you." His voice was calmly reflective. "Some of you may have heard that my poor father was taken ill a few days ago. He's in hospital. He's not in a good way.

278

"I would like all of you here, and those of you watching at home, to please send your prayers to that fine man. I thank you all for taking the time to listen to me today. I planned to stay longer, and spend more time with you all, but, my father needs me. I love you all! God bless you."

Daniel choked up on the last words then slowly turned from the audience and, overcome with emotion, staggered off the set, and out of their view.

*

Daniel had never seen such auras before. The blues were electric and pulsating. He saw that more than half the audience was in tears, the rest were euphorically behind every bullshit word he'd just spoken.

He always knew that he could 'blue tap' the audience and maybe get some positive reactions.

He had no idea, however, that he could feed them rehashed, political dogma, and that they would eat it up like brand new, freshly baked cookies.

This opened up a whole new set of options.

*

He was overwhelmed at the energy and passion he had instilled in the studio audience. What he couldn't see were the reactions of the home audience.

*

The home viewers were emotionally on fire. They were screaming at their LID screens. Yelling out of their windows, some danced wildly in the middle of their living rooms. They had felt the blue light.

Whether in the studio, or at home, it was clear that Daniel's audience did hear him, and they agreed with everything he said.

Daniel had *tapped* (literally) into a gusher.

Now, he just needed to open the valves, just a little bit more. Then the people would be clear about his message. It wasn't just a little fixing that the country needed.

It needed a complete sea change.

*

Daniel's speech on *The Nick Chavez Show* went viral. In the first twenty-four hours, there were over twelve million hits. By Monday the number was over fifty million.

And that was just on YouTube. On social media, it had been shared to numbers so big, they couldn't be tracked.

It wasn't just trending.

It was a phenomenon.

Daniel was suddenly being approached by every talk show in America. From the morning sector, right through to the late-night comics.

He knew he had to plan his next step very carefully. He didn't want to screw things up by premature overexposure. He wanted it steady and controlled.

Too much too soon, and everything could peak and wane before even getting the right traction.

After some serious contemplation, and a few lines of some primo Columbian happy powder, he decided that he needed professional advice.

It was funny that his dad should have thrown Mayor Starling's name at him as a threat the other day. The fact was, she would be the perfect person to give him some early pointers.

She took his call immediately, and before he could get a word in, she rambled on almost incessantly about how amazing he had been on that show. She raved about his passion, his obvious patriotism, to say nothing of his ability to hold and electrify an audience.

She then apologised, in advance, for what she was about to say. She knew it wasn't what he was calling about, or even something he would consider, but she, and the others in her office, all believed that Daniel had a calling. A mission even.

They all felt he needed to become part of government. He knew the issues and she believed he had what it took to get elected, then he could help resolve them.

"I'm not sure how well suited I would be for local government," he replied humbly. "I'm very flattered but maybe I can help more in the background."

"Fuck that!" the mayor of Los Angeles threw back at him. "Who's talking local government? Sid Harding is going to step down as California senator in a matter of days. It's cancer, but that's not been announced yet.

"There will be a special election within three months. You need to be our candidate."

Daniel was, for one of the first times in his adult life, lost for words. He knew he wanted a seat at the table. He just never imagined being invited to sit at one of the best tables in the house.

At least not yet.

"I don't know what to say. I'm not ready. I haven't done anything to warrant a shot at higher office."

"Don't be so naïve! It's nothing to do with warranting. It's to do with personality, drive, appeal, and the thing you have, that I haven't seen in decades, the ability to captivate an audience. Besides, you were a millionaire by twenty-one, you have proved to the city that you are an extraordinary deal maker and businessman. What part of 'not ready' do you think relates to you? I personally believe that you, Daniel, were born ready!"You also happen to be the luckiest son of a bitch I have had the pleasure of knowing and working with. Don't discount luck when talking politics!"

Daniel drew a deep breath. "So, what would be the next step if I did choose to explore this option?"

"First of all, there is no IF. The timing of this is beyond fate. You explode onto social media and TV as our US senator for California drops out. No, this is your time. I'm going to make some calls and talk to Jeff Range at the DNC.

"While I am doing that, I want you to call Paul Tector. He's the best political PR person in the country. He's in town helping draft Senator Harding's retirement statements.

"Hold the line, Suzie will give you his contact details."

Daniel was suddenly listening to hold music.

It was Emerson, Lake and Palmer's 'Lucky Man'.

CHAPTER
FOUR

Daniel met Paul Tector the following day for lunch. He had been surprised when Paul said to meet him at the Horse and Groom pub in Santa Monica.

It was one of the most authentic 'old style' British pubs on the west coast. Darts, warm ale and good old pub grub. It was a fun place. Daniel had just assumed that a mover and shaker would opt for something a little more chic and expensive.

Daniel had also expected Paul to 'look the part' of the best political PR rep in America. He didn't. At minimum he had expected something that smacked of DC power. Dark suit, Savile Row shirt, five-hundred-dollar tie. The usual.

Instead, the man sitting across from him was younger than he was, was wearing cargo shorts, a faded Led Zeppelin T-shirt and flip flops.

That's as far as the casual side went.

The man was razor sharp, highly eloquent, and held Daniel with steely grey eyes that seemed to never blink.

They both took a moment to order. Neither consulted the food-stained menu (also authentic). They both ordered a pint of Guinness and fish and chips.

"I watched your TV thing a couple of times," Paul stated bluntly. "I think Sandra – sorry, Mayor Starling is right. You have something to say, and what's far more important, you have the whole package with which to sell it."

"Thank you," Daniel replied.

"You can cut the humble pie crap with me. You know you have it, and you know exactly how to use it. The moment you did the first Chavez show, you were like a heat-seeking missile. You knew your target, and you knew how to enter the coordinates into the guidance system. You knew precisely what you were doing. That second appearance may just end up changing history.

"If you choose to continue down this road, and let's not blow smoke up each other's respective backsides, we both know you will, we have to determine what you are today, and what we need you to be tomorrow. You're young. That's a blessing, and a curse. The new guard will love you for it. The old guard will not. We could dress you up like a rich senator, with pin stripes and Ferragamos, but that optic could say, if you'll pardon my The Who reference '*Meet the new boss, same as the old boss*'. We don't want that.

"We could go youthful, and keep you in jeans and sweats, but that could read, 'not serious enough for the big leagues'. It's a tough call, but I already have a sense on the best *you* to go with.

"You are rich and successful. You should look like money, but only casually. Oxford button-down, no ties, penny loafers, maybe even no socks. Black or grey slacks. Expensive jacket, but not a blazer. Something along those lines. We want you to show some class, but not separation from the people. They need to feel you are one of them, but maybe just a little smarter, and a little more 'in the know'.

"Driving over here, I was thinking about some hook. Something that would make you look different but still say, 'I am a patriot and I'm here to save the country'. Something that stands out, but still keeps you grounded. Something that becomes your 'thing'. What about a baseball cap? Blue. A blue baseball cap. Maybe even with a slogan on it."

Daniel stopped drinking his Guinness mid gulp. "You had me up until the baseball cap. What sort of moron, in this day and age, would wear a baseball cap with a slogan on it?"

Paul burst out laughing. "You're right. Not even sure where that came from."

"The one thing that I don't want to do, and quite frankly, will not do, is change who I am." Daniel was suddenly in dead serious mode. "Otherwise the whole exercise is pointless. I will only move forward on my terms, and my terms only. As far as stage dressing, with the exception of the hat thing, that's fine. But I won't be told what to say.

"The reason you are here today, is that my words and appeal seem to have resonated with the public. If we dilute that, by my having to feed them some party script, they'll know it, and I will know it. To be completely blunt, and not remotely humble, I can only sell my message in my way."

Paul was studying him closely.

"You know what? You keep spouting pearls like that, and I do believe you could just end up as president."

Daniel took a long swig of his dark brew. "Is that as high as I can go?"

Paul nodded his approval of the other man's unabashed hubris.

"We're gonna have a fucking blast!" Paul clinked his beer mug against Daniel's.

Both men drank, but their eyes never left each other.

*

The two sat in the pub for three more hours, going over every aspect of how to formally launch Daniel onto the American stage. One of Paul's biggest caveats was that until Daniel was up to speed on what being a senator actually meant, he was to hold off from any more public speaking opportunities.

After another Guinness, Daniel reluctantly agreed.

By the end of the meeting, Daniel's brain was swimming. Partially because of the Guinness, but also, by the complexity of the planning that went into starting a bid for public office.

As they were saying goodbye, Paul added one small nugget.

"You'll get a pass for a senate run, but if you do decide to go for the big chair, get a wife. Ease up on the TMZ talent, and get an intelligent woman to support you. If you find a pretty one, even better"

"Do you think I actually need the support of a woman?"

"I doubt it. But if you want any women in the country to vote for you, you'd best marry one. Also, when you find the right one, never stop broadcasting just how much you depend on her, and that you couldn't do any of it without her support."

"I'd better start looking," Daniel replied with amusement.

"For fuck's sake, look in a different pool from the one you've been swimming in. The nation doesn't need a first lady that thinks the Constitution is a new party hotel in Vegas.

"Aim for class and a brain. It'll be a new experience for you, but give it a try."

Before Daniel could say anything else, a black SUV pulled up at the kerb. Paul got in.

A tinted back window rolled down, and Paul's face appeared.

"Get an Uber. A DUI wouldn't be a great way to start the campaign!"

The window rose back up.

*

As predicted, Senator Sidney Harding formally notified the senate leadership two days later that he was resigning, effective immediately. The public spin was simply that he wanted to spend more time with his family.

*

Paul kept in close touch with Daniel. He advised him that he and the DNC had decided that what Daniel desperately needed was someone to hold his hand, and keep his dick dry until his full campaign team was in place.

"I'm sending someone out there immediately. We'll refer to her as your aide," Paul announced.

"What the hell is an aide, and what do I do with one?" Daniel responded.

"Consider her your PR compass for the next few weeks. I will give you as much time as I can, but there's a shit storm brewing in DC. I'll fill you in on that when I see you next. It could even be good for you, down the road.

"The Dems will be sending a team to LA in a few days. Listen to them. They'd eat their own children for the party. In fact, I think one of them actually did.

"Robyn Watkins, your 'aide', is flying in tonight. She's staying at the Canon Wilshire. She has your number. I have just texted you hers. Get together tomorrow. Please listen to every word she says. She has two degrees from Harvard. Political Science and Congressional Law. For the next three months, she is the only woman you will be seen with in public. You can screw around again once you get elected."

"What's she like?" Daniel tried to sound casual.

"She's like the smartest person you will ever meet. That means she is going to be good for you, if you listen to her. That also means that she will not be dazzled by your big blue eyes, and end up facing the headboard, while you drill for oil at the other end. Understood?"

"Got it!"

The next morning, Daniel was in the lobby of the Canon Wilshire Hotel, waiting for Robyn to appear. If there was one place where he didn't mind being kept waiting, it was at the CW.

It was a truly beautiful hotel. Built in the late 1920s, its exterior was 'Grand Deco'. Depicted in the movie, *Pretty Woman*, it was still *the* place to stay in LA, if you wanted old-world charm, class and service.

There were plenty of five-star hotels that catered for the young and wealthy who wanted to be seen at a rooftop pool bar partying with celebrity gangbangers.

The Canon Wilshire did not choose to cater for that particular clientele.

Daniel watched as the established rich and powerful glided through the lobby, heading out to do battle with the Los Angeles elite.

He was facing the main elevator lobby, so could see each carload as they emerged.

He already had a sense of what Robyn was going to look like and as the next car disgorged its human cargo, he saw that he was right.

Five-foot, dark hair pulled back tight, manly suit, white blouse buttoned all the way up. She was a little heavy and her eyes were also a little too close together. It wasn't that she was unattractive. She was just – blah.

Daniel sighed as she approached him. Then again, she was here to help. She didn't need to be a knockout.

Daniel stood up and held out his hand. She shook it with a limp wrist. Her palms were sweaty.

"I'm so sorry I'm late. I overslept, then I couldn't seem to work the shower. There were so many knobs. Please forgive me, Mr Withers. It won't happen again."

It took Daniel a moment to catch on.

"I'm not Mr Withers." He tried to keep the relief out of his voice.

The sound of a woman laughing behind him made him turn around.

That was the moment that Daniel's life changed forever.

CHAPTER
FIVE

Robyn was almost as tall as him, though the three-inch heels definitely played a part. She, like the blah woman, was wearing a manly business suit, but hers was probably Balenciaga, plus, the highly educated Harvard alumni had a rockin' body.

Daniel finally managed to raise his gaze from the below-neck playground, to her face.

Perfect. Classically beautiful. Not pretty. The angles were too strong. Her eyes were almond shaped, with just a trace of an upward slant. Maybe some East Asian in her blood.

Then there was their colour. Emerald green with flecks of gold.

He wanted to dive into those eyes, right there and then.

Though still laughing, she held out her hand.

"That was very impressive, Mr Trapp." Her voice was silky with just a trace of a rasp. Think Demi Moore in the eighties.

"I can see that it's going to be interesting working with you."

"Thank you." Daniel gave her his best smile.

"It wasn't a compliment. Let's find somewhere we can talk."

She headed off towards the Regal Bar. Good choice. They would have complete privacy this early in the day.

Daniel tried, with every molecule of his being, to not check out her ass as she walked away. Clearly a few molecules weren't giving it their all.

Great ass. Great legs.

Daniel couldn't help himself. He gave her a tiny, almost insignificant *tap*.

No blue appeared.

The woman was perfect. She was gorgeous. But she had no aura. Nothing. Not even a shimmer. He tried a second *tap*, but with a little more spin on it. A double *tap* so to speak.

Nada!

Robyn realised that he wasn't following her.

"You coming?"

Daniel gave her his version of a winning smile, then caught up with her.

Fuck! Daniel thought to himself. Here was the most beautiful woman he had ever seen, and he was going to have to work without a net.

No help from the *tap*.

He wasn't sure he even knew how to behave around a woman without his little helper. He was even more uncertain about how a woman would react to him, totally *tapless*!

Maybe he could get her drunk and go the old-fashioned route.

Classy to the end!

*

For the next week straight, Daniel and Robyn were inseparable, except, much to Daniel's disappointment, during the overnight hours. She would then return to her hotel room, and he to his condo.

He had tried to get her drunk over one of their working dinners, but found that she could, quite literally, drink him under the table.

He had taken her to the infamous Tonies Beanery on Santa Monica Blvd, and had plied her with their house version of the inimitable Mai Tai.

After a countless number of the lethal concoctions, he could hardly stand. She on the other hand, chose to walk back to the hotel almost three miles away. Something about the magic of the night air.

In LA!

No one walked anywhere in LA!

He attempted to be vaguely chivalrous, and offered to accompany her, but after falling out of the restaurant door, then tripping on the kerb, she advised him that she would feel much safer without him.

She did, however, tuck him into an Uber, and sent him home.

He had no recollection of getting home, but did remember spending the early hours of the morning puking so much, that he could have sworn he brought up a shrimp he'd eaten the previous week.

When he duly reported for work the next morning, he had a slight case of the shivers, was deathly white, and his skin felt slick and oily.

Robyn appeared looking healthier and more beautiful than ever.

Clearly not having sex with him was doing wonders for her.

Daniel felt like he was dying.

*

At the end of the exhausting week, he decided to try one more attempt at inebriated seduction and took her to Tex in West Hollywood.

The clientele was primarily gay, which freaked him out a little, but it was still one of Daniel's favourite restaurants.

Tex started life as a tiny Tex-Mex joint which just happened to serve the best margaritas in the world, plus some seriously good fajitas. It caught on big time.

You just couldn't get in.

Instead of expanding the place by enlarging the building, the owners cleverly doubled its size with wood-framed green plastic tenting which could be rolled back in summer and anchored down in the winter. Heat lamps took care of any chill. The extra space was on two levels, and was filled with gigantic birds of paradise plants.

The place was packed every night of the year.

On Cinco de Mayo the patronage doubled and even included a mariachi band. There is video taken from outside the restaurant on the fifth, showing the tenting actually expanding and contracting to the music.

*

When Daniel pulled up in his vintage Porsche Cayenne, the valets recognised him (or the bright yellow vehicle), and flung open the doors for the couple.

Usually one had to wait sometimes hours to get in, but being a regular who tipped unlike any other regular, they were seated immediately.

Robyn loved the place. He had told her where they were going earlier in the day, so she had, for once, swapped the designer executive wear, for jeans and an untucked man's dress shirt.

All eyes were on her. The women wanted her and the men wanted to be like her.

Daniel took the alpha role as he was a regular, and ordered a pitcher of their double-strength margaritas.

They devoured it within minutes, as well as two bowls of the home-made tortilla chips and salsa.

Daniel was about to order another, when Robyn stopped him.

She looked up at the waiter and asked if they had Heradura Silver.

They did.

She ordered four shots and two Pacificos.

Once the waiter left, she turned and smiled knowingly at Daniel.

"If you're gonna try to get me drunk, then get me drunk. Enough with the fruit drinks!"

And so began the showdown.

Somewhere in between eating shrimp and beef fajitas, a Tex special burrito and a shredded chicken tostada, they consumed eight shots and four beers a piece.

Daniel found an entirely new and unforgettable way to impress Robyn.

Just after paying the bill, and as Daniel was struggling to get on his feet, two girls in their twenties stepped up to the table and blocked him from moving any further. He couldn't make out their features, but could plainly see their shimmering blue auras.

"We saw you on TV. You were amazing," one of them fawned.

Daniel tried to smile then opened his mouth to speak, but instead, managed to projectile vomit over both young women.

Amazingly, neither seemed to mind in the least. Daniel could only watch through his tequila-filtered eyes, as the pair worked at cleaning his own vomit off themselves. All the while, still showering him with adulation.

The one part of the debacle that he would never forget was the image of Robyn still seated, howling with laughter, as tears ran down her face.

In the Uber home (the yellow Porsche remained behind) she turned to him and, still laughing, said, "You really are a prince among men, aren't you!?"

He tried to nod but passed out cold instead.

*

They only had two more days together before the DNC advanced candidacy team was scheduled to arrive.

There was still much more work to do before then.

Robyn had schooled him on every aspect of the senate operation, its history, its mandated function, its actual function and the painful reality of what it really took to sit among the other ninety-nine senators, and get anything done.

On their last day alone, Robyn led him outside the hotel, just as her ordered Uber pulled up.

She wouldn't tell him where they were going, but once they turned off Sunset and passed the Bel Air gates, he knew.

He turned to her with a look of hurt and anger.

"Why?"

She took hold of his hand. "Because they haven't heard from you since it happened."

"I don't want to see them. Driver, turn around."

"Bill." Robyn addressed him by his name. "My friend here doesn't want to visit his parents, but he's going to, so please don't listen to him."

The young black Uber driver stared at Daniel in his mirror. "There's no excuse to not visit your family, Mr Trapp. They're the only real truth in your life."

Daniel sulked in the back.

"By the way, I saw your big speech on TV."

"What did you think of it?" Robyn asked.

"Sounded like the same old rhetoric to me."

That took Daniel out of his self-pitying funk. He then noticed that Bill had a slight aura, but it was pale red. Not a trace of blue.

"You watched it?" Daniel asked with growing concern.

"Yes, sir. Watched it on YouTube just the other day. Can't see what all the fuss was about, if you'll pardon the honesty."

"Not at all." Daniel actually meant it.

He had just learned a very important technical fact about his *taps*. He knew they affected people in the flesh, and also those at home, via the cameras. He had heard all the hype. Yet this guy watched the show a full week later, on YouTube, and the tap hadn't done a thing.

It was like old analogue video. Each time a new copy was made, a generation was lost.

The same principle must apply to his taps. When recorded, they fade with time!

Talk about a good Uber experience.

He was gonna get five stars!

He had just found out a vital piece of information about his power.

It had to be served fresh.

CHAPTER
SIX

Christy answered the door. She looked like she had aged ten years in the two weeks since he'd seen her.

She smiled weakly and gave him an all-enveloping hug.

Daniel introduced Robyn, and the three walked into the main lounge.

Mary had been working on a HUD, LID tablet and had three screens in the air around her. When she saw them enter, she reduced the images and stood to greet them.

"Mum, this is Robyn."

"I know, honey. We talk almost every day."

Daniel shot Robyn a puzzled glance.

"Where's Dad?" Daniel asked.

"In the garden somewhere. He knows you were coming."

"I'm sorry I haven't – you know – been around since—" Daniel tried unsuccessfully to express himself.

"I'm sorry too!" Mary grabbed his hand.

Daniel nodded guiltily.

"He's doing okay. Let's track him down, and you'll see."

Mary led the way through the den, to a set of massive French doors that opened onto the rolling acreage of manicured lawn.

"I'll stay here," Robyn suggested. "You guys go ahead. Maybe Christy and I can have a cup of tea or something."

Mary looked at her with silent thanks.

*

They found Henry behind the tennis court, standing under a truly massive Moreton Bay Fig tree. He was looking up at the gnarled branches with an expression of serene reflection.

He looked thinner and his face seemed to have more shadows than Daniel remembered. He also hadn't shaved in a few days, which was unheard of for him.

"Magnificent, isn't it?" He turned to face them as they approached. "We used to have one just like it when I was a boy. I spent many a summer climbing the damn thing. I used to just love sitting on the higher branches and watching the world go by.

"I always wanted to just stay up there and leave all the trouble way below me."

"How are you, Dad?" Daniel asked. All he could see was a deep red and grey aura, swirling around his father's head and shoulders.

"I'm good, Daniel. Very good. I hear you might be dipping your toes into politics?"

"Something like that."

"We watched your TV thing a couple of days ago."

"And?"

"You know me. I don't understand politics. I like the factual stuff like science. You always know where you stand."

"Your father's been asked to join CERN full time. Their new anti-matter catchment housing is complete, and they're ready to start the testing," Mary announced proudly.

"Dad, that's great. When will you go back?"

"I don't know. I've got a few things on my mind at the moment. Once I've dealt with those, your mother and I will head back across the pond."

Something about the way Henry answered electrified the hairs on the back of his neck.

He didn't know what to say.

"If you need any help with the politics thing, get your mum involved. She knows everybody!"

Henry then turned away from them, and resumed gazing up at the majestic tree.

Mary and Daniel made their way back to the house.

"He seems good," Daniel offered.

"No, he doesn't. He's not Henry any more. The doctors say he's fine and that the old spark will return, but you saw him. It's sort of Henry but at the same time, not."

Mary stopped and turned to face him.

"I'm going to ask you a strange question. I've been hesitant about it, but to hell with it. I have to. Please don't think I'm crazy, okay."

Daniel nodded but at the same time felt his guts churn. He knew what she was about to ask.

"That day in the living room – did you do something to him?"

"What do you mean?" Daniel tried to sound surprised.

Mary stepped up close to him, and looked him in the eye.

"Did you do something to your father?"

"No. Of course not. I don't know what you even mean."

"Don't you? I would really love to believe that, Daniel. Please make me believe that."

Daniel took her in his arms and held her tight. "I swear on my life that I have no idea what you are talking about."

Neither could see the other's face. Daniel had his eyes pressed tightly shut as if trying to avoid the reality of the conversation.

Mary's eyes were wide open.

Daniel had not made her believe.

After a few moments they broke away, like boxers being warned by the ref.

Daniel looked back one last time, and saw that his father was still staring up at the higher branches. Daniel really hoped that somehow he would come around and become the Henry they all knew and loved.

#

That was the last time he saw his father alive.

CHAPTER
SEVEN

Christy volunteered to drive them back to Robyn's hotel. During the trip no one spoke. At all. It was tense. As she pulled the car under the hotel portico, Christy waved off the valet and sat there for a moment.

"Your parents need you, Daniel. This is a very difficult time for them. Can you please try and make more of an effort to be around?"

Daniel reached for the door handle then hesitated.

"I'm sorry for what they are going through, and yes, I will try, but the next few months are going to be crazy. I'm running for senator."

"I'd heard. I think you'll probably win, but we're talking about your father."

Daniel opened the door and just before stepping out, said, "I know he's my father. I also know that you are basically the housekeeper, so, I'm not sure you're in a position to tell me how I should interact with my family."

Christy reacted as if she'd been slapped. She had been a part of his life almost since birth. She had always felt like a family member and had always been treated as one. Until that moment.

Daniel walked away from the car and entered the hotel.

Robyn looked over to her. "Sorry."

She then followed Daniel into the building.

*

Though they managed to complete the last of Robyn's instructions on 'How to become a senator in three easy months', Daniel had been distracted, and had had trouble focusing on their last day.

Robyn finally closed her laptop.

"Let's finish up over dinner. I'll order something sent to my suite and we can work there."

"Whatever."

"There's no WHATEVER allowed at this point. As of tomorrow, you will be fast-tracked to the candidacy, and you will need to be on your game like never before.

"You will be interviewed a hundred times. You will shake thousands of hands, and you will make countless public speeches. You have three months to persuade the whole damn state that you are special, and that they need you, and only you.

"Let me tell you something, buckaroo! Sulking and self-pity is not going to help. Save it, store it away, bury it. I don't care, but by first light tomorrow, you are the alpha. So, put on your big-boy pants and get a grip. Understood?"

Daniel took a deep breath, and reluctantly nodded. "Got it."

"Good. Be at my suite at seven. We have a lot to do."

"Can't wait," Daniel mumbled.

"God help us." Robyn shook her head.

*

He was at her door at seven o'clock sharp. Feeling completely unmotivated about another long night being schooled in senatorial bullshit. He had thus dressed for the occasion.

Baggy jeans, a vintage tie-dyed Grateful Dead T-shirt and a pair of leather sandals.

He was expecting Robyn to give him shit about it, but instead, upon opening her door, she took one look at him and smiled appreciatively.

"Nice!" She seemed sincere, which really baffled him.

Then she flung open the door. She was wearing almost the same clothing vibe, but she went with the Doors instead of the Dead.

He walked into her suite and immediately picked up on the fact that the living room coffee table wasn't piled high with folders, plus there wasn't a laptop in sight.

"What happened to the classroom?"

"It's in the other room. But first, something to drink." She gestured to the small wet bar at one end of the luxurious sitting room.

On it was a silver ice bucket with a bottle of Perrier Jouet poking out of the top.

"I thought you had this big rule about no drinking until class was over?"

"Tonight, you're learning something different."

She breezed by him. He picked up the distinct fragrance of Joy perfume.

She never wore perfume.

She should. She smelled fantastic.

Robyn nodded to the waiting champagne bottle. 'Will you do the honours?"

She walked back into what he assumed was her bedroom.

He was getting a really strange feeling about all this. He felt he was being set up in some way, but, for the life of him, he didn't know how.

He dutifully opened the gold foil at the top of the bottle and removed the cork with practised ease.

He poured two glasses and carried them to the coffee table.

After Robyn didn't reappear for a while, he called out that the champagne was getting warm.

"Be right there!"

She emerged wearing one of the fluffy hotel robes. In her hand was a Jamaican-sized spliff.

Robyn hadn't bothered to tie the robe too tightly and Daniel could plainly see that under it, was nothing but Robyn.

"What's going on here?" His voice cracked.

"This is your final lesson. If you are to be a real player, you need to learn how to act around a woman."

"That's one thing I don't need to learn!" he boasted.

"I am not talking about to banging brainless Twinkies. I am referring to romance and style."

"I'm pretty sure Paul didn't have this in mind." Daniel was sounding a little nervous.

"Of course he didn't. But having watched you stumble around trying every means to get me to bed, it was, quite frankly, getting embarrassing. Someone needed to teach you the finer points of seduction."

"What's that got to do with politics?"

Robyn burst out laughing. "Actually, absolutely everything! That's why I decided to add it to the curriculum."

She gave him a serious nod as if that explained everything.

"Wait a minute! You can't stand me. I don't get this."

"Don't fuck it up, Romeo. Just stick to my script tonight."

She sat next to him on the couch and lit up the mega joint. She took a massive hit, held back a cough, swallowed, and finally breathed out.

"Oh yeah!" She grinned as she handed it to Daniel.

There was a gentle knock on the door.

A voice called from outside in the hallway.

"Your dinner, madam."

She rose, almost weightlessly, from the couch, and opened the door.

"I'll take it from here."

The waiter clearly smelled the ganga, saw her attire, the guy waiting on the couch, and understood the situation. He handed her the leather billfold. She signed the room service ticket and added twenty percent.

She then dragged the trolley into the room.

She returned to the couch, but on her way to being seated, gently kissed Daniel's ear.

It lasted less than a second, yet was the most erotic sensation he had ever experienced in his life.

He started to reach for her. She stopped his progress by placing her hand gently on his chest.

"My script, remember!" She gestured to the joint. "Take a hit. It'll help you relax."

He took a big one.

He felt immediately relaxed.

"Close your eyes," she whispered throatily.

He closed his eyes.

She leant over and softly kissed his neck. He tried to join in, but she pushed him back into the couch.

She again kissed his ear, this time using her tongue to trace its edges.

Daniel had a boner the size of one of Elon Musk's old starships. But it was pointed down into his jeans, instead of standing proudly facing the heavens. It wasn't comfortable.

He tried to adjust it without disturbing Robyn's fine work, but couldn't quite get the angle right.

Robyn, sensing his dilemma, slowly reached down and unbuttoned his jeans. She reached into the folds of the denim, and took gentle hold of the trapped phallus. She managed to reposition it, facing upward so it could join the party.

She then moved as if to get on her knees, but instead stood up and walked to the room-service trolley.

"Go put on the other robe. It's in my bathroom. I'll fix us some plates."

Daniel looked at her as if she had suggested rappelling down the hotel wall.

"You want to eat now!"

"Absolutely."

"You did notice that I'm sort of ready for something other than food, right?"

"If you are referring to your rather beautiful, and nicely sized penis, then yes. It was hard to miss. However, I plan to make use of it later on, but first, we feast."

Daniel looked devastated.

"And I promise you—," she whispered, "the wait will only make it better."

"As long as I have your word."

He somehow got to his feet, and for some reason tried to hide his protruding cock under his T-shirt while holding the sides of his jeans together.

He felt clumsy. He looked clumsy.

She watched him leave, smiling the whole time.

*

When he returned, he was wearing the matching white terry cloth robe. For some reason, the garment made Robyn look indescribably desirable. Yet on him, it looked too small and was entirely unflattering.

Robyn had served up a selection of goodies from the trolley. He'd been concerned that under the silver plate covers would be luxury nonsense like caviar and all that crap.

Instead, she seemed to have known all his favourite finger foods, and had the hotel prepare them specially.

Bagels, sour cream and smoked salmon, barbequed pork ribs, curly fries, Asian salad with dried cranberries, and chicken satay with extra peanut sauce.

Washed down with Perrier Jouet.

Heaven.

There was nothing slow and erotic about their eating.

They ate like conquering Vikings.

They sat facing each other. Both took pleasure in watching the other slake their hunger. Their eyes stayed locked on each other as they ripped, sipped and dipped.

Their plates finally empty, Robyn walked over to the trolley and reached under the starched white linen tablecloth. She opened a small freezer compartment underneath.

Daniel wondered how the hell she knew it was even there, then decided that if he started questioning any of the goings on that night, he could end up a gibbering mess.

He just needed to keep to her script.

She withdrew two frosted bowls filled with what he immediately recognised as Ben and Jerry's Chunky Monkey ice cream.

He was starting to wonder if the night really could get any better.

Then she reached into a heated compartment and produced a small pitcher of melted dark chocolate.

She placed his ice cream before him, then slowly drizzled the black molten delight over the top.

She sat down and did the same for herself.

They both thought to raise a piled spoon in a toast to each other.

When they had finished, Robyn took Daniel by the hand and wordlessly led him into the bedroom.

She let her robe fall to the floor, then stepped over to him. She reached inside his robe and gently cupped his balls in her hand.

She kissed him gently on the mouth. Then kissed just the bottom lip, then the top. She kissed him passionately with her tongue finding his.

She slowly knelt before him and parted his robe.

She took him between her lips. First, she focused just on the engorged tip, then slowly took almost the entire length of him within her mouth.

Daniel's knees were literally quivering.

She rose back up and again kissed him. Harder this time.

Daniel reached out and felt the moistness between her legs.

"No. My script." She slid off his robe, then playfully pushed him down onto the bed. She crawled onto him and licked each of his nipples until they were almost as big as hers.

She then worked on his legs and inner thighs, her tongue sometimes licking, sometimes sucking, sometimes biting.

Daniel had never felt anything close to these sensations. He usually opted for the bare minimum of foreplay before spreading the gams and sliding right in.

Robyn moved again to his penis, this time using her tongue below his ball sack and slowly, agonisingly slowly, worked her way back up the shaft.

All he could do was groan.

At the point when he didn't think his pleasure sensors could take any more, Robyn slowly lowered herself onto him. She moved down until he was completely inside her.

Daniel wanted to thrust and climax, but each time he tried, she rose off him then after a few moments, lowered herself again. It was becoming clear that his job was to just lie there and take it like a man.

Before long, Robyn began to lift and lower herself faster. Her breathing became laboured. Her chest and breasts reddened. She began to groan and pant.

Daniel tried to keep still, but by that point was thrusting upwards each time she descended upon him.

He was enveloped in her heat and wetness.

She suddenly arched backwards and trembled. Daniel arched upwards and trembled.

They both cried out, as their joint climax transcended them to an alternate dimension.

*

Later, as they lay in each other's arms, smoking more of the Jamaican beauty, Daniel rested on an elbow so he could look at her.

"What was that?"

"That, my dear, is called passion. See the difference?" she teased.

"Oh yeah! But I still don't get why you're doing this – with me?"

"Are you complaining?"

"Hardly!"

She sat up and looked down at him. "Let's just say that I enjoyed it as much as you did, and hope we can do this a lot more."

"Well, if we have to, we have to. Just promise me that one day you'll explain why you changed your mind about me."

"Who said I did?" She winked.

"You see. I just don't get—"

"Do you really want to talk?" She guided his hand between her legs, so he too could feel the intense heat.

He slid down the bed and let his tongue help quench the fire.

CHAPTER
EIGHT

The next day was just as chaotic as Robyn had predicted.

*

He had snuck back to his place super early, and had reappeared at the hotel in the aforementioned big-boy pants.

Robyn appeared in one of her stylish business suits, but Daniel now knew what all the curves actually looked like underneath the expensive silk.

They sat in the lobby for a few moments before Paul walked in from the street. He was also dressed in far more businesslike apparel.

They both got to their feet as he approached.

"Holy shit!" Paul blurted out, just a little too loudly. "Daniel! I gave you one specific instruction. Don't fuck her. And as for you—" He faced Robyn. "Since when do you jump in bed with your projects?"

"Shut up, Paul. It was part of his instruction."

"Well, if he does end up in DC he might as well learn how to get properly fucked, I guess."

"May I ask a naïve question?" Daniel looked confused. "How the hell did you know?"

"Simple. Robyn is glowing and you suddenly look like a grown man. Come to think of it, why am I bitching? We wanted you to gain a little maturity. Anyway. No time for chit chat. We're expected in Century City in fifteen minutes, so let's do this thing."

"Bet your ass, I am," he replied in perfect John Wayne.

As they exited the hotel, a shiny black SUV pulled up right in front of them.

The DNC had rented space in the Century Plaza Towers in Century City. The towers, though substantially shorter, looked eerily like New York's ill-fated twin towers.

They pulled up in front of the entrance and were greeted by a young intern who'd been given the assignment of escorting the three up to their business suite.

They were led to a suite of offices on the eighteenth floor. The place had a vacant feel, despite all the upscale rental furniture that was still being moved in. In the back of the suite, was a decent sized conference room. Fifteen complete strangers studied Daniel as he walked in. They were looking at him like someone trying to decide which lobster to pick from the tank for dinner.

He could tell from the auras that most weren't that enamoured with him being the candidate option.

Daniel really didn't want to be bothered spending the next few days trying to impress a bunch of pompous prigs.

As he was introduced to each person, he tapped a little blue into their lives.

By the time he was able to finally sit down, all eyes were still on him, but now they seemed more positively intrigued than before.

They stayed in that stuffy room for almost twelve hours straight, basically setting up a timeline of action points. What to announce, when to announce it and how to announce it. Blah, blah, blah.

The only interesting part of the meeting, as far as Daniel was concerned, was when the DNC communications director started pontificating on exactly what Daniel was to say at his live announcement, and subsequent interviews.

Paul interrupted the young, bespectacled woman, and reminded her that Daniel was the only person who would decide what he was to say.

The woman actually laughed at him, then condescendingly reminded him of her own self-importance. She also focused her intense little eyes at Daniel, then blew a bong-load of smoke up his ass.

"Mr Trapp. Please understand, that I truly believe that you will be elected senator, and I know you have a way with words and people. The thing is, there are specific messages that have to be included in anything you say. I know that you are new to all this, but you will be representing the Democratic Party of America, and therefore have to follow the party protocols that go along with that honour. So, let's get back to what we will need you to say. Let's start with the launch announcement."

She smiled at Daniel with a look of defiant superiority.

Daniel laughed as he stood up.

"Paul. Hope we speak soon. Robyn, I hope we speak sooner."

He then headed for the door.

The DNC chairman, who was seated at the head of the table, looked utterly stunned.

"Where the do you think you're going, young man?"

Daniel gave him a toothy smile. "I've just decided to run as an independent – old man!"

He left the room and could be heard laughing as he walked down the hall.

He got to the elevator bank and pressed the down button. As he watched the indicators for the four elevators, he bet to himself which one would get there first.

You gotta get your fun where you find it.

Just as elevator three arrived (Daniel lost the bet), Paul and Robyn jumped in after him.

"That went well," Robyn said.

"Were you serious back there? Independent?" Paul wasn't seeing the funny side yet.

"Why not? I can't work with that bunch of jackals."

"You need them. There's no way to build the momentum without the machinery they already have in place. They're plugged in to the Democratic voter lists, the donors, the unions. Everything you will need to win that seat."

"But what if I didn't need them," Daniel asked.

"You do, and if you go solo, you'll lose."

"But what if he really doesn't need them?" Robyn asked with a fresh twinkle in her eye.

The conversation stopped as they reached the ground floor. The moment they exited the elevator, Megadeth blared out of Daniel's pocket.

He was pretty sure he didn't want to hear what his mum had to say.

*

His father had been found in his favourite childhood place, high up in his Moreton Bay Fig tree. He had somehow nestled himself among the highest branches then, using a professional box cutter, slit his wrists. Not the amateur way, horizontally across the arm, but vertically from the hand, halfway up to the elbow.

His blood had dripped through the branches, forming what looked like dark red icicles as it dried.

Mary gave him the news, but asked that he not come to the house.

He understood.

*

The funeral was held at Forrest Lawn Cemetery overlooking Warner Bros Studios. On a clear day, you could even see beyond that, to Magnolia Blvd where Henry's dreams had first been realised.

It was a full house in the white chapel. Friends and colleagues from CERN, Google and MV were all in attendance.

Daniel did not go in the limousine with his mother. Instead, he went in a town car with Robyn. She also sat with him at the front of the chapel, next to the other family members. Christy was in the same row.

David Chen gave the eulogy, and a few others said their piece.

Daniel knew that all eyes were on him, and that people were wondering why he hadn't spoken.

He didn't want to speak.

He didn't know what to say.

After the last speaker descended from the pulpit, and just before the priest continued with his part of the service, Daniel suddenly got to his feet and stepped up to the microphone.

He looked out at the attendees, and realised that he knew most of them. They had been part of the life that Henry had brought him into.

"Henry wasn't my birth father." His voice was strong, clear and sombre.

"He was so much more. He and Mary were devoutly non-parental. They were very good at it, and enjoyed that way of life. My birth mother and father died in a tragic accident that brought Mary and Henry to the hospital that was caring for me. They stood at my incubator and their hearts opened. Without debate or regret, they changed their entire lives just to give me a home."

Daniel's voice started to crack.

"Having Henry as a father was like living with the smartest teenager in the world. He never quite grew up, despite managing to create one of the greatest technological breakthroughs of our time.

"He was a physicist, and never for one moment stopped questioning matter and our place among it. Life with Henry was like being on a roller-coaster that never stopped.

"Henry and his bride, my mother, Mary, made a wonderful home for me. A home that I wouldn't have had

319

with my birth parents. A fantastic life, that I wouldn't have had with my birth parents. Opportunities, that I wouldn't have had with my birth parents."

He had to pause to wipe his eyes with the back of his hand and take a steadying breath.

"Henry decided to take an early leave from this realm and from us. We will never understand or know the torment that must have been hiding within that wonderful and caring man.

"I can only hope that wherever you are, you are surrounded by never-imagined physical wonders and mysteries for you to ponder, and maybe even solve."

Daniel began crying openly. "I have lost, not just a parent and a friend, but a huge piece of who I am.

"He was my mentor.

"My compass.

"My dad."

*

Daniel had to steady himself as he walked back to his seat. All eyes were on him. All felt his loss and his pain.

All except Mary.

Mary had not been moved by his speech.

Not one bit.

As the service ended, they played his father's favourite song. 'Are We Human or Are We Dancer' by The Killers. Everyone slowly walked out of the chapel, and on to the graveside service a few hundred yards away.

*

Later, back in their car, Robyn patted his hand.

"You okay?"

Daniel dried his eyes with a tissue from a box provided by the car service. He then drank the contents of a small plastic water bottle, then turned and smiled at her.

"Actually, I'm feeling pretty good."

CHAPTER
NINE

Daniel called Paul from the car.

"You okay?" Paul sounded like he actually cared.

"Yeah. I'm fine."

"Good, 'cause the DNC have been on my back since you walked out. I talked to the director and gave him a very simple ultimatum. Do it our way or find someone else. I also pointed out that you were almost certainly going to win the seat, no matter which party you ran with."

"And?" Daniel sounded bored.

"They agreed. They still want to schedule your time, and drag you from one end of the state to the other but, as far as messaging, it'll all be you."

Daniel didn't seem at all surprised at the news. "There's one more thing. That cunt with the glasses – she's gotta go."

Daniel heard Paul laughing down the phone.

"What?"

"The other condition I made with them was that I would be acting communications director for your campaign. They accepted that as well. Apparently, they all think she's a cunt and couldn't wait to kick her back to DC."

"Nice! So, what's next?"

"What's next is for you to make the big announcement as we discussed. You're booked to be on *Late Night With Matt Hardy* as his guest tomorrow. They tape at 2 p.m. on the Universal Lot. Robyn and I will rehearse you tomorrow morning on a dummy set in Hollywood."

"Sounds good. Do I need to come back to Century City today?"

"Nope. It's unlikely you'll have to come to the Century City offices again. Once you announce, we will move into your own campaign offices.

"Tomorrow afternoon you will formally become the candidate and thus become public property. Everything you say, do or even wear, will be scrutinised by the pundits. You sure you're ready for this?"

"I keep telling you. I was born ready!" Daniel smiled.

"Take the night off. It will be the last one you'll have any control over!"

Daniel ended the call and turned to Robyn. "I presume you already somehow knew?"

"A little. What I didn't know, I could garner from that call. You excited?"

"Of course. I get the night off! Who wouldn't be excited? Can we continue my education?"

She gave him an exasperated expression.

"Please, miss?" He used his best British schoolboy voice.

She rolled her eyes, but couldn't help smiling.

*

They both knew that it would be the last night before he would be under the microscope, or at least a telephoto lens.

It was also the last time that Daniel could get away with any extravagant behaviour.

Daniel called Van Nuys and arranged for a modest private jet.

That was the great thing about having access to private aircraft. You could fly to San Francisco for the best Chinese food in America, be back in LA in time for dessert at the Four Seasons, and continue your sex education class at the Canon Wilshire. All on the same night.

*

Daniel, Robyn and Paul arrived at nine sharp at a clapped-out-looking soundstage in the bowels of Hollywood. It was on a run-down side street off Santa Monica Blvd, on the wrong side of Highland.

There was no security gate, just a door in a wall and a questionable-looking buzzer.

Robyn was the only one brave enough to touch the thing. It made a crackling sound, then nothing. Eventually, a security guard opened the door from the inside.

The term security guard may have been a slight exaggeration. The man was in his eighties, if he was a day. He looked like alcohol was a frequent friend, and never too far away. His eyes were rummy, and his breath was something you'd expect to find at the gates of hell.

Then again, the soundstage certainly wasn't what anyone would consider heaven.

They followed the wheezing geriatric down a dreary hallway. Its walls were covered with faded one-sheets, promoting a variety of unheard-of B movies from a time that land forgot.

They emerged onto the stage itself, and felt akin to Alice after her dabble with hallucinogenic 'shrooms.

Sitting in the middle of the poorly maintained stage was a highly modern talk-show set with a massive backdrop LID screen, showing LA at night.

It was an exact reproduction of the *Late Night With Matt Hardy* set.

There were five unmanned cameras, and even a bandstand set up off to the right. They would be using none of those.

There were a couple of technicians standing by, surrounded by a team from the Century City office.

Bud Calderon, the director of the DNC, who had earlier called Daniel 'young man', greeted them all warmly.

He made a special effort to take Daniel aside, and apologised for their bumpy start together. Daniel patted him on the arm and said, "no harm Pops"

The others looked on to see Bud's reaction.

The older man just smiled.

"You're gonna be a handful, aren't you?"

"I'm certainly gonna do my best."

At that, Bud laughed openly.

"Shall we get started?" he suggested. "Paul, you are Matt. You sit behind the desk and Daniel, you are gonna have to play yourself I'm afraid."

Daniel smiled at Bud. He was getting to like the old fart.

The two men took their places on the set, got comfortable, then Paul started.

"So, of course we all know you as LA's youngest real estate mogul. You also seem to be dating every gorgeous starlet in the city. So, tell us, what's up with this new crusade of yours. We all saw you on the Chavez show and were pretty much blown away."

Five hours later, Daniel walked onto the real set. The dummy one really had been identical, only here there was a live audience, the host was the actual Matt Hardy, and the bandstand was full of kick-ass musicians.

Once Daniel was seated, Matt Hardy looked over at him and smiled his famous toothy smile.

"So, Daniel, what the fuck? One minute you're a lothario real estate mogul, the next you're giving an epic political speech on daytime TV. Care to tell us what the hell is going on?"

Daniel laughed. "I'd be delighted. It's true that I've done well with real estate."

"And with every available model in LA!" Matt interrupted.

The audience burst out laughing.

"Don't forget the actresses!" Daniel added.

The crowd laughed again. A few even applauded. There was even one woo-hoo. Daniel wasn't surprised at the positive reaction. He'd blue-tapped them the moment he was on stage. He had waited a few moments before doing the same to the home viewers through the camera's eye.

"Being successful doesn't make someone blind. I see what's going on. I talk to people. I listen. I know that when I was growing up, it was easy to be proud of our country. Domestically and internationally. But over the past twenty years or so, something changed. The political system that was put in place by our Founding Fathers to ensure the balanced and honest running of our government has come off the rails. Loopholes to the Constitution have been found, then widened into six-lane expressways. Integrity has become secondary to cronyism. Lobbying, which I feel was always questionable in its ability to remain incorruptible, has become a model of efficiency in openly bribing our elected officials."

The audience started applauding. It grew and grew and formed into screaming cheers.

Daniel waited for them to settle down.

"I feel that someone, finally, has to step up to the challenge and rein in the circus in DC. That someone has to be willing to, not just bring the dark dealings into the light, but make changes that will guarantee future votes. We have become more separated and partisan than at any other time in our history, except for the period leading up to the American Civil War. Is that really how we want to live our lives? Do we want to actually get to the point where a civil war is the only way we can communicate our grievances with one another? I say no. I say we're better than that! I say that if we want to bring America back from the brink of corruption, and self-serving government, we have to be better than that! The only way that is gonna happen, is when we unite as one country again and go back to giving a damn about what has happened to our country! There can be no more apathy. We, as Americans, have to take responsibility over the decisions that come out of our government. We need to reclaim our country! Today!"

The audience went crazy.

It took Matt almost two whole minutes of air to quieten them down.

"I can't really disagree with what you've said but where is this white knight that is going to lead us from the dark side?" Matt finally managed. "We know who the players are, and I haven't seen one that I think is gonna put a dent in the machine."

Daniel leaned forward in his guest chair. "Funny you should ask!" He paused for effect. "I am proud to announce here tonight…"

The audience suddenly had a glimmer of what was coming, and though still silent, an electric energy had begun building among them.

"… that I am going to run as Democratic candidate to be the next United States Senator for California."

The audience rose to their feet as one and started a slow clap which, beat by beat, got faster and louder till it filled the stage, the building and the entire state of California.

CHAPTER
TEN

The next six weeks went exactly as Paul and Robyn had advertised. He gave speech after speech, sound bite after sound bite, interview after interview. It was a robotic existence.

He would wake up at five and have a working breakfast with his team. He would then be bundled into a car, bus or plane and taken to another part of the state that under normal circumstances he wouldn't have visited on a dare.

He'd stump in the middle of a farming community at nine, have lunch in a diner in a working harbour, drink a date shake with tribal leaders outside Palm Springs, then attend a black-tie thousand-dollars-a-plate donor dinner in San Diego.

The next day, and the next, and the next, he'd repeat almost the exact same schedule, only in different parts of the state.

The only good part was that Daniel left every single attendee, at every single event, feeling strangely positive about the young candidate from Los Angeles.

Funny how that could happen.

He slept, or rather fell unconscious, in a different hotel or motel almost every night. Alone.

He had had no intimate contact with Robyn since announcing, then again, he didn't have the strength to spit, let alone bonk. He had to satisfy himself with the occasional wink from her after a stump speech or gala dinner.

Daniel had also done the politically unthinkable, and poured over fifteen million dollars of his own money into online presence and local TV spots. It became nearly impossible to go a day in California without seeing his face, or hearing his voice.

Finally, when Daniel wasn't sure he could handle one more day of gruelling self-perpetuation, the time arrived for the grand finale of the whole shebang.

*

The live-streamed senatorial debate.

*

Daniel was to debate his Republican rival, Tam Malburg. The ex-Governor of California.

The man was a career politician. Slick, slimy and very good at debating his opponents into the ground.

Daniel's team had been prepping him for the big

event from day one. He knew that they all felt that if he was going to screw the pooch, this was when it would happen.

He felt sorry for his crew. They needn't have worried. Daniel was ready for Governor Malburg.

He had a special tap already in the chamber.

The usually lively and ultra-personable Malburg was gonna come down with a last-minute case of the blues!

*

The debate was held in The Kodak Theatre in Hollywood.

Better known for hosting the Oscars, when there still were Oscars. Low ratings, corruption and racial inequality finally put the awards show out of its misery ten years earlier.

The Kodak was a big auditorium. It was chosen because this was going to be a big debate.

Daniel had reached rock star status wherever he went, and everybody wanted more of him. Malburg, on the other hand, had been considered by many as the best governor the state had ever had, and was still fondly referred to as Pappy by almost everyone in California. The debate was expected to be viewed by tens of millions, either via stream or broadcast. In a rare move usually reserved for presidential debates, all California affiliate network channels would cover the debate live.

The host and moderator for the event was CNN's venerable news anchor, Chris Cuomo. Now in his seventies, he still looked fit and ready to keep the two candidates in line.

Malburg walked on stage first, to rousing applause. Daniel then walked on stage to screams, hooting and even tears.

The candidates shook hands, then positioned themselves behind their respective podiums. Malburg stage left, Daniel stage right.

Cuomo announced that each candidate would have ninety seconds for their introduction, then the Q and A, after which, each man had three minutes to sum up.

After winning a coin toss back stage, Malburg would go first.

He didn't hesitate to go straight for the jugular.

"I have been a politician in this fine state for over thirty years. I have served in the state senate, and as your governor. I bring years of hard-earned experience to this campaign.

"My opponent, on the other hand, has served in no public capacity whatsoever, and brings a whopping three months of experience to the campaign.

"I have spent my career focusing on improving life for all Californians. My opponent has spent his career focusing on making money, just for himself. I have dedicated myself to public service. Mr Trapp has dedicated himself to greed and sexual promiscuity."

*

Daniel decided he'd had enough of the old blowhard and triple red-tapped him in mid-sentence. He was amazed at the results.

*

Malburg suddenly started slurring his words. The right side of his face started to droop. It almost looked like it was melting. All this was enhanced on the giant LID screens above the stage.

He grabbed the sides of the podium, looked confused and scared, then collapsed onto the hard stage floor.

People screamed. Some ran out of the hall. Cuomo calmly called to the stage manager to get an ambulance there. Stat!

Malburg was rushed to Cedars Sinai Hospital, where it was determined that he had had a massive stroke. He was being kept alive by machines. The doctors didn't know if he would live. If he did, it was unlikely that he would ever be able to talk or even breathe on his own.

California was in shock. It was bad enough that such a tragic thing had happened to Pappy. The fact that everybody witnessed it live, made it exponentially worse.

Daniel had been whisked away from the Kodak, moments after the incident.

He later offered his condolences via every medium possible. He expressed his personal sorrow that such a horrific thing could happen to such a fine man.

*

In reality, he was delighted.

He now had no opposition for the senate seat. He was also extraordinarily happy with the knowledge that his taps had the power to not just depress another human but could actually do physical damage on the spot.

The tap had become a far better weapon.

*

With less than ten days till the election, forces were trying to delay it, postpone it, or cancel it all together. There was a public outcry.

Daniel's team advised him that the election would proceed, and that the Republican Party would doubtless field someone. As all balloting was fully electronic, adding or deleting a name to the ballot took less than ten seconds.

Paul told Daniel that it didn't matter who the RNC brought into the fray, they didn't stand a chance. There simply wasn't the time to get their name out there, and capture the necessary recognition, and thus, votes.

Paul actually started planning for Daniel's acceptance night speech, and subsequent swearing in, in DC.

The team's elation lasted for just over sixteen hours. Then the sky fell.

Hard.

*

Malburg's wife announced that she would run in place of her husband for the senate seat.

During Tam's entire career, Lanny Malburg had worked diligently at his side. As California's First Lady, she shepherded in more social programmes than even her husband. She had been a second circuit judge in California, and had fought ardently for trial and prison reform. She was a heavy hitter, and was also adored as much, if not more, than Tam.

She didn't need to get voter recognition. She already had it, in spades. Her husband's voters were happy to just move their votes to her.

Daniel's camp was in crisis. There would be no debate, no public side-by-side appearances and they knew that if Lanny was smart, which she was, she would just lie low until voting day.

The polls still showed a close race, but it was frustrating his campaign team that they couldn't come up with some way to slant the chances a little more in their favour.

Robyn unknowingly came up with the solution. She joked that Lanny had lunch every Thursday at the Bel Vu Hotel. Maybe they should put something nasty in her food.

Robyn had a dark sense of humour!

Daniel had a darker sense of reality.

*

The following Thursday, as Lanny made her way to the patio restaurant, she passed a young man with a full beard and heavily tinted sunglasses. He gave her a big smile and raised his glasses as he passed.

Lanny noticed that his eyes were an extraordinary shade of blue.

That was the last thing she ever saw.

She collapsed on the manicured pathway, only feet from her favourite lunch spot.

The post-mortem determined that she had suffered a catastrophic brain aneurism. Likely brought on by high blood pressure, and stress over her husband's stroke.

*

California went into a state of mourning. Flags were at half mast. The election took a back seat in the minds of most Californians.

One week later, with minimal fanfare, and lower than expected turnout, Daniel won the seat, beating out a practically unknown county supervision (that the RNC had shoehorned in at the last moment), a member of the PETA party, and an independent, who was running on the promise of eliminating all cars in the state and retuning it to horse-drawn vehicles only. The strange thing was – he came in second.

*

Daniel's election night party was intentionally subdued, to honour the Malburgs. His speech was brief and included his deep regret that he had won under such unfortunate conditions.

Before sneaking out of the dirge-like event, Bud Calderon took Daniel aside and actually gave him a hug. He also whispered, "Daniel, my boy, you are one lucky motherfucker."

Robyn and Daniel returned to her hotel and with solemn and sympathetic faces, made their way to her suite.

Then the real party began.

CHAPTER
EVELEN

Robyn and Daniel travelled to Washington a few days ahead of the swearing in. They wanted to find a DC residence that afforded security, privacy and understated elegance, as befitting his new role as a US senator.

Their realtor showed them tons of places up Connecticut Ave, the trendy, but still funky Adams Morgan, Dupont Circle and Kalorama. All great areas, but none gave them that tingly feeling they were looking for.

The realtor then suggested they give the Citygate a try.

The infamous complex that was featured centrally in the downfall of one American president, was situated right on the Potomac, next door to the Kennedy Center, and at the start of the Rock Creek Parkway.

It was built in the 1960s, and didn't have the more modern feel that most people wanted. What it did have however, were large rooms, river views, great security and only a three-minute walk to Georgetown, where the best bars, restaurants and shopping were located.

The realtor found three units that were currently for rent. One was only a one bedroom so it didn't qualify. The other two were oversized two-bedroom units. One had a city view and was located in the Citygate West on Virginia Avenue, the other had a sweeping river view, a wraparound balcony, and was situated in, what most felt was by far the better building, Citygate South.

It also had the benefit of being completely furnished. As an extra bonus, it had a second parking space underground, which was basically unheard of in the nation's capital.

Daniel signed the lease there and then. They moved from their hotel the following morning. Funny how credit, background checks, and co-op approval, seem to vanish when you are the freshman senator from California.

Though not officially 'dating', Robyn and Daniel had become inseparable, and were going to try being grown-up enough to actually start living together.

Robyn had filled a void in Daniel that he never knew he had. She somehow made him feel whole. He had always lived a very self-centred existence, and been perfectly content to continue on that path. Robyn brought an entirely new dimensionality to his life. He was able to share his thoughts and dreams, at least the ones that didn't involve murdering his competition.

As a bonus, Robyn turned out to be a fantastic cook. She was as enthusiastically experimental in the kitchen as she was in the bedroom.

The only problem with the relationship was that Daniel couldn't completely get past the nagging question of why a woman like her was with a guy like him.

The fact that she was 'untappable' made it even more of a conundrum. In a weird way, he had always been more comfortable with girls who were with him basically against their wills.

That made more sense.

Every so often, he still felt the need to ask her why him. In each instance, she would just smile and coyly reply that maybe one day she'd tell him.

*

The swearing in was somewhat of an anticlimax. Being the only senator elect was unusual. Normally there was a whole gaggle of senators being sworn in after a general or midterm election.

As he was there as a result of a special election for only one position, he was the sole participant.

The ceremony took place in an antechamber to the actual senate floor. There were few guests and no press. It had a Freemason-ish feel about it.

The president of the senate read the oath of office, and Daniel acknowledged it.

That was it.

*

Paul, Bud, Robyn and Daniel celebrated quietly at the Round Table Bar inside the stately Blake Hotel just down Pennsylvania Avenue.

Daniel, with a lot of help from Bud and Paul, had pretty much completed staffing up his freshman senator's office. Robyn had, after a surprising amount of persuasion, agreed to be his communications director.

Some of the other key posts were filled by people that had worked on the campaign. Others had been recommended by Paul and Bud. In all he had a staff of twenty-two.

Daniel had desperately wanted Paul to take a leading role in his office, but Paul had much bigger fish to fry.

He was still working with the DNC on something 'unbelievably big'.

He dangled the same hook as before, that what he was working on could directly impact Daniel and his upward trajectory. But refused to say anything else at that point.

Bud listened, and simply smiled knowingly.

The bastards! Daniel was dying to know what they were hatching, but neither would give even a hint. Due to the complexities of scheduling in the upper echelons of DC politics, Daniel had had to be sworn in ten days before the senate actually returned from recess.

He and Robyn decided to take a few days, and head back to Los Angeles to finish up the final details for the sale of his company. It felt strange handing his baby off to someone else, but as a sitting senator, he could not continue to have management interest in any for-profit endeavour.

Besides, his plans were now far loftier than converting old buildings.

He had his eyes on converting an old country!

*

As they drove along 66 towards the jet park at Dulles International, Daniel nudged Robyn who had been staring out at a Metro train that was moving alongside them at the exact same speed.

"What?" she asked distractedly.

"I thought that maybe on the way there, we could stop over somewhere."

"Sure."

She went back to watching the train.

"Where?"

"Las Vegas."

She turned away from the window and stared at him with a baffled look.

"Why in God's name do you want to stop there?"

"You've never been!" he declared.

"For a reason. I can honestly say that Las Vegas has nothing whatsoever of interest to me," she stated.

"Not even a twenty-four-hour wedding chapel?"

He casually dropped a ring box in her lap.

She stared at him like it was some stupid joke. She then saw on his face that it wasn't.

She reached for the box and opened it. It was empty.

She looked at him questioningly.

"They also have the best jewellers in the world, also open twenty-four-seven. I thought we should choose the ring together. I'll ask again." Daniel smiled at her. "May we please stop in Las Vegas?"

Robyn's eyes welled up with tears as she looked into his eyes.

"Are you sure about this?" she whispered.

"Robyn Watkins, will you do me the honour of marrying me, and becoming the future First Lady of the United States?"

"Only if you promise to actually become president."

"Deal!"

They kissed, much to the delight of the driver. He'd never been witness to a marriage proposal before. People had tried to consummate their commitment plenty of times in the back seat, but a proposal – now that was a first.

From what he could tell from the front seat, she was some looker too.

The lucky bastard!

CHAPTER
TWELVE

They landed at Henderson Executive Airport, on the outskirts of Vegas. A black SUV was waiting for them.

They were driven along non-touristy back streets then ended up in an underground, discreet entrance to the Emperor's Palace Hotel.

A VIP hostess was waiting for them. They were ushered into a private elevator which took them up to a crazy, over-the-top, luxury suite. It wasn't their idea of decor, but it certainly was striking and memorable. Whoever had designed the suite had no fear of colour whatsoever.

Every wall was a different hue. Every expensive-looking chair held a different pattern. One wall in the bedroom was a giant LID screen. It covered the entire wall.

Every room also had floor-to-ceiling windows that looked out over the vastly overbuilt Las Vegas valley.

There was a time, before Daniel was even born, when one could still see giant swathes of the desert that encircled the city proper. Now, it had built itself out to the surrounding mountains, and even crept halfway up those.

*

They had a super quick shower (platonic), dressed in classy casual (him in grey slacks and a dark blue shirt, Robyn in black trousers with a long-sleeved white Oxford button-down). They then took the private elevator to the Emperor's Palace shops.

The indoor mall was vast. Its multistoried wings branched out in seemingly random fashion. The majority of the shops were pure tack. They were designed solely to grab tourist dollars, with super high turnover.

Daniel knew his way around the Roman-themed maze, and with him leading, they emerged in what had been the original centre of the mall, when it was originally opened.

It still had its reproduction Trevi Fountain, and its sky-blue domed ceiling that was lit in such a way as to portray time changing from day to night, in an hourly cycle. It was said that the paint they used had had gold flecks in it, which gave the ceiling its realistic 'outdoor sky' feel.

Daniel led Robyn to the Rodeo's jewellery store. It had a prime location facing the gurgling fountain.

Robyn was already suffering from sensory overload. First the suite, now the Roman mall with its darkening interior sky, then the sight of every ultra-luxury store on Earth, all encircling a working marble fountain.

Daniel noticed her condition and squeezed her hand.

"I told you. You had to see Vegas at least once."

"Is it all like this?" she managed to ask, as three Roman soldiers walked by. All naked from the waist up, and all ripped.

"No, of course not. This place is subdued compared to some of the others."

Rodeo's gilt-edged double doors silently slid open as the couple approached. The manager greeted them, and it was clear that Daniel had called ahead. They were led to a private room at the back of the store where a selection of engagement rings was waiting for them to view.

The manager, who strangely enough looked exactly like a jewellery sales manager, started describing each ring in ludicrously specific, and quite frankly boring, detail.

"Now this one is a VVS," he pontificated. "It has a fantastic blue-white clarity. You can see how the classic brilliant cut and platinum mounting brings out the—"

"May I try that one?" Robyn interrupted, pointing at an emerald cut diamond ring, at the back of the display pad.

"Why, of course. I hadn't shown you that one yet, as it does have just the faintest inclusion, and the colour is not perfect." He removed it from the black felt pad, and held it out to her.

"You can see just a trace of yellow in the colour which some find off-putting. I personally feel it makes it more unique."

Robyn held the ring at various angles, trying so see the yellow shade.

"Let me show you in the showroom. The lighting is much closer to true daylight."

He led the pair to the front of the store and against the huge glass window display. The light was indeed crisper and more natural.

Robyn held it out. She could see the yellow, but actually liked it. It looked like champagne.

She slipped it on her ring finger. It was a perfect fit. Grinning, she held out her hand to Daniel.

"It's beautiful."

The manager became distracted as a couple of men, clearly very drunk, stared at them from the other side of the glass. They began pointing and making obscene gestures at Robyn.

The manager looked with frustration at a small desk tucked away to the right of the entrance. A security guard was checking out a leggy cocktail waitress in an ultra-short toga, serving someone by the fountain.

The manager cleared his throat. The guard immediately got to his feet. The manager gestured subtly with his head towards the two losers on the other side of the security glass.

"The joys of being open twenty-four-seven!" the manager joked.

Daniel laughed.

"Oh! I do apologise. Did I say that out loud?" The manager gave them a cheeky wink.

He showed them back to the private viewing room, as the security guard asked the men to please move on.

They resisted.

As if by magic, four hotel security officers appeared from nowhere. They, none too gently, escorted the pair out of the mall area, and presumably out of the hotel. The

346

security response was way too well orchestrated. Clearly wrangling inebriated visitors was a regular thing.

Daniel and Robyn agreed on the engagement ring, then chose their wedding rings. Simple platinum bands, with rounded edges. Robyn watched Daniel haggle with the manager. It was amazing to see. As far as she was aware, Rodeo's didn't discount their merchandise, yet Daniel got them to take a whopping forty percent off the price.

With the engagement ring on her finger, and the wedding rings in Daniel's pocket, they went in search of pre-wedding libation.

They ended up next door at the Belladona Hotel. They settled on a private and exclusive Italian-themed terrace, right at the water's edge. The terrace, the lake and the surrounding building façade, were supposed to look like a mini version of Italy's Lake Como.

It was the best seat in town for Belladona's water and laser show. It had recently celebrated its fiftieth birthday. The show had been stunning when it had first opened. Now, with the water shooting twice as high and holographic characters (Henry's technology) dancing amidst the spray, it was even more breathtaking.

They drank champagne cocktails and Jäger shots. Both had decided that inebriation was the only way either of them was going to survive a Vegas-styled wedding.

Or any wedding for that matter.

As the time neared for the nuptials to begin, they staggered out of the Belladona, across the skywalk to the Hotel de France, and took a back escalator down to the wedding chapel foyer. They were both surprised at how restrained the place actually looked. To be fair, Daniel had actually done some serious research. The hotel chapel was known to be much more subdued and formal than most of the Vegas offerings.

They were already registered, and their licence had been electronically sent directly from the town hall. The days of having to stand in line at the twenty-four-hour wedding licence office were a thing of the past.

Kind of a shame.

Gone were the days of standing in line behind a couple dressed in monkey suits, behind an Elvis impersonator standing next to a girl in a tutu. It was a big part of the Vegas heritage.

Now it was all done on an app.

*

They were seated in a comfortable lounge bar, while the previous ceremony concluded. They were offered champagne but opted for Cuervo shots and a beer.

Suddenly, it was time. A side door opened and a middle-aged man with a truly awful comb-over and a slight limp greeted them like long-lost friends.

He ushered them into a small twenty-seater chapel. A tasteful, non-denominational, abstract painting dominated the wall behind the altar. Flowers adorned each row. Two large vases filled with green roses stood on either side of the apse.

"Welcome, Mr Trapp and Miss Watkins. Are you here today to take the bonds of marriage? Do you have a witness?"

"Yes, we are, and no, we don't," Daniel replied solemnly.

"Oh yes you bloody do, mate!" Giles exclaimed as he and his wife, Emma, stepped into the chapel from a side door.

Daniel was so stunned, he actually staggered in place. Then again, that could have been the booze.

"How the hell—?"

"How do you think, ya prat!?" Giles nodded to Robyn.

Daniel turned to her in total disbelief.

"But how?"

"Where do I start? The confirmation texts from the limo service, the hotel, the chapel! If you plan on surprising someone, don't leave your LID lying on the bed at the time that everyone's gonna confirm stuff!"

Daniel could only shake his head.

The four quickly exchanged hugs and hellos.

The minister then cleared his voice to get their attention.

"I guess we do have witnesses," Daniel announced.

"In that case let's proceed."

The service was ridiculously quick, and would have been even faster if Emma hadn't had a sneezing fit in the middle. She swore that it was because of all the flowers. The others doubted her claim, as they were pretty sure they were all artificial. Especially the green roses.

They kept that to themselves.

*

Giles and Emma had another surprise for the couple. They had booked a table in the lofty Tour D'Amour restaurant that sat atop the hotel's three-quarter-size replica of the real Eiffel Tower.

The maître d' clearly expected them and showed them to one of the highly sought-after window booths. Their view faced down the length of the Strip, then out into the dark void beyond the Vegas lights. You could just make out the 15 Freeway, as it rose out of the valley in the far distance. Only the pinprick of head and tail lights mapped its existence.

They ate and drank like kings. At one point, Giles, who was somehow even more drunk than Daniel, staggered to his feet, shushed the entire restaurant, then toasted the freshman senator from California and his brand-new freshman wife.

The other diners applauded the couple. Free drinks began arriving at their table.

Somehow, these too, were consumed.

The grand finale was when the maître d' wheeled in a silver trolley, on which was perched their wedding cake. It was a four-tiered, chocolate-on-chocolate triumph with a miniature White House on the top.

Robyn and Daniel held the cake knife together and made the first cut. They then insisted that everyone in the restaurant, staff included, got a piece.

They all did.

The foursome closed the restaurant, then stumbled back down to the lobby. Giles and Emma were staying in the Hotel de France, so their journey to bed was the easiest. They agreed to meet the following day for brunch at the Hotel de France Brasserie.

Daniel and Robyn made their way to the skywalk that crossed Flamingo Ave, then joined the one that went over the Strip, and ended up at the Emperor's.

It was 3:15 a.m. and the walkways were almost completely devoid of foot traffic. Halfway across, they saw two people walking the other way, coming towards them. For a moment, they were relieved to see others out so late.

The relief vanished when Robyn recognised the pair. They were the two men that had been watching them through the shop window at Rodeo's.

The bigger man was white, scrawny, tall and mean-looking. The other was black, musclebound and his face expressed nothing but hate.

Both were wearing hoodies.

The black man's hoody was plain grey, with no logo or design. The white guy's was black, with a gold phoenix rising from what looked like a turd.

Both lowered their hoods as they approached, almost as if wanting their victims to recognise them.

They each had one hand in their hoody's centre pouch.

Robyn whispered an aside to Daniel. "Don't do anything stupid. Just give them what they want."

"I have a better idea. Watch this," Daniel boasted drunkenly.

The men were still twenty feet from them. Daniel tapped each of them hard and fast and repeatedly.

The black guy tried to get his gun out of his hoody, but his entire body began twitching as if struck with a violent attack of palsy.

The white attacker grabbed both sides of his head and began screaming at the top of his lungs.

His partner kept trying for his gun.

He finally got it out of the front pouch, but his twitching had worsened. He tried to aim his weapon, but his arm was jerking ultra-violently. He fired a volley of shots but all headed off in random directions.

He began to cry and to shake his head, as if to ward off a swarm of insects.

He tried one last time to fire his gun.

He succeeded, however it discharged at the same time as an exceptionally big spasm.

He managed to shoot his accomplice under his chin.

The top of the mugger's head erupted in a plume of blood, brains and gore. Oddly, in the background, The Mirage Hotel's fake volcano attraction seemed to be mimicking him, as it erupted at the same moment, spewing a plume of bright red lava high into the air.

The man crumpled like a dropped sweater.

The black guy went insane. He started involuntarily jumping and dancing in place as his head-shaking became extremely exaggerated.

Suddenly, there was a loud cracking sound.

His head froze at an odd angle. An impossible angle. An angle that would not exist on a living person.

He tried to speak but only gurgled, then attempted to take a step.

His entire body seized completely, and he fell forward like a plank.

He was dead before he hit the stamped concrete flooring of the skywalk.

Daniel took a relieved breath, seeing that he had succeeded in vanquishing the threat.

He looked proudly to Robyn.

She was on the ground, leaning against the walkway wall. She looked up at him. Confused.

Daniel's first thought was that she was unhurt.

She was going to be okay.

It was just the shock.

Though there was a small tear in her white shirt, dead centre between her breasts.

A red stain then appeared around the tear, that wasn't a tear.

It was a hole caused by a 9mm slug.

A red tide now covered Robyn's shirt.

She tried to talk, but was too weak.

Daniel knelt in front of her. "What, my darling?" Daniel asked through his own tears.

Robyn managed to whisper her last words in that lifetime.

"But, I was supposed to help you!"

Daniel looked into her eyes.

Those beautiful emerald green eyes.

He saw their light dim, and then dull.

He saw the life pass from her.

*

He felt his own life, or at least what had been his life, also pass from him.

CHAPTER
THIRTEEN

The LVPD investigators determined that it had been an attempted mugging, gone wrong. If the one mugger hadn't had the sudden epileptic seizure, they felt that things could have been much worse.

They believed, and expressed in the final report, that Daniel was extremely lucky to have not himself been shot and killed.

*

Robyn's service was held in the tiny town of Deale, Maryland, where she had been raised, and her family still lived.

The small church was nestled amidst rolling green hills on one side, and a remarkably scenic small-boat marina on the other.

The church was old, and the term rustic would be way too grand an adjective.

Dilapidated would be a closer description, yet it was still a working house of God. Considering it was positioned where it would take a broadside from any storm that swept across the Chesapeake, it was lucky to be standing at all.

Robyn had been baptised in that church, took her first Communion in that church, and was now being remembered in that church.

Her parents, friends and DC work colleagues were all present, as was Daniel and Giles. Emma had had to return to the UK to fulfil her magistrate duties.

*

Mary and Christy did not attend.

The service was long, though Daniel hardly noticed. He hardly noticed much of anything any more.

*

The graveside service was thankfully very brief. A cold wind had arisen, and was sweeping in from the Chesapeake.

The priest's voice could hardly be heard over the clanking of loose rigging on the hundreds of sail boats moored only a few hundred feet away.

*

Daniel didn't feel anything.
Then he realised that really wasn't the case.
He felt something.
He felt hate.

Hatred towards everyone.
Hatred towards life itself.
He didn't know what to do any more.
He no longer had a concrete plan.
He just wanted others to feel as he did.
He wanted others to feel his pain.
He wanted the entire country to feel his pain.
Maybe even the world needed to share in his misery.

CHAPTER
FOURTEEN

Daniel returned to the Citygate but no longer felt any of the earlier joy, of when he and Robyn had found the apartment together. Now it was just a place to eat, sleep and shit.

A shell.

He dutifully, though dispassionately, attended the opening day of the senate after they returned from recess.

The president made a short speech, both welcoming Daniel to the floor, but also expressing his shock and sadness for what had happened just days before.

Daniel went through the motions of work. He was given a few committees on which to sit, as was usual for a freshman senator. These were not the grand and well publicised ones like Defence or Appropriations. These were the 'starter' committees for newbies to cut their teeth on.

He got the committees on Ageing and Small Business Entrepreneurship.

He wasn't going to change the world with those, but they did keep him busy. They also showed him how the whole process actually worked.

They were, in their own way, good training.

*

Three weeks later, Bud called and asked if he could come by the Citygate and have a chat with him.

When he arrived, he was shocked at the state of the place. It looked like a college dorm instead of a senator's home.

He pulled out his phone and made one call to his personal assistant. He arranged a cleaning service for Daniel. Starting immediately.

Daniel was about to object but, frankly, couldn't be bothered.

"How are you doing – really?" Bud knew the answer already.

"How do you think?" Daniel replied bluntly.

"Like shit, I would imagine." He sat on the cream-coloured couch without being asked. "Got any booze?"

"I think there's some in the kitchen. Any preference?"

"I'll take a bourbon, if you have it."

Daniel walked off, and could be heard rummaging among glass bottles. "How about a Scotch?"

"That'll do."

Daniel reappeared with an open bottle of Glenfiddich and two glasses. He poured two ridiculously large drinks.

Bud raised an eyebrow but said nothing.

He took a sip of the amber liquid.

Daniel took a gulp, then another. He emptied half the glass.

"Do you remember when Paul told you that something big was about to happen in DC?" Bud was watching him closely.

"Vaguely."

"Well it's about to explode, and I wanted to talk to you first."

"I'm not sure there's much you can say that would mean anything to me right now." Daniel took another huge gulp.

Bud studied him for a moment, trying to decide whether to proceed or not.

He really only had one choice.

"The president and the vice president are going to announce within the next few days that neither will seek a second term," Bud declared.

"But why? They've been campaigning non-stop for almost a year!" Daniel was, in fact, stunned by the news. "What the hell happened?"

"A series of audio recordings came into our possession recently. The content, if made public, would have doubtless led to their impeachment and removal from office."

"Doubtless?"

"Doubtless!"

"My god, what the hell did they do? Take a personal cheque from the Russians?" Daniel joked.

Bud looked at him with surprise. "You have no idea how close that statement is to the truth."

Daniel could only look back in amazement.

"They are both resigning, specifically so that the details will never be known publicly. That's the deal that's been made."

"But you know."

"There are a few of us who do, but this dirty little secret will remain just that. If any of us were to leak the facts, especially in an election year, it could shatter the entire belief structure of our democracy. It would certainly be the end to the Democratic Party."

"Why are you telling me?" Daniel was truly puzzled. "This sounds like one of the biggest cover-ups ever."

"That's why they are both resigning, effective immediately. That's why we would like you to run for the office of president."

"You have to be kidding. The election is in six months. It's too late for me to even be added to the primary ballots in half the states!"

"Exceptions within the party can always be made," Bud stated.

"I've just lost my wife," Daniel reminded him. "Paul always insisted that any candidate that wasn't married wouldn't stand a chance."

"And he was right. Except…" he chose the next words carefully, "… to be completely blunt, the only exception to that rule, would be a candidate who'd been recently widowed."

Daniel looked at the older man with utter incredulity.

"Are you shitting me!? Are you actually telling me that my wife having been shot to death could be an advantage?"

"You want it straight or sugar-coated?"

Daniel's expression said it all.

"No sugar then. Being married displayed the fact that you are a family man. That you are not gay and that you are able to commit. You fulfilled all of those concerns by marrying Robyn."

"For eight hours!" Daniel reminded him.

"Doesn't matter. The boxes were ticked. Now, you have the additional benefit of national sympathy. Not just at her loss, but sympathy over the way she died. Did you know that her death, and your grief, have been the number one trending news items since it happened? The public are behind you in a way I've never seen before. If you were to make violent crime reduction a major part of your campaign, you'd become exponentially more likely to be elected."

Daniel looked at him with a mix of revulsion and awe.

"You really are a cold, calculating motherfucker."

"This is politics. Of course I am. How about you? Do you want to make Robyn's death count for something?"

"How long do I have to form an exploratory team?" Daniel could hardly believe that he was considering it.

"You have exactly no time whatsoever. The DNC has done the exploratory work already. You poll higher than anyone else currently in the race. We've taken the liberty of booking the Google Center, in Minneapolis, for your first campaign rally next Friday."

"You were pretty confident I would agree?"

"Quite frankly, yes."

"That's a fucking big venue!"

"You're applying for a big fucking job!"

"It's also a completely red state. Shouldn't I focus on the friendlier ones?"

"Only a complete idiot would do his campaigning only in the friendly states. You need to win over the disenfranchised and undecided. And you have to do it fast!"

"Great. So, straight into the lion's den!" Daniel shook his head.

"You can't tame them if you don't get into the cage with them."

"It doesn't sound like you've left me with much choice."

"That's not true. You can sit here and drink yourself to death, or become the most powerful person in the world. That is the choice."

Daniel nodded his understanding.

"By the way, I asked Paul to join us. He should be here any minute."

Daniel's LID beeped. He saw that it was a text from the lobby security. Paul's photo was above the lobby request whether to let him up or not.

Daniel touched the ADMIT button on the security app.

*

The three of them talked for the next two hours straight. There was no time for subtlety or waiting for a slow day. The second the White House announcement was made about POTUS and VPOTUS, the DNC was going to saturate global media about Daniel.

They all felt that this would be an election won online and in mega stadium venues.

They didn't have the luxury of being able to have their candidate campaign the way he did in California. The Democratic Convention was only two months away.

They had a hell of a lot to do.

*

The announcement, that the president and vice president were not going to stand for re-election, came two days later at four twenty-seven in the afternoon.

*

At four twenty-nine, Daniel's candidacy for president was announced via every medium available on the planet.

Polls estimated that by five o'clock, nearly seventy-five percent of the American population were aware of the two breaking stories.

Daniel's was trending two to one, against the White House piece.

*

In the St Cloud house, Mary was entertaining a group of influential friends for lunch, ahead of her run for a seat on the district council.

Almost everybody's phone chirped, beeped or made an animal sound as the first item broke. There was hushed silence as they grabbed their LIDs and read about the president and vice president. A few seconds after recovering from the news, the second phone cacophony interrupted their conversations.

Heads looked down again as they read the second news item.

As Mary returned from the kitchen where she had been checking on the dessert, she was met with all her guests staring at her, some almost in awe.

"What!?" she asked in complete innocence.

About an hour later, as the guests were saying their goodbyes and congratulations (again), Mary pulled Councilman Ben Stevens aside.

"Do you still have somebody who does those little research projects you want kept quiet?" Mary asked in a lowered voice.

"Sounds like it's too late to investigate your son!" he teased.

"No kidding!" She laughed with him. "Actually, I was wanting to track down an old friend I haven't seen in decades. She used to live with her husband in Vermont."

"Well that sounds too easy. I'll have Jane Hayes call you tomorrow. She can find just about anybody, so long as there's a breath in their body, or a trail on why there isn't!"

"That would be great, thank you." Mary patted him on the arm. "Not a problem. Thank you for a great lunch, and congrats on your news. I couldn't get my lazy ass son to run to the store, let alone run for president!" He laughed.

Mary laughed too, until the front door was safely shut with the guests on the other side of it.

Her face took on an expression of equal parts fear and hate.

CHAPTER
FIFTEEN

Daniel stepped out onto the stage in Minnesota and gave the crowd a big wave.

The place was packed to the rafters. The press section had had to be enlarged at the last minute because of the unexpected global interest.

For his inaugural speech in the quest to become the most powerful person in the world, he had decided to dress like one of his personal heroes.

Blue jeans, black polo neck and white trainers.

A little casual for such a momentous occasion, yet Steve Jobs had, at one point, changed the world in the same relaxed attire.

While the audience applause continued to fill the twenty-thousand-seat stadium, Daniel carefully studied the aura representation.

It was mixed about fifty-fifty. Blue and red. It only then dawned on him how incredibly odd that his aura perceptions were the same colours as those of the two political parties. He decided that that was just another indication that he was living his destiny.

Before he spoke his first words, he gave the giant hall a welcome blue tap. He immediately saw the ratio change to seventy-five blue against twenty-five red.

As he stepped up to the microphone he gave one littler tap to the live audience and one big blue wave tap to the press corps and their cameras.

"Hi! I'm Daniel Trapp, and in case you hadn't heard, I want to be your next president."

The crowd went crazy.

Daniel talked to them for over an hour, about all the things that he felt were wrong with how Americans were now living, and how badly they were being treated.

He focused heavily on violent crime.

After laying the groundwork in their minds, Daniel changed tack. He returned to one of his earlier speeches when he had told the audience how close they were to civil war, and that he was the person to bring the nation back from the brink.

This time however, his words hinted at a darker option.

"We all know that there is more disparity between the party messages, than ever before. The Right are so far to the right they can't even see centre with a telescope. The Left are so far the other way that they make socialism sound like a capitalist's playground.

"I have said before that we have to find a common ground and work outwards from there, but, and it's a big but, what if there really is no common ground? If half of the country can only see the sky as blue while the other half swears it's pink, who is right? Is one side actually wrong or do our eyes differ in the colours they can perceive?

"If you have an evenly divided nation that cannot agree on the most basic everyday issues, then how the hell can lawmakers determine what laws to make?

"Since I was born, we have gone from one mass shooting a week to two mass shootings a day.

"Every day. Yet, can we agree that hand guns and assault weapons do not have a place in the hands of the general public?

"No. We can't. So, another twenty students were killed in their school yesterday. Couldn't be the guns, could it?

"'Oh well. That shit happens'!" Daniel used a goofy voice for emphasis.

"Last week, a black church in Georgia was firebombed by a known group of white supremacists. Nineteen people died. Couldn't be because of racism being ignored, could it? 'Oh well. That shit happens.'

"The western states have, for the past five years, not had a day when at least one large-scale fire wasn't burning out of control. Also – in Florida, the Keys are now under water more than two hundred days a year. Can't be global warming though, could it?"

Daniel held his mic out to the audience, like a rock star letting the fans sing the verse.

And amazingly, they all repeated his verse. Twenty thousand people cried out –"Oh well. That shit happens!"

*

Daniel let the stadium's massive size echo their words. He didn't speak. As his reverberated message faded away, the silence became deafening.

*

"Maybe the time has finally come when we have to realise that perhaps we, as a nation, are no longer fit to have complete freedom of choice.

"Maybe we, as a nation, cannot be left to decide what's best for us and the country purely by popular consensus. "Maybe we, as a nation, need to all move to centre again, even if that means we do away with the archaic model of the two-party system.

"I say to you here – let's make America whole again.

"I say to you at home – let's make America whole again. "Everybody!

"Make America whole again. "Make America whole again."

*

The crowd picked up the chant. Slowly at first. Then, more joined in.

Finally, the entire audience took over the chant.

Daniel stopped chanting himself, and just watched the audience from his vantage point above them.

Looking down.

Just the way he liked it.

*

"Make America whole again!"
"Make America whole again!"
"Make America whole again!"

*

Daniel walked off the stage smiling, as the chanting continued in the auditorium.

He walked past Paul, Bud and other shell-shocked party members who had been standing in the wings.

He gave them a big thumbs-up.

"Got 'em!" he laughed and headed for the dressing room and a few shots of Mescal, before security brought him a selection of some of the prettier young female audience members.

*

The result of his inflammatory speech was as bizarre as the speech itself.

Half the nation appeared to blindly agree with his views, while the other half vehemently decried Daniel for his blatant verbal desecration of the Constitution, and of long-held American values.

Yet the polling on the following day showed a massive swing in Minnesota from Republican to Democrat.

Street interviews after the Minnesota rally showed individuals of all ages, races, all colours, all religions, ardently defending 'their' candidate. Though when asked for specifics of what exactly Daniel Trapp had said that so enthralled them, none of them could verbalise what those were.

Instead, they became more defensive of the candidate, and pushed back against the interviewers calling them biased and unfair.

The DNC found themselves in a very peculiar situation. They did not agree with any of Daniel's closing statement in Minneapolis, yet they were gaining in the polls because of them.

Bud and Paul had tried to get Daniel to understand that he couldn't just blurt out any random thoughts to please an audience.

Daniel pointed out that, not only could he blurt out whatever he felt would 'grab' the crowds, but that every presidential candidate in the last six elections had done exactly that. Furthermore, what made them think that his thoughts were random? He made it completely clear that he knew exactly what he was doing and saying.

He then informed them that he had scheduled another campaign rally for the following week, at Sun Stadium in Tempe, Arizona. He suggested they 'swing by and check it out'.

The party decided to do just that. They'd see how the candidate behaved, then decide if his wings needed to be clipped. If, God forbid, they had backed the wrong horse entirely, they were running out of time to harness someone else from their underwhelming stables.

*

Between the Minneapolis and Arizona rallies, Daniel made appearances on every late-night show, every morning news magazine, and even did a walk-on, on *Saturday Night Live*.

He got booed as much as cheered.

Overnight, he somehow became one of the most polarising figures in the country.

His private behaviour was also anathema.

It was as if he was reading a book on how to become president, then doing the exact opposite.

His Citygate apartment had become his 'PARTY headquarters' as he liked to call it.

Security had had to modify their app in order to send him live video, so that he could preview the women who randomly appeared at the building's security. He could then decide their 'fuckability' rating. Anyone over an eight was granted immediate access.

The press had a field day over this, and tried to make hay with article after article about his disgraceful and degrading behaviour.

Fifty percent of the country felt this was just another indication that he was completely unfit to be a candidate. They were certain, at the rate he was going, that he would burn out long before the finish line.

The other fifty percent loved the dream Daniel was living. They felt that his recent tragedy somehow gave him the right to mourn in his own way. If partying till dawn was his way, more power to him.

He could do no wrong.

CHAPTER
SIXTEEN

Daniel flew into Tempe in a black executive VTL limo with TRAPP in gold lettering plastered to the side of it.

When it landed, he stepped out into the desert sunshine and was immediately met by twenty scantily-clad cheerleaders, hired to escort him inside the venue.

Daniel was learning the art of the grand entrance!

There were as many people outside the stadium who couldn't get in as there were inside the sixty-thousand-seat arena. Most were screaming love and devotion for the candidate.

A few poorly planned protest groups tried to have their voices heard, but failed. One group was actually attacked, and twelve of the protesters ended up in hospital.

When Daniel walked on stage, the audience started chanting.

*

"Make America whole again."
"Make America whole again."

*

Daniel noticed immediately that the majority of the crowd were wearing bright blue baseball caps with the slogan embroidered on it.

He made a note to apologise to Paul. Clearly the man had known what he was talking about when he had suggested the hat thing.

Daniel stepped up to the podium. The giant LID screen behind him changed from a close shot of him, to a graphic showing a golden eagle, near death, by the side of a toxic river, partially draped with a frayed American flag.

*

"These are dark times, my friends…"

*

He spoke for over two hours. His speech in Tempe made the one in Minneapolis sound light and fluffy in comparison.

The darker he portrayed America's current condition, the more enraged and yet enraptured the audience became.

When he took the stage, sixty percent of the people were glowing blue. When he left, ninety percent had the blue aura.

Their aura colour was oddly close in hue to their caps.

What was truly amazing was that he had only lightly

tapped the crowd. They had changed colour mostly on their own.

Not the case for the viewers outside or at home. The cameras got the full twenty-four-carat, grade-A-certified tap.

He told America that there was only one person who could remedy the ills of the country, and especially its lack of an intelligent, honest and compassionate government.

He also again berated any system that permitted a complete stalemate of national consensus. He railed that such a state automatically guaranteed stagnation and deterioration of the fragile democracy.

At one point, he stepped away from the podium and went to the edge of the stage.

"You do not have to simply take my word for what I am saying here today," he announced with his arms spread wide to the crowd. "Look to the polls. In less than a week, I have already turned sixty percent of the nation blue. Imagine what I could do in four years, let alone in eight!"

They stood and cheered.

They naturally thought he was referring to party preference when he stated he had turned them blue.

He, of course, hadn't been referring to that at all.

He had meant exactly what he had said.

*

He had just admitted to millions of Americans that he had basically been mind-fucking them into submission.

They responded by giving him an ovation, like nothing anybody had seen outside of Germany a hundred years earlier.

He stared out at the crowd who one minute were chanting his mantra, the next his name.

On cue, the house lights were brought up to full, so he could see his audience and applaud their belief in him.

He could make out the faces of the individuals in the crowd. The farmers, the housewives, the doctors, the lawyers.

All walks of life.

All disillusioned.

All needing a saviour.

He knew that he was that man.

Or at least, that he could make them believe he was.

If nothing else, he knew he could save them from themselves. After all, it was better that they die in revolt, than live in impotency.

*

For a brief moment, Daniel had a different view of the audience. Instead of the eager, red-faced, energetic mass, all he saw was death.

They were seated facing him. Row by row by row.

Sightless.

Their corpses, decomposing into the faded orange fabric of the seats. Their brightly coloured clothes had dulled and had partially rotted into the grey green ooze that had once been living flesh.

The only part of them that didn't reflect death and decay was their caps.

The bright blue baseball caps, with the slogan MAKE AMERICA WHOLE AGAIN, looked brand new. They were still perched on their heads. The lifeless heads atop decaying corpses.

The message, though, was still clear.

Daniel realised at that point that he may have lost his mind. The creeping tendrils of insanity had possibly taken hold of his brain. Then again, he justified – you had to be crazy to want to be president. Didn't you?

Daniel closed his eyes tight, then opened them again.

He was back among the living.

For now.

CHAPTER
SEVENTEEN

The DNC held an emergency meeting the following morning. The situation had, in one week, gone from questionable to apocalyptic. Their candidate wasn't just 'off message'. He was pitching the end of democracy. The end of the two-party system. He might as well have burned a copy of the Constitution live for the whole world to see.

They all agreed that he had to go.

But, they also all agreed that he was polling higher than any Democratic Party candidate in modern history, and that was after only a couple of weeks.

Daniel had harnessed the frustration and suppressed lunacy of a sector of America who had never before had a champion. This newly franchised voting block was a volatile, forgotten mass, that was suddenly in a position to swing the election in whatever direction their new hero wanted.

They discussed the ramifications if Daniel were removed as their candidate and what that could mean to the party and to the election.

The options were bleak and unacceptable.

They came to a frightening realisation that, if they wanted to win, Daniel was the only person, at that moment in time, to get them into the White House.

They then came to what historians would later refer to as 'their party's doomsday protocol'. They decided their only option was to let their horse run freely. Then after the election, they'd tighten the reins and bring him back into the fold.

To the men and women around that conference table, on that day, it sounded like a doable, win-win scenario.

*

Daniel didn't do any of the usual types of campaigning leading up to the Democratic Convention.

He just held mega rallies. He started filling hundred-thousand-seat stadiums.

His adoring public grew in size at a startling and frightening rate. The rallies became vast ego chambers in which Daniel could bath in the raw, electric energy of his maniacally devoted fans.

His speeches became more dire, while his solutions became less evident.

By convention time, his only solution, devoid of any detail or rationale, was that he was their only answer.

*

The Democratic Convention was held on July 9th at Philadelphia's Alibaba Center, and before it even began, everyone knew where the bulk of the states' votes were going to go.

In the days leading up to the vote, the invited speakers all praised the young candidate from California. They praised his refreshing views on politics, his emphatic rejection of 'politics as usual'. And his fresh 'masterplan' for America's future.

Daniel had cleverly harangued alumni with whom he had gone to school at Le Lac, to speak on his behalf.

He was able to produce presidents and prime ministers of dozens of countries. Leaders of industry and even of various religions.

He brought his favourite bands to the convention. He brought the Mormon Tabernacle Choir. He brought the entire Dallas Cowboy cheerleading squad, who performed a custom, and extremely raunchy, routine to Aerosmith's 'Pink'.

The reps from the bible-belt states felt it a bit much, but hailed Daniel's gusto and diversity.

Despite every attempt by the DNC to take some control over the proceedings, Daniel simply took over the staging and turned the four-day convention into a massive party in his honour.

By the last day, everyone was exhausted and had pretty much forgotten the point of the gathering.

The actual vote count to determine who would lead the Democratic fight for the White House was an absurd anticlimax.

As each state representative took their mic and announced their numbers, it was clear by the time they had reached Georgia (it goes alphabetically), that there was only ever going to be the one candidate.

Daniel took every state.

*

After winning the candidacy, he walked on stage, surrounded by the party leadership, as well as a bevy of gorgeous young women who all assumed were there to add their beauty to the photo op.

The audience loved his devil-may-care arrogance.

The DNC elite, though on stage with him, were now realising that they had zero control over their candidate.

Their original idea of giving him enough rope to win, then bringing him to bear once he took office, was starting to look like a pipe dream.

They collectively prayed that his speech would not rattle any more of the country's framework, and that they could all go back to DC and try to come up with a solution as to how the hell they were going to work with their new president.

*

Then their candidate stepped up to the microphone.

"My friends, my fellow countrymen, my family and colleagues, this has been an amazing week. A week that has seen me cement my position as your candidate for the Office of President of these United States.

"A week that has seen praise. A week that has seen unity. A week that has seen this party rid itself of doubt. Rid itself of infighting. Rid itself of indecision.

"And most importantly, rid itself forever of its inability to unite solely for one candidate.

"A week that has shown America and the world that there is only one candidate, and one party.

"For that, I thank you all.

"We are all exhausted.

"We are all spent.

"There is nothing more to say tonight.

"Instead we will all retire to our homes and take pride in what we have achieved here.

"November's election was decided here tonight.

"The future of America was decided here tonight.

"The future of the world was decided here tonight.

"God bless you all."

*

It was the shortest acceptance speech in history. The DNC was quietly delighted, and at the same relieved. Somehow, they had got through the last day of the conference without Trapp causing any irreparable harm to the country. The crowd remained in the massive hall and cheered till they had no more voice to give.

Daniel was whisked away into a waiting motorcade, with three of the girls that had been on stage with him. They were driven directly to the Crystal Hotel, then escorted up to the lavish presidential suite.

With the Secret Service having now taken control of the candidate's safety, the entire floor was made secure with agents posted along the hallway and outside the suite door.

The moment they were alone, one of the girls produced some Acrylic Z. The latest non-addictive and yet highly potent meth alternative.

They each broke a capsule under their noses.

The rush was intense.

The euphoria, long lasting and soul elevating. The four stripped off their clothes and jumped onto the double king bed.

Almost as if rehearsed, the girls found their positions as Daniel lay on his back floating high above the universe.

Two of the girls were each licking one of his testicles, as the third girl, a natural southern redhead, sat astride his face. She moaned deeply, as she moved her hips slowly back and forth across Daniel's quivering tongue.

Daniel decided he wanted to take their pleasure up a notch. He also wanted to experiment. He gave them all a huge blue tap. Their auras were already blue, but he thought they should be allowed to reach a higher plane of colour and emotional sensitivity.

For a brief moment, their auras actually flashed to a darker blue but then immediately dulled.

The redhead spasmed violently. Daniel thought she had had a major orgasm. But then he suddenly tasted urine, and was pretty sure he could smell shit.

The girl then tipped to one side, and fell off him.

The other two had stopped licking.

Daniel clawed his way out of the melee, and saw that all three girls didn't seem to be breathing. The two blondes still had their tongues out, but both now had blood-specked drool dripping from the sides of their mouths.

Daniel could see that the redhead had indeed evacuated her bladder and bowels.

Daniel spat and spat and spat.

Then he screamed for the Secret Service.

The girls were rushed to the nearest hospital. The two blondes were dead on arrival. The redhead was in a coma and not expected to live.

The doctors were quickly able to determine that all three had had massive brain aneurisms. Veins in their heads had popped like tiny balloons.

The only cause they could determine, was extreme vascular pressure brought on by the Acrylic Z.

Daniel was briefly questioned by the police but cleared of any wrongdoing.

The synthetic drug wasn't illegal.

In fact, the officers, after a tiny tap, felt that the senator was the real victim that night.

He was airlifted to DC in his 'Trapp' branded VTL limo, then driven straight to the Citygate.

*

Paul was waiting for him in the lobby.

They rode up the elevator in silence.

Once in his apartment, Daniel walked directly to the kitchen.

"I suppose you heard?" he called back to Paul.

"Yes. That's why I am here. I am on your list of emergency contacts."

"I didn't kill those two girls." Daniel reappeared with two hefty glasses of amber liquid. Paul took one reluctantly.

"Three actually. The third girl died while you were in the air."

"The redhead?"

"Her name was Alison," Paul tossed in.

"Whatever."

"Did you know any of their names?"

Daniel shrugged as he downed the booze.

"I still didn't kill them."

"Don't bullshit me, Daniel. How much of an idiot do you really think I am? You do realise that at some point it's going to be noticed that people around you seem to be dying from brain aneurisms and strokes. It just might raise a red flag."

"If anything, the girls went out on a blue flag," Daniel chuckled.

Paul just stared at him in horrified amazement.

"What happened to you?"

"What do you mean what happened?" Daniel barked. "Maybe having my wife die right in front of me could have had some effect – huh!?"

"She was shot because of what you did to the muggers' brains!"

"That's a lie!" Daniel practically screamed.

The two drank for a moment in complete silence.

"You know I could kill you right here, don't you?"

Paul looked over at him with an expression of sadness mixed with revulsion.

"Yes, I do."

"In fact, I could walk up to someone in the middle of Dupont Circle and kill them. And you know what? I'd get away with it."

"This will end badly, you know!" Paul whispered.

"Not for me. Not yet anyway. I have a destiny. I have the power."

"All men of great evil felt that way at some point."

"So, you do at least give me credit for being great." Daniel again chuckled.

"No. I don't. I think you've snapped. Or maybe this was always you, we just didn't see it."

"And now it's too late!" Daniel replied.

Paul put down his glass and started for the door.

"See you in Vermont?"

Paul hesitated, then replied without looking back.

"No. I gave my notice on the trip back from Philly. You're on your own now." He quietly shut Daniel's apartment door behind him.

"Bullshit." Daniel could be heard in the hallway. "Everybody worships me. I will never be alone!"

Paul shook his head as he walked the curved Citygate hallway for the last time.

CHAPTER
EIGHTEEN

The death of the three girls made global news. It was front and centre online, on TV and on what remained of the print press. Daniel would have liked for the whole thing to have just blown over but not surprisingly the story had legs.

It wasn't going to go away until his voice had been heard.

The party, remarkably, was able to convince him to take the situation seriously, and for him to give one interview on the subject.

Daniel decided on Nick Chavez. He felt a kinship to the man who had started the ball rolling.

It was determined that Daniel would fly out to LA and have the interview take place on the Chavez set but in a huge coup for the host it would go out live to the world.

Daniel arrived early, and was sulking in the studio green room, when one of his Secret Service agents knocked on the door.

"I thought I said I didn't want to be disturbed!?" he yelled back.

"Your mother's here!" the agent replied calmly. Temperamental candidates were a dime a dozen as far as he was concerned.

Surprised, Daniel opened the door. Mary thanked the agent then walked past Daniel and sat in one of the guest chairs.

"To what do I owe this honour?" Daniel asked sarcastically.

"Can't a doting mother visit her famous son when he's in town?"

"Unlikely, without a reason, don't you think?" he parried.

"I just wanted to see you. It's become a rarity and you never know what the world holds in store do you?"

"I truly have no idea what you're talking about."

A gentle knock on the door was followed by the stage manager's voice.

"Five minutes, Senator!"

"Thank you," Daniel shouted back.

"I've got to get ready," he stated flatly to Mary. "Why don't you just say what you came to say and get it over with. The one thing I don't need today is another message of rebuke from my mother. Then again, you're not my mother, are you?"

"As you so eloquently stated, I am not your mother. You killed your mother, and father, and Henry and many more that I'm aware of. God knows how many others you've actually killed or at least mentally destroyed."

"Do you want to be next?" he asked as casually as one would when offering a cup of tea.

"I'll leave you now. I won't be seeing you again. At least not in the flesh. I just wanted you to know something very important."

"Get on with it then."

He turned to her and was shocked to see her aura. It was bright green. He had never seen one that colour and for the life of him, didn't know what it meant.

Mary walked over to him, leant in and gently whispered, "You are a fucking monster, and I'm afraid to say, are no longer part of the plan."

The words hit him like a sledgehammer though he didn't really understand why.

"I don't know what that means." He looked at her with defiance and curiosity.

"That's what's so terrifying about this whole thing. You never knew what any of it meant. You were given a gift, yet even from the womb, you turned it into a weapon."

"That's enough!" He looked to the door. "Jimmy!"

The agent opened the door immediately.

"Get this nut job out of here," Daniel ordered.

Jimmy looked confused.

"Your mother?"

"She's not my mother. She never was!"

Mary gave him one last look then exited the room. Moments later the stage manager was back at the door.

"We're ready for you, Senator."

Daniel followed the man through a labyrinth of hallways until they finally arrived at stage four and the Chavez set.

Instead of the usual host desk and talk-show seating, it had been modified to consist only of two facing chairs positioned in front of a row of vertically arranged American flags.

As the show wasn't going live for another few minutes, Daniel walked on set alone, and took a moment to get settled. Nick then arrived and shook hands with him, and told him he had no intention of badgering him. He was only going to do a brief lead-in then let Daniel do all the talking.

Daniel nodded his understanding at which point the stage assistant announced, "Thirty seconds."

The two men sat silently till the assistant voiced the count.

Five,

Four... Then the silent finger signals of:

Three,

Two,

One.

Nick was true to his word and introduced the senator and presidential candidate then mentioned the Philadelphia event in rare brevity, before giving the stage, or at least the chair, to Daniel.

"Thank you, Nick. It's a pleasure to be back in LA and here on your stage again."

Daniel's voice was calm, controlled and held a perfect mix of authority and humility.

"The tragic deaths of Alison, Britney and Candie will weigh heavily on me for the rest of my life. People have asked me whether I feel responsible and the simple answer is, yes. I do. Of course, I do."

Daniel managed to get his voice to crack.

"Those sweet girls came to me for an evening of fun and excitement, and it ended in complete tragedy. I had no idea the girls had ingested that..." He pretended to search for the name. "Acrylic Z. In fact, until that night – that night that will forever haunt me, I had never heard of that drug. Don't get me wrong. I have not lived the life of an angel. But I had never heard of these synthetics of which, I am told, Acrylic Z is one. These obviously highly dangerous and deadly drugs are, amazingly, completely legal. Anyone can buy them.

"They are the government's last-ditch solution to the government's never-ending war on methamphetamine addiction, but to what end? Three beautiful, intelligent young women, who all had incredible futures ahead of them, were struck down by this government's approved, lethal, synthetic amphetamine.

"Here is another example of what I have been saying about the criminal mismanagement of our great nation.

"Our leaders won't take away guns, won't put an end to racism and – *and*, not only won't rid our great country of drugs and their dealers, but instead, basically go into the business of being drug lords themselves. First, they legalised marijuana. A gateway drug as we all know. Then cocaine became initially government regulated, then it too became legal. Then it was meth, one of the most destructive scourges this country has ever seen.

"Our government's answer to a veritable plague upon our homeland was to create its own versions of the drug – and naturally, then legalise those as well.

"There was a great soundbite slogan over half a century ago. It said 'Just say no'. It was aimed at kids, to try to get them to not take that first step towards addiction.

"What has our great government done since then? I'll tell you. It has removed almost all barriers that prevented drug use. Its slogan should be "Just say no – to the dealers, and buy from us!".

"Well, in my book that isn't a solution. Having our government convince us that the only answer to drug abuse is to have them, our elected leaders, become the manufacturers and dealers themselves, is absolutely insane!

"When did everything become so completely crazy. It can't continue. No country can live without a strong and indomitable framework of basic human morality. Our impotent and self-serving government has to be wiped clean and rebuilt from scratch.

"We, the people, have to take back the mantle of holding our leadership responsible for the safety, well-being and prosperity of every living American!"When that day happens, maybe we can look back, and say that Alison, Britney and Candie did not give their lives in vain. Just maybe they brought this despicable situation to the forefront of the American consciousness, and helped force the long overdue reboot of our corrupt, inept and obsolete government."

There was no live audience but the crew applauded and cheered loudly enough to fill the sound stage.

*

The director chose that moment to dissolve to a still of Daniel's face. A single tear of passion rested on his cheek.

Nick leaned over and patted Daniel on the knee.

"Amazing. Fantastic speech. I just don't know what else to say."

Daniel stood and patted the other man on the shoulders as he walked past.

Daniel's Secret Service detail escorted him back towards the dressing room. They too congratulated him on his perfect messaging at such a difficult time.

Daniel waited before he was in his dressing room to start laughing. He couldn't. The tears really were running down his face.

CHAPTER
NINETEEN

Daniel's VTL limo landed next to the Huawei Center in Montpelier, Vermont. A massive crowd was waiting to greet their champion.

He signed a few blue caps, shook a minimal number of hands, then was led into the vast structure.

A few minutes later he walked on stage from the darkened wings to applause that was so loud it seemed to actually vibrate the giant, closed, retractable roof.

He was wearing his Steve Jobs outfit, but had added one of the blue caps. He looked ridiculous, but the crowd loved it.

He started speaking, but noticed almost immediately that there was a commotion in one of the aisles leading to the raised stage.

An elderly woman was trying to wheel herself closer to the stage, but Trapp fans were blocking the aisle, and had no intention of getting out of the way for some old biddy.

Daniel stopped his speech, and pointed to the woman, then faced the crowd.

"We have here a perfect example of how our great nation has crumbled into disrepair and disrespect.

"We have here a wonderful, great, older American, who simply wants to be able to see and hear me more clearly. I find that a noble intent.

"Yet there are those of you who would stand in her way and block her path.

"What happened to helping your fellow man? To sharing the load? To working together as a whole?

"I want all of you people who are standing in her way to start acting like the Americans who carved this country out of bedrock, and lift her up here. I want this great woman to have a place on my stage."

His instructions electrified the group in the aisle. Twelve men immediately took hold of her wheelchair and gently hoisted her into the air. Looking like a modern version of Egyptian slaves, carrying their pharaoh's throne, they walked her right past security and up the narrow steps to the stage.

They hesitated, not sure quite where Daniel wanted her to be placed. He smiled, and pointed just off to the side.

They gently lowered her to the wooden surface. Made sure her quilted comforter was snuggly tucked in and that she was comfortable. They then walked by Daniel on their way back to their seats. Each man saluted as they passed.

"Thank you, men!" Daniel called after them.

The audience cheered them back to their seats.

Daniel removed the wireless mic from the podium and walked over to the woman.

He knelt down on one knee and spoke into the mic, while looking at her heavily wrinkled face and twitching hands beneath her quilt.

"Is this a better seat for you?" he asked with a big grin.

He held the mic out for her to speak into it.

"Yes. Thank you, it's perfect, Daniel."

Something about the woman jarred some cobwebs in the very attic of his mind. Her voice was ancient but still held sort of a hereditary memory.

"Do I know you?"

He held the mic close to her mouth, so all could hear.

"Not directly, no…"

The entire audience laughed.

"But you did murder my son, Zeke, and his wife. Your real mother."

The sound of over sixty thousand people, all gasping at once, was uniquely chilling.

Daniel was so stunned by her words that he couldn't move.

Glenda Darnell stopped fiddling under her quilt and produced an old-looking, rusted, large calibre revolver. Her tiny hands shook with its weight.

Despite the shaking and her growing inability to physically hold the heavy gun, she managed to pull the trigger.

Just once.

Only once.

Once is all it takes with a forty-five.

She had aimed for his chest, but the kick had raised the barrel.

If she had been twenty feet away, the bullet may have actually gone over Daniel's head, but at three feet, the bullet tore through the right side of his skull, filling his bright blue cap with bone, blood and most of his right frontal lobe.

Glenda Darnell never made it off the stage. Six Secret Service agents shot her a total of twenty-seven times.

Her face, head and upper torso seemed to somehow become dismantled like a portrait in a Picasso painting, before crumpling into a bloody heap.

The force of the bullets had actually given the wheelchair life, and even when the shooting stopped, the chair continued its backwards, curving journey to the edge of the stage.

In what everyone later described as slow motion, the metal, rubber and bloodied pile went over the edge and danced down the steps, sending body bits and blood in all directions until it finally reached the arena floor, and stopped moving.

There was a momentary hushed silence that consumed all the air in the arena.

*

Then one woman screamed.

EPILOGUE

The clinic was sheltered from the rest of the world by almost a mile of paved driveway. It was flanked by manicured lawns, majestic old-growth woods and topiary, finely trimmed into the shape of exotic animals.

Mary's driver hadn't uttered a single word since they left the city, ninety minutes earlier.

He didn't feel it was his place to speak, which was fine with Mary. This wasn't the time for small talk.

The black SUV pulled up to an imposing marble and stone entry.

A livery appeared in full uniform and opened Mary's door.

She walked into the building and was met by Herman Schneller. The director of the clinic.

There was no introduction, and again, no words were spoken as she was escorted to one particular doorway.

Herr Schneller opened the door for her.

She stepped in.

The door closed silently behind her.

The room was large and decorated in pale pastels.

The lighting was subdued, and somehow provided no shadows.

There was only a single bed in the middle of the room and a solitary hospital chair by a large bay window.

The bed was empty. The chair was not.

Mary walked over to the figure, held upright by padded straps.

Daniel was facing out of the window, yet saw nothing.

The right side of his head had healed, if you can call it that. There was a huge concave crater where a quarter of his brain had once rested.

The bullet had almost surgically removed his right frontal lobe. He could breathe on his own, though was now blind, paralysed, mute and incontinent. His brain showed some function on the scans, but none was visible with the human eye.

This was the first and only time Mary would visit. She looked at him with a mixture of loathing, pity and regret.

She was amazed at his aura.

Prior to the shooting it had always been a royal blue. Now it held every colour imaginable. All intertwined as the palette vibrated, sparked and danced around his useless, destroyed head.

Mary had seen this type of aura once before.

The Down's syndrome child at Daniel's pre-school had one that was similar.

Without the ability of the brain to function in a linear mode, the aura was free roaming and able to defy normal auratic patterns.

Also like the child at the pre-school, Daniel was smiling. Nobody knew why. Including Daniel.

Yet he smiled.
All day.
Every day.

*

The doctors all agreed that he was extraordinarily lucky to have survived the assassination attempt.

*

Mary knelt down closer to him and whispered.

"I just wanted you to know that I have been asked to take your place."

She looked at his face with its drooped features, hoping to see some reaction.

There was none.

She stood back up. Took one last look at him, then left the room.

*

There was total silence in the SUV as they drove sedately back to the wrought-iron entry gates.

Once through the gates, her Secret Service detail started their vehicles, and took their positions in front and behind her SUV. The small motorcade then began the long drive back to the city.

ACKNOWLEDGEMENTS

I would like to thank my wonderful and patient wife, Clare, for giving me the physical and mental space I needed to write this book as well as the love and encouragement to make me believe I could actually finish it.

I also want to thank Craig Leener, friend and superb author, for unwittingly becoming not only my muse while writing this book, but also my grammar punctuation and dialogue coach.

Finally, I would like to thank my friends Wendy Stanford, ands Joshua Morfin who read the rough drafts and gave me their thoughts and impressions. Their positive input got me through the darker days.

 Matador

For exclusive discounts on Matador titles,
sign up to our occasional newsletter at
troubador.co.uk/bookshop